RAISING CONFIDENT CHILDREN

Dr Samir Parikh is an eminent psychiatrist who has been working in the field of mental health over the past two decades. He is the Director of the Department of Mental Health and Behavioural Sciences at Fortis Healthcare. Under his guidance and leadership, the Department of Mental Health and Behavioural Sciences works to provide comprehensive mental health services, including conducting specialized programmes for the community. He has been a speaker at various national and international forums on mental-health issues. He is amongst the most well-known experts of the country on mental-health issues. He has previously authored *Let Him Not Sink: First Steps to Mental Health*.
Twitter: @dr_samirparikh

Kamna Chhibber is a clinical psychologist. She is currently the Head of the Department of Mental Health and Behavioural Sciences at Fortis Healthcare, and holds an MPhil in Clinical Psychology. She works within an eclectic frame for the treatment of clinical and other related problems in children, adolescents and adults. She has been instrumental in developing the Fortis School Mental Health Program. Through her blogs and interactions with media, she has been working towards making mental health a priority for all.
Twitter: @kamna_chhibber

Mimansa Singh Tanwar is a clinical psychologist. She is a Cognitive Behavioural Therapist working in the clinical space using evidence-based treatments with adolescents, parents, couples and families. She holds an MPhil in Clinical Psychology. As the Lead Clinical Psychologist, she provides clinical supervision and assistance to psychologists to enhance therapeutic care across centres. She also leads the Fortis School Mental Health Program with a sense of passion for enhancing the mental health in children at schools.
Twitter: @mimansasingh

RAISING CONFIDENT CHILDREN

A 52-Week Guide

Samir Parikh
Kamna Chhibber & Mimansa Singh Tanwar

Published by
Rupa Publications India Pvt. Ltd 2019
7/16, Ansari Road, Daryaganj
New Delhi 110002

Sales centres:
Allahabad Bengaluru Chennai
Hyderabad Jaipur Kathmandu
Kolkata Mumbai

Copyright © Samir Parikh, Kamna Chhibber
and Mimansa Singh Tanwar 2019

The views and opinions expressed in this book are the authors' own and the facts are as reported by them which have been verified to the extent possible, and the publishers are not in any way liable for the same.

All rights reserved.

No part of this publication may be reproduced, transmitted, or stored in a retrieval system, in any form or by any means, electronic, mechanical, photocopying, recording or otherwise, without the prior permission of the publisher.

ISBN: 978-93-5333-572-4

First impression 2019

10 9 8 7 6 5 4 3 2 1

The moral right of the author has been asserted.

Printed at Parksons Graphics Pvt. Ltd, Mumbai

This book is sold subject to the condition that it shall not, by way of trade or otherwise, be lent, resold, hired out, or otherwise circulated, without the publisher's prior consent, in any form of binding or cover other than that in which it is published.

CONTENTS

About the Fortis School Mental Health Program   ix
Message from Dr Samir Parikh   xi

SECTION ONE: UNDERSTAND YOUR CHILD AND YOURSELF
1. Building Confidence in Your Child   3
2. Your Child is Unique   7
3. Assess Your Child's Self-Esteem   12
4. Use Art and Play to Understand Your Child   16
5. Let Your Child Be an Explorer   20
6. Know Your Parenting Style   25
7. Factors Influencing Your Parenting Style   29

SECTION TWO: THE GUIDE TO GOOD COMMUNICATION
8. The Role of Your Non-Verbals   35
9. Pick Your Battles—Choose Your Noes!   39
10. Create Space for Self-Expression   43
11. Hone Your Listening Skills   48
12. Maintain Eye Contact during Conversations   52
13. Choose Your Words Wisely   56
14. Make the Time You Spend with Your Child Count   60

SECTION THREE: BUILD EMOTIONAL WELL-BEING
15. Identify Your Child's Emotions   67
16. Help Your Child Identify Emotions   72
17. Empathy for Better Connectedness   77
18. Create Space for Emotional Conversations   82
19. Accept Your Child's Self-Expressions   86
20. Model Self-Regulation of Emotions   90

21. Walk with Me	95
22. Acknowledge Your Child's Abilities	100

SECTION FOUR: BUILD CONFIDENCE THROUGH PROBLEM-SOLVING

23. Solving Problems with Your Child	107
24. Persistent Corrections Can Breed Self-Doubt	114
25. Negotiate to Persuade Instead of Being Coercive	119
26. Work to Nurture Self-Awareness	124
27. Reinforce the Efforts	129
28. Support Your Child through Failures	135
29. Create Internal Drive through Goal Setting	141
30. Encourage Perseverance	147

SECTION FIVE: WATCH OUT FOR THESE PARENTING SYNDROMES

31. Parents, Watch Your Reactions!	155
32. Do Not Criticize the Behaviour	160
33. Don't Banish the Mistakes	166
34. Nagging Leads to Shutdown	171
35. Comparison Depletes Self-Confidence	176
36. Restrain Parental Expectations	181
37. Refrain from Body-Shaming	186
38. Balance Instructions with Requests	191
39. Tone Down the Excessive Pampering	196
40. Embrace Your Limitations	201

SECTION SIX: PARENTING WITH A SENSITIVE APPROACH

41. Help Your Child Face Fears Head-on	207
42. Consistency Is the Key	214
43. Create Opportunities to Hone Skills	220
44. Teach Assertiveness	225

45. Help Your Child Build Social Skills to Develop Healthy Relationships	231
46. Let Go of the Assumptions	237
47. Stimulate Creative Thinking	242
48. Develop Critical Thinking in Your Child	247
49. Evaluate Performance, Not Your Child	253
50. Share Your Stories	258
51. Be a Gender-Sensitive Parent	263
52. Be Accepting of What Comes Your Way	269

ABOUT THE FORTIS SCHOOL MENTAL HEALTH PROGRAM

The Fortis School Mental Health Program, since its inception, has been extending its services to students, teachers, parents and all other stakeholders involved in a student's life. It is a platform that promotes psycho-social health and well-being of school-aged children through the provision of therapeutic, preventive and rehabilitative services. The programme focuses on enhancing the life skills of children and adolescents to help them cope effectively with the challenges of life and preparing them for most contingencies.

The programme has a dual focus—a strong impetus on clinical aspects of working with the young population of the country, as well as building resilience through workshops and seminars. The multi-disciplinary team of experts comprising psychiatrists, clinical psychologists, counselling psychologists, psychodynamic psychotherapists, special educators, occupational therapists and sports psychologists, work collaboratively to ensure the best service provision under one roof for all child- and adolescent-related mental health needs.

Simultaneously, the programme focuses on working with school settings to promote positive mental health. The development of life skills is integral to work done through the Fortis Prosocial Peer Moderator Program, while skill acquisition and knowledge development are the cornerstones of the Fortis School Counsellor Forum. The Fortis Bully-to-Buddy program focuses on building a school system that is bully free and the Fortis Advocacy Program works to engage students to become flag bearers of the message of mental health across media. Additionally, Fortis Psych-Ed is an annual psychology quiz for school students which orients students to an active engagement with the subject.

Through its presence across the country, provision of services within schools and associations for programmes on a no-cost basis, the Fortis School Mental Health Program has been effective in creating a positive narrative for mental health.

Instagram: fortismentalhealth
Facebook: Fortis School Mental Health Program
Email: mentalhealth@fortishealthcare.com
Fortis 24x7 Helpline: +918376804102

MESSAGE FROM DR SAMIR PARIKH

Through the years as I have continued to work with children, adolescents and their parents, I have observed a shift in parenting styles. The changing social environment, increasing demands placed on the youth, reduced time that is available with parents, diminishing social support structures, increased nuclearization of families are all contributing to these shifts which have also made parenting a challenging task.

Most parents have expectations from their children and harbour a vision of what skills and attributes they would like to inculcate in them. In striving to ensure these goals are achieved, parents can often feel confused or unsure about the mechanisms they need to put in place to move forward. Confidence is one such attribute which has great significance in today's times. Confident children are perceived in a positive light and seen to do well in the future as self-belief is associated with navigating through challenges and finding success.

Building confidence is not about having conversations that are centred around the concept of confidence or telling children that they need to be confident. In contrast, its development involves a complex interplay of various components, skills and techniques that need to be imparted by parents.

This book is written as a guide that can be implemented in 52 weeks with a specific aspect being a focal point for each week. The different elements that have been discussed are integral to helping a child grow into a confident and self-assured adult. It is an aid for parents to keep taking the right steps towards raising confident children!

Section One

UNDERSTAND YOUR CHILD AND YOURSELF

1

BUILDING CONFIDENCE IN YOUR CHILD

Confidence, a highly valued attribute, is not simple to inculcate. Hard work and continuous efforts are key ingredients. When mixed with the right parenting approaches, these attributes help children evolve into confident adults.

From the time your child is a few months old and begins to interact with the outside world, parents begin to observe the child's behaviour towards others. Seeing them interact with people, objects or their own selves in novel ways that take you by surprise, is a constant source of fun and joy. Every child is unique. Some children take longer to engage with others, while some are comfortable from the start.

SETTING THE CONTEXT

During your child's first pre-school performance, you observe three children who are exceptionally expressive and enjoying themselves on the stage. Two others are singing in a low tone, hesitant in their actions, and another child refusing to go on the stage at all. You also notice another child standing reluctantly in front of the audience, seemingly frozen on stage.

Any of these could be your child. Though of course, you would be ecstatic to see your child be the expressive one, comfortable and confident, making the audience gush. If the case was reversed and your child could not get on the stage, or refused to sing, not coming across as happy and confident, your inner self would raise a voice of concern. Most parents in such a situation would think, 'I really need to do something to make my child more confident'. Concerned, worried and anxious, you would discuss with your spouse, just before falling asleep, 'I think I will enroll her or him in a drama or dance class. That will certainly help take care of the shyness. I am confident (s)he will do well the next time.'

PARENTS' DESIRES

Parents want children to be confident and equipped to deal with the challenges of the outside world. For this, we attempt to provide them with stimulating experiences and opportunities. However, more often than not, in our continuous efforts to stimulate our child, we become too insistent, pushy, nagging and intrusive. This usually happens because our own fears and concerns mask our ability to really understand our own children as our actions are now being directed by our emotions.

Parenting is no doubt challenging. It is not merely about instincts and experiences but is also an art that requires the application of the right skills based on a scientific understanding of what can and does work for your child. This brings us to the most important question—do we know the exact age by when a child develops self-confidence? Let's find out!

THE DEVELOPMENT OF CONFIDENCE IN CHILDREN

Self-confidence and self-esteem emerge in children by the age of four. At this age, children are able to formulate their own judgements like, how happy they are at school, who would they like to play with, or who would they like to be friendly with. By this age, their conversations are mostly about how well they recited a poem in class, or what did (s)he say in a game when playing with friends.

The focus is more on self-performance and pride, but they lack the cognitive or thinking ability to combine these aspects into a global sense of self-confidence. At this early stage, when children are very sensitive to information that comes their way, a highly critical and controlling approach by the parents towards the child's behaviour, can lead to a feeling of guilt and inadequacy in the child. In contrast, children whose parents take an approach of patiently encouraging the child's explorative behaviour and acknowledge their specific achievements, tend to develop a stronger and stable sense of self-worth and mastery over learnt skills.

From the age of six through the teen years, self-confidence takes a more organized form. A child's self-evaluations become specifically associated with academics, social and physical competence, finally translating into an overall self-image. Since children also tend to make social comparisons as they get older, self-confidence can dip in a natural progression, only to rise again with positive experiences, both comparative and otherwise. Parents who lay emphasis on the child's individual self-growth and improvement at this stage are able to foster competence and self-assuredness in their child.

BUILDING CONFIDENCE

Confidence is about a child's trust and faith in her or his own abilities. Parents play an incumbent role in nurturing self-confidence. Consistent mirroring of your child's good qualities can sow the early seeds of confidence. How you extend your trust in your child transforms into the trust that they imbibe in themselves. Making presumptions and prejudices about their behaviour can lead to the development of fragile self-belief, causing the child to look for validation externally. This can breed feelings of insecurity, especially since external feedback can be inconsistent.

During teen years and early adulthood, the ability to form meaningful relationships, physical appearance and sense of identity, contribute towards the building of self-confidence. This is reflected in an adolescent's self-belief and future goals. Adolescents seek independence in their actions and choices. Parents who give adequate space, allowing their adolescents to make their own choices, have a collaborative process in place, and provide support through the challenges they face, have children who are resilient.

CULTIVATE THE RIGHT APPROACH

As parents we oscillate between knowing what's best for our child and protecting them from failures that may come their way, and believing that it is important for them to learn through their own failures, negotiating the difficult world out there. The fact is that there is no one-size-fits-all approach that is applicable, and we need to know how much to protect or expose an adolescent to a challenge. For some adolescents, multiple failures can lead to a cycle of self-defeating thoughts. Similarly, children of overprotective parents can lack self-belief and can find it difficult to manage themselves in an adverse situation.

Through the course of this book, we will highlight the steps that will aid you in your journey of building confidence in your child.

HIGHLIGHTS

- Understand the importance of building confidence in the development of your child.
- Confidence can be built through developing adequate self-belief.
- Over- and under-stimulation of a child's self through activities can cause lack of self-trust.
- Mirror positive qualities that your child displays to help develop self-belief.
- Acknowledge your child's specific achievements without comparisons to others.
- Avoid making presumptions and demonstrate your trust in your child's abilities.

2

YOUR CHILD IS UNIQUE

We are not all peas of the same pod. There is much that is unique in us as adults and the seeds of this uniqueness are sown even before we are born. Embrace this fact, cherish it and let it help your child grow.

Parents have, in their minds, ideas of what or how they would like their children to be—their ways of thinking, of doing things, responding to situations, their traits and characteristics, and so on. What makes your child become the person (s)he is to be, is defined by many diverse factors, each of which uniquely combines with others to create a novel constitution that represents your child.

WHAT THIS MEANS

Often parents experience societal pressures and cultural forces, both consciously and unconsciously. This influences their parenting choices. This, in turn, impacts the desires a parent harbours and the images they derive about how their children should be. Everyone values a certain trait or attribute, which parents, in turn, wish for their child as well.

You notice a young child being socially adept and you wish your child was like that, or your best friend's child does exceptionally well in academics and you begin to wonder about your ward. Though it is true that often what individuals observe helps them challenge their own selves, this can also be a dual-edged sword. You need to find ways to guard yourself against relentlessly engaging in expectant behaviour, and instead, find ways to accept and maintain the understanding that your child is unique.

Given the unique elements that each child possesses from birth, combined with the environment they have, parents require a personally tailored approach that is considerate towards your child specifically. Even the construct of self-confidence develops in a manner that is unique to your child. If you have more than one child then the process can be potentially different for each of your children and it would not mean that one child is better than or worse off than the other or that either of them does not have the potential to be confident in the future.

As a corollary, this reflects and reinforces the need for parents to have a relaxed approach when it comes to helping their child develop confidence in themselves. Since no one technique or strategy is going to fit all children, who come with their own set of inherent abilities which need to be further shaped, taking a comfortable and nurturing approach is of great value and support to your child. This is in stark contrast to constant push from your side to change your child or mirror expectations that create a feeling of deficit in your child.

FACTORS THAT MAKE YOUR CHILD UNIQUE

There is much that goes on with your child besides what they are born with, which contributes towards making your child unique. Let's take a look at some of these aspects:

1. *What nature contributes:* The nature-nurture debate has occupied our minds since time immemorial. There is much that nature contributes to your child. Some things are preset and it helps to know that these elements would remain an intricate part of your child forever. In case of a disability, parents tend to blame themselves. One must understand that a child's physical growth and mental development is also one such preset element that has already been determined.
2. *The responsiveness of the parents:* Early research spoke of the

role a mother's response has in the development of the child. This includes temperament, attachment and all other aspects of a child's thinking and behaviour. With changing family structures and parental roles in society, the focus has shifted to the responsiveness of both parents to contribute to the child's development. Responsive parents, who are attuned to their child's needs, particularly during infancy, provide significant scaffolding to the child, which is crucial to the child's growth and development.

3. *The role of the family:* The family a child is born into plays a large role in shaping the way a child thinks, the habits (s)he develops, the way (s)he responds to situations, the learning the child has, the understanding the child develops about what works and what does not, the rules of society and how people tend to act and react. The family acts as a pit-stop before the child goes out into the world and an interface with the world once (s)he enters it. The family plays a significant role in buttressing a child—providing protection and support—which enables the child to go out and explore the world. This is a key element in developing confidence.

4. *Adverse life experiences:* Even for a very young child, adverse life events can have a significantly deteriorating negative effect on personal qualities like temperament and personality. As parents, providing a protective environment is crucial for a child to grow and develop into confident adolescents and adults. Children who have experiences of loss, trauma, abuse, adverse environmental conditions or any other negative event, can be significantly impacted by it. They often develop low self-concepts in addition to the negative impact on self-confidence.

5. *Experiences with friends and at school:* Beyond having responsive parents, the quality of experiences a child has in her or his early years also contribute to the beliefs they develop about themselves, and their confidence in interactions. The more positive the experiences, the higher the likelihood of the child developing into a confident child. Negative events slowly but steadily corrode the sense of self in the child. The consistent

vigilant presence of a parent through the varied phases of a child's growing years can ensure that you can help your child develop confidence.
6. *Additional skills that a child develops:* All areas of a growing child's life have a potential to impact their confidence positively or negatively. What sets your child apart is the other things that (s)he engages in. Art, music, dance, sport, play, theatre, horse riding, or any other additional skill can change the child's personality and temperament. Children who have proficiency in multiple areas of functioning, not necessarily including academic success, are seen to be confident children. This is also contingent upon the role that you play as a parent and your positive attitude towards these alternate skill areas.

UTILIZE A MULTI-FOCUSED APPROACH

Building confidence in your child comes through the application of multiple principles. The unique set of characteristics and traits that define your child can be best harnessed by capitalizing on their strengths and simultaneously working on their weaknesses. A multi-focused approach that allows parents to determine what works best is thus warranted in such a situation.

Understanding your child and recognizing that their uniqueness is the main contributing factor to selecting a methodology to work with, is going to aid you in applying the suggested strategies in this book. We would be focusing on taking a multi-pronged approach to raising a confident child!

HIGHLIGHTS

- Keep in mind the uniqueness of your child.
- Be flexible and nurturing when working with your child on building her or his confidence.
- Remember the multiple influences that contribute to making your child unique.
- Consider a multimodal approach that takes into account varied aspects of what makes your child unique.
- The same approach will not work for multiple children. So be ready to keep fine-tuning your approach.

3
ASSESS YOUR CHILD'S SELF-ESTEEM

A child's developing self is like a sapling that requires adequately balanced sun, water and pruning to grow into a tall and strong tree. Some plants bloom best under the shade, while others require more sunlight. Nurturing it with the right ingredients by sensing its needs make the roots strong enough to weather the winds and stormy days.

The foundation for your child's self-concepts is laid from the day (s)he is born. Your communication shapes it through your responses, the eye contact you make, the validation you provide and the positive strokes you give. The inherent respect that these reflect, translate into what the child mirrors in her or his behaviour.

An additional role is played by the permissiveness incorporated in the parenting approach. Allowing children to make their choices and not consistently buffering them from making their mistakes, enables the development of the ability to assess situations and make judgements. It reduces a strong dependency on the parent. There is a fine line between allowing learning through experiencing, and becoming critical or harsh with your child. A harsh approach can create a pattern of being over critical of oneself.

Many parents believe that to develop confidence and esteem in a child, the focus should be on good scholastic performance and robust social interactions along with engagement in extracurricular activities. If a child performs well in these areas, parents believe that (s)he possesses good self-esteem.

Ask yourself 'Are these factors sufficient to assess self-esteem in your child?'

DEFINING HEALTHY SELF-ESTEEM

During early childhood, children focus more on egocentric conversations, tasks and discovery, which makes it difficult to measure a young child's self-esteem. When they enter pre-teen years, their self-evaluation is based on how they perceive themselves, how peers and adults view them, their ability and openness to engage with challenges and the efficacy with which they are able to implement the tasks given to them. As they progress further, the manner in which they cope with adversities also adds to their self-esteem.

Adolescents who are aware of their strengths and limitations and possess the ability to acknowledge their own qualities, work on their weaknesses as a continuous part of the growth process. This helps them develop healthy self-esteem. It is important to understand that having robust self-esteem is not governed by perfection in all domains. An adolescent may be good in a specific skilled area and not in others, and yet have good self-esteem.

Equipped with this knowledge about oneself, the child is able to take extra steps and necessary risks to achieve goals efficiently. Simultaneously, a positive feeling and self-evaluation provides internal validation to the child and helps develop a reduced need to look for external reassurances. This further contributes to developing effective coping skills to deal with hardships in life.

RED FLAGS THAT HELP IN ASSESSING SELF-ESTEEM

As is evident, even if at the outset a child shows exceptional qualities and capabilities, it is possible for her or him to harbour a feeling of worthlessness within, reflecting in the form of low self-esteem. Some common subjective expressions that can help you assess if your child has low self-esteem include:

1. *Self-critical approach in performance:* Children often define their self-esteem based on their performance in academics or other areas of interest. These evaluations often fluctuate as the child's performance can and does vary, be it in academics or in areas like sport, music or art. The more these fluctuations impact the views that children harbour about themselves, the more it affects their self-esteem. Children who tend to be very critical with their own selves and continuously reassess themselves can be struggling with low self-esteem.
2. *Negative evaluation of self and others:* Common negative beliefs and self-defeating thought patterns like 'I am incompetent and not good enough', 'I don't think people like me', 'I know I will not be able to perform well', 'I am not good looking', 'This was just luck' are signs of a child with poor self-esteem. Further, children who engage in forms of aggression or blame and disrespect others may also experience low self-esteem.
3. *Self-doubting thought patterns:* Having a negative belief system, where there are continuous doubts about one's self, one's ways of doing things, being around others, thinking and feeling, can be a strong indicator of low self-esteem. It is usually seen that in such a circumstance a child experiences self-doubt even in areas of strength, often fluctuating and self-correcting or seeking reassurance. Avoidance of difficult situations frequently becomes a natural response.
4. *Deficits in social skills:* Making friends and sustaining the friendships can be difficult for children. Children who struggle with either making friends or maintaining their friendships can experience significant self-doubt and feelings of being different from others around them. These can contribute to low self-esteem as well.

THINGS YOU CAN DO AS A PARENT

The good news is children are not born with self-esteem but they can be given the right skills to develop a healthy one!

1. *Aid your child in broadening the areas that form a part of her or his self-definition:* Go beyond the performance-based methods of characterizing the self. Instead, help your child incorporate virtues like care towards others, honesty, loyalty and hard work as attributes of her or his self. Children often overlook the importance of such traits as contributing to a strong personality.
2. *Work with your child on her or his negative belief system:* Help your child understand the lack of any evidence to support the generalized negative self-perception they may have. Encourage them to develop more positive thought processes towards self and others.
3. *Provide your child with opportunities to acquire adequate social skills:* Help your child determine ways to initiate and maintain peer relations. Work with her or him through conversations, demonstrations and role plays. Help in building skills for being assertive, resolving conflict and making decisions which also aid the development of healthy self-esteem.

HIGHLIGHTS

- Healthy self-esteem is defined by competency, confidence, positive self-evaluation, ability to form connections and good coping skills.
- Don't be over-protective or excessively harsh as both impact self-esteem.
- Watch out for the red flags that can be an indicator of low self-esteem.
- Provide the right skills to aid in the development of healthy self-esteem.
- Actively work with your child through conversations, demonstrations and role plays to develop skills that enhance self-esteem.

4

USE ART AND PLAY TO UNDERSTAND YOUR CHILD

A child is like a blank canvas. You can fill it with colours of strength, character and kinship through your playful parenting. Enter into your child's world of imagination; undoubtedly it is a better one.

Playfulness is an innate characteristic of being a child. The playful cooing of an infant, the morning marathons with your toddler before school starts, the big hugs as they go to school, the joyful story times and the silent walks—all represent a child's natural exuberant way of connecting with parents and the environment.

Play gives a child the power to explore, engage and discover the outside world. The child's imagination acts as a tool to connect, communicate and to express her or his will and emotions. It also helps them understand a world full of adults. Through make-believe play where a child mimics the mother in a loud voice saying, 'Oh no! You have to finish your dinner,' or as (s)he plays peek-a-boo when you are getting late for office, the child is finding ways to involve the parents and engage them in her or his world.

As adults grow, they lose the essence of play, perceiving it as boring or non-relatable, though they recognize its importance for the child. Parents often wonder 'How can (s)he play with toys all day?' or 'How does (s)he have the energy to talk and share so much at the end of the day?' It can seem quite exhausting, requiring a lot of energy.

Let's take a look at why play is important and how it can help either of you bridge gaps with your child.

THE TRANSITIONS IN A CHILD'S USE OF ART AND PLAY

At each age and stage a child uses different means of art and play to communicate with parents and the outside world. An infant starts with unoccupied play, moving to solitary play and onlooker play. The child then moves to parallel play before engaging in associative play with other children, where even though they do not have a common goal, they still play together. The most complex and advanced stage of play is cooperative play, where groups are organized and there is teamwork and leadership in the play.

Similarly, it is observed that younger children most often like to use puppets or dolls, engaging in imaginary and pretend play, and even role playing with their parents. You will often be an audience when your child enacts a fight with a sibling or a friend, and says mean things, while simultaneously feeling bad and hurtful. Or the child may take it a step further to share how an adult or teacher responded to that situation. You may notice your child mimicking a doctor who gave an injection.

As a child grows older more refined forms like painting and writing enter, which enable a child to connect with deeper emotions and thoughts. These transitions happen very naturally and smoothly as the child's cognitive and emotional abilities change.

THE PURPOSE OF ART AND PLAY

Art and play have enormous utility, purpose and meaning in a child's life, her or his growth and development. These help a child articulate thoughts, ideas, feelings and emotions. (S)He learns to share and showcase inner experiences using different mediums like art, stories, puppets and role-play. Play helps a child recover from emotional distress, solve problems and develop a strong connection with parents. This creates the foundation for healthy self-concepts and instills confidence in the child.

Play gives the child a sense of power, replacing feelings of helplessness into a sense of reassurance and security through imagination and creativity. When your child learns to use colours, filling them in shapes, sometimes going outside the lines or using red instead of green for leaves, (s)he is thinking out of the box. (S)He is learning to challenge norms and develop her or his own thought process about what is and what can be. As you participate in the art and play with your child, reassuring and cajoling them to do more, you teach your child to trust her or his own self and explore unhindered.

The creative process which is inherent in art and play enables the development of thinking, problem-solving and decision-making skills, which are core life skills for sustenance of health and well-being.

TRANSFORMING PARENTING MOMENTS THROUGH PLAYFULNESS

Parenting, that integrates and utilizes the advantages that art and play can provide, has the power to enrich the parent-child relationship, besides helping you raise a confident child. Let's look at a scenario where your child is resisting taking a bath in the morning, before school. As days go by, even your tender prodding turns into a screaming-crying match, making it frustrating for both of you. As things continue, both of you feel stuck and powerless. A harsh remark may also be used, which makes your child feel further distressed.

Now there are two alternatives in front of you—to continue in the same vein, or to use play in resolving this daily nightmarish ritual. If you continue in the same way, the problem only persists. Now try using play. Imagine, as your child enters the bath, you playfully turn the water into a monster which is showering weapons. You challenge your child that if (s)he wants to win and beat the monster, then the only way is to dance under the shower. You change your tone, imitating a monster, raising your voice in a playful manner, making the expressions of a monster to engage your child and ease the tension associated with the situation currently. Now, your child responds, taking the first tentative step under the water, and then joining you in a dance as you both playfully wade through the situation.

Play helps you reconnect with your child when it is lost during tense situations. The moment anger and frustration is replaced by fun, love, care and connect, you transform a difficult moment. You may do it through play, art, stories, drama, music, songs or any other creative mechanism.

PLAY FOSTERS CONFIDENCE

A child engages in play because it is fun, but that does not dissociate it from the development of confidence. As a child explores the environment, moves around in a space, engages in pretend play, pushes the boundaries to be imaginative and creative, (s)he gains confidence. Your presence in your child's playful moments helps her or him be more exploratory, which pushes towards developing independence. As you gently expand the area of play for your child, or suggest other ways in which (s)he can play with the same paints or blocks, the child grows in confidence. Your enthusiastic participation and responsiveness to your child's play, communicates that you value and believe what your child is doing. Remember to not push or create too many structures which inhibits your child from engaging in free play.

HIGHLIGHTS

- A child's world involves playfulness which is their way of communication and articulation.
- Art and play, in their varied forms, provide an alternate medium to connect.
- Enter your child's world by being involved in her or his art and play.
- Playful parenting helps diffuse tense situations into playful moments.
- Playfulness embraces and enhances a child's self-concepts instilling confidence and competence.

5

LET YOUR CHILD BE AN EXPLORER

By exploring through my hands, eyes and mind,
I will discover the world within.
Let me be an explorer,
To embark on my journey of life.

From the day children are born and begin to make sense of the surroundings, they realize that there is so much more to explore around them. They explore the sounds like that of a fallen spoon, the rattle and beating of hands on the table. They also discover the various tastes of food items and even those that are non-edible items! They feel the texture of objects, recognizing them as hard, soft, rough or prickly. They seek and admire the beauty around them and learn to make connections. Innately, children are curious and inquisitive, continuously trying to know more.

Usually at an early age, parents let children crawl, run, touch, throw and feel things as a part of their play. They recognize the developmental impacts of such exploratory behaviour. As they grow older it becomes difficult to provide the same level of freedom, as rules and expectations start coming into the picture. A parent worries, expresses concern, warns and withholds the child from continuously experimenting, to ensure safety, as well as to teach good behaviour. It becomes difficult to just let the child be. And to preserve your energy you stop them with 'No, No! You are not supposed to touch that bowl!', 'Please stay away from the bucket!' or 'Can you hurry up and walk home?'

However, it is through this innate characteristic that children learn and thrive. It is essential to understand the role that curiosity plays in shaping a child's inner self. Learning through self-discovery enhances knowledge about the environment and their own selves. This continuous conscious relation between the inner and outer world, promotes greater self-awareness, connection and confidence.

SELF-DISCOVERY AND EXPLORATION CRITICAL TO SELF-GROWTH

When engaging in the process of self-discovery, a child is exploring the moment. Her or his focused attention to discover the world through sensory processing, transforms the playful manipulation of the object into a learning experience. A child isn't always able to find and use words or language to express what was seen or learnt. Parents play a crucial role in helping the child acquire the necessary vocabulary by generating associations between what (s)he sees or feels and the words. For instance you state, 'This is a blanket and you seem to like how soft this is,' to help your child define why (s)he likes an object.

Learning happens when the child directly interacts with the environment and this is facilitated by the parent. As children grow, their inquisitiveness takes the form of a 'tell me why' phase. Your child attacks you with lots of questions like 'Why is this hot?' 'Why do we have to brush everyday?' or 'Why do I have to drink milk daily?' It can be a frustrating, hair-pulling experience at times. Yet, your patient engagement in their curious world can harness their ability to keep seeking answers either with your assistance or using other means to generate solutions.

Children do need to be nudged to become active learners. Parents can play the role of active observers by not reflexively stopping a child from exploring the object at hand, patiently waiting before formulating an opinion about your agreement to the situation. Nevertheless, even if you end up impulsively refusing, only to later realize that you could have avoided saying a no, you can always rescue the situation with 'Well on second thought, it might be a good idea if we both see what to do with this!' You can further enhance your child's visual and sensory learning by using rich language and an encouraging tone. Ask your child additional questions like 'What are you seeing? Do you see its colour? What shape do you think it is? Would you like to taste it?'

Always keep in mind that children have a short but sharp attention span. As they focus on an object, they grasp and store in their memory, everything that they understand about it.

MAINTAIN THE MOTIVATION TO EXPLORE

To preserve a child's self-motivation to acquire knowledge, it is imperative to nurture the skill of self-exploration and learning. A child's mind is a clean slate, and if everything is written on it by a parent or an adult through the medium of conventional methods of transmitting knowledge and values to children, it restricts their potential to grow into independent beings with unique thoughts and views. It is more relevant for parents to be facilitators, adding value to the child's learning process by engaging in their play and enhancing their creative thinking and perceptual understanding.

It is a known fact that children develop stronger instincts through self-exploration. They are able to sense their inner needs and potential threats in the environment better through this process. They also learn to make independent choices and understand the limitations of their abilities to solve problems and explore. Undoubtedly, children require parental monitoring and you need to put measures in place to ensure safety and security. However, letting the child take some calculated risks is important for the abilities to develop further. Such an approach helps the child develop better mechanisms to protect the self and also keeps them motivated to learn and do more.

MAKE YOUR CHILD AN EXPLORER FOR LIFE

It is well-known that play is a natural way for children to discover and learn while having fun. It helps to find ways to sustain this playful process of self-learning in children for life. A parent needs to consciously avoid imparting excessive knowledge, instead of helping the child learn through experiences and play. For children to be motivated learners, parents can play a crucial role by being cognizant of their approach.

1. *Create a free space for self-exploration:* To foster curiosity in your child, give your child a free space to play and discover. Refrain from using phrases like 'Don't spill again', 'Don't open that box, I had cleaned it just yesterday', 'That's not for you to play with. Stay away' that curb the child's need to explore. Make sure you keep away the things that you don't want your child to touch. As long as the child is under your supervision and away from any potential harm, let the child enjoy the moment. Be a part of her or his play by joining in the fun. Ask 'Do you want to know what this is? Come I will show you' or say, 'You can surely play with it, just be careful'.
2. *Be an active observer:* Observe your child carefully while at play to see how (s)he handles the objects, what are the things that are of interest to her or him, and how does (s)he solve problems. Don't intervene immediately to offer help or support. Give your child ample time to play mindfully with the object. Facilitate learning by providing support when (s)he feels stuck by giving new information and knowledge about the object being explored.
3. *Know when to back off:* When the child is engaged in a task requiring her or him to analyse and solve problems, it is tempting for parents to give instructions or offer help without being asked for. Parents can get impatient or want to prevent a mistake. So they might say something like, 'No that's not how you do it, I will tell you'. Children of parents who let them get behind the steering wheel and don't hover around or create pressures on them, develop better competence. They have a higher sense of awareness of what they can or cannot do well.
4. *Provide exposure to exploratory activities:* Introduce your child to books, puzzles, mazes and games like treasure hunt. These are a great way to promote curiosity, exploration skills and problem-solving. It also develops enthusiasm in your child to work on

challenges and accomplish tasks in a fun, exploratory way.
5. *Tap into their interests:* By encouraging a child to pursue interests, even if they may seem quite unique like card collections or eraser collections, you are keeping the child's curiosity and desire to learn, alive. Exploring an area of interest maintains the child's need to discover more in relation to that interest.

LET GO OF YOUR FEARS

To let your child explore freely you need to let go of your own fears, worries and anxieties. A parent's fears can prevent the child from exerting her or his will across different situations. It may not be possible for you to let go of all fears instantaneously, but being aware of what stops you inhibits the ease with which you can let your child explore.

A heightened state of awareness can create the space for conscious withdrawal of the boundaries you may erect around your child out of fear. Realistic appraisal of the possibility of hurt or harm as your child continues to explore the environment, people, relationships, abilities and the self, is critical to the freedom (s)he can have in knowing and learning more.

HIGHLIGHTS

- Children are innately curious beings.
- From an early age, children embark on a journey of self-exploration through play.
- Promote self-discovery as an active learning approach in children for self-growth.
- Acquiring knowledge through self-exploration makes your child a motivated learner.
- Act as an active observer and facilitator, nudging your child to grow and learn to build competence and confidence.

6

KNOW YOUR PARENTING STYLE

Parenting is the journey to being a better human, a journey that involves unconditional love, care and concern, by nurturing a child into becoming a healthy member of the society.

Like any journey, parenting is subsumed by its own ups and downs. Questions about how much to worry, how much to love, how much to hold and when and where to withdraw your hand, continuously plague a parent. Each time you share your experience or worry with a friend, parent or group, you get multiple views, opinions and stories of a better way for parenting your child. But how do we define what the best parenting approach is.

Previously, we spoke about every child being unique and the various factors that contribute to form a child's self. The next question for us to answer is, 'If the interaction between nature and nurture is bound to shape my child, how do I measure that my parenting approach is suiting my child's needs?' As complex as it may seem, we shall explore the various dimensions of parenting, and the effects these can have on your child.

UNDERSTAND YOURSELF AS A PARENT

It is a known psychological fact that children learn most through observation, and during this process they introject elements of their parents' personality. Awareness of your thought process, behaviour and reactions in a given circumstance can help you understand who you are as a parent and how it contributes to your child's developing personality and temperament.

The Authoritarian Parent

Many of us have been exposed to an approach where parents make decisions for their children with expectations of strict adherence to rules and clearly defined accepted ways of behaving. This is usually accompanied by the use of punishment, in the belief that it teaches children to behave well. In this style of parenting, parents believe that right and wrong is structured and clearly demarcated, leaving no ambiguity for the child. 'Do as I say because I know what is best for you!' best represents this style.

The Permissive Parent

This is an alternative approach where children are given minimum to no rules and the child is left to her or his devices. This kind of permissiveness provides very limited boundaries and definitions to the child. 'Do what you deem as correct and make your own choices' best represents this style of parenting.

The Authoritative Parent

This is based on a balanced approach, which provides children the opportunity to explore their environment, while parents simultaneously provide boundaries, define what is okay and what is not, and gently guide the child in the right direction, while continuously being responsive to the child's needs—physical, emotional and psychological. This style of parenting provides children the scaffolding and the right environment where expectations are balanced by the provision of support and understanding. 'Make your choices and remember I am here to support you, but also remember there are things which you know are not okay for us as a family' best represents this style of parenting.

Helicopter Parents—The New-Age Phenomenon

We also see around us a version of parenting that is very emotionally driven. Guilt forms the foundation of this style of parenting, where either one or both the parents use guilt as a tradeoff to obtain the desired behaviour from the child. An anxious parent can often become over-involved, taking excess responsibility for children's experiences, particularly their successes and failures, almost making the child feel smothered. Helicopter or hovering parenting, where over-indulgence is the underlying theme on account of competitive pressures, is gaining prominence over the last few decades. This can result in lowering of confidence and self-esteem, poorly developed coping skills as well as increased anxiety amongst children. Despite being a well-informed parent, the pressure to be involved and the need to facilitate everything, is the basis of this intrusive approach.

AGE-APPROPRIATE PARENTING MODIFICATIONS

Growth is a continuous process. It necessitates the need to change oneself as a parent, as your child attains her or his milestones. Being an emotionally available and responsive parent from infancy to early childhood is imperative. However, during the elementary school years, parents can diverge in their ways of parenting. Parenting styles can focus on and give importance to multiple aspects like discipline or education, responsiveness or sensitivity or general welfare and protection. How a parent transitions between parenting styles and techniques, is critical for the smooth transitions of a growing child, and this contributes to the development of her or his self, personality and overall well-being.

The failure of a parent in adapting to changes can affect the parent-child relationship adversely, particularly in the teen or adolescent years. Rigidity in the parenting approach can affect how a child's self is nurtured. Both the child and the outside environment are variables contributing towards change and growth. Parenting, as the third variable, also requires to be tempered. When all interacting factors are in sync with each other, there is space for healthy and complete growth of your child.

PARENTING ATTRIBUTES THAT LEAD TO HIGH CONFIDENCE

No singular rule can be put in place when it comes to choosing a parenting style for your child. The ability to have a flexible approach is key. Several research studies demonstrate that a parenting approach, which gives the child space to explore, discover and express themselves with reciprocal engagement by the parent, contributes to the development of high self-confidence in children. Being emotionally responsive during infancy and then being firm, yet providing increasing exposure for unstructured exploration in the preschool years, provides a strong foundation for the child to develop confidence.

During the elementary years, a stable environment that permits age appropriate autonomy, decision-making and problem-solving enhances confidence. In the adolescent years, as the teen goes through a process of forming her or his identity and experiences low esteem, a focus on building social and emotional health of your child would help build better resilience. Respecting your adolescent's feelings and struggles and providing them with the right skills to effectively deal with emotional changes as well as to maintain social relationships, will help them regain their confidence. In further sections of the book, we will explore the steps towards building high levels of confidence in your child.

HIGHLIGHTS

- Recognize your parenting style.
- Refrain from using authoritarian or emotional parenting approaches characterized by coercion, guilt and lack of autonomy.
- Avoid resisting transitions in your parenting style.
- Being a self-aware parent is the key to being a healthy parent.
- Provide space to explore, be emotionally responsive, show respect and provide skills to your child.

7

FACTORS INFLUENCING YOUR PARENTING STYLE

There are varied influences interacting with each other in a dynamic manner, which shape us to become who we are as individuals and also who we are in the multiple roles we play in our lives—friend, partner, family member, colleague and even a parent.

Parenting is not an attribute or skill set that people are born with. It is imbibed and integrated into our self-system, nurtured and developed within our beings, and shaped by varied experiences. Given the complex interplay of factors that is responsible in the ultimate style of one's parenting, it helps to understand these elements.

An accurate and comprehensive knowledge of the factors influencing parenting styles enables the process of situating the person within diverse contexts from which (s)he comes. It also helps to understand how doing things in certain patterns has emerged. These methodologies or styles of parenting can be significantly divergent from people around, from what has been read in books or seen in media. Consequently, this also enhances the ability to change and further shape the existing style of parenting.

THE FACTORS INVOLVED IN CREATING PARENTING STYLES

It would be easy to presume that parenting is innate and that individuals usually have a way of being a parent and responding to a child. Not many would give a second thought to the way they are as a parent, to assess and evaluate where these patterns may emanate from. Let's take a look at some of the elements that are intricately involved and implicated in the development of an individual's parenting style.

1. *The parenting style adopted by your family:* Your family has a strong influence on your parenting style. What you observed growing up, as the most common method of parenting, disciplining, shaping behaviour, bringing in values and creating learning experiences, can either be the exact manner of your parenting, or it may push you to go in the opposite direction. Your beliefs and feelings about how you were parented strongly penetrate into your incorporated parenting style. Often people choose to tread somewhere in between, employing those elements which they thought worked best, while eliminating or substituting others, which they did not appreciate or felt were detrimental and unhelpful.

2. *Your attachment style, personality and temperament:* The predominant manner in which you form attachments, and your temperament, impresses upon the nature of your parenting style. Parents who tend to have a responsive manner of attachment, harbour a sense of security and safety in their children, enabling the child's exploration of the environment in an assured manner. Parents who tend to be less consistently responsive to their child, do not create a predictable environment, often leaving the child confused. Those parents who tend to be distant in their manner of attachment have a parenting style which may reflect strictness, demanding close adherence to rules and reduced emotional responsiveness to the needs of the child.

3. *Your perceptions of what is acceptable in your peer group:* Frequently, the choices people make are determined by the extent to which they believe these choices would be acknowledged, validated and accepted by their peers. The approach you take towards the process of parenting is one such area that is strongly influenced by the social fabric you

are a part of. The acceptable standards and methodologies of parenting get discussed in groups, comparisons may be drawn and emphasis laid on doing things a certain way. This too becomes a mechanism that influences your parenting style.

4. *The culture to which you belong:* Culture, despite the changing world-views that individuals have, pose a significant influence on the approach you adopt to parenting. For instance, in India it is culturally appropriate and at times even mandated, to leave children under the watchful eye of their grandparents or other responsible adults, instead of enrolling a child in a crèche or daycare. These systems are changing and more people are agreeable to the idea of their child going to daycare or a crèche. This phenomenon is also a reflection of the change that urban Indian society is going through.

5. *Your perception of environmental threat:* The changes that surround you within the social environment play a determining role in your parenting approach. Perceptions about the safety of your environment contribute to the extent of your control on your child's movements, the activities (s)he is involved in, as well as the people your child chooses to associate with. This modern-day element is gaining much prominence in the mind of parents as they choose their methods of parenting.

BRING FLEXIBILITY IN YOUR PARENTING STYLE

Parenting styles are not cast in iron. They are malleable and can transform if you decide to put your mind to it. To be flexible in your approach, you must begin with understanding yourself. The more you know about your own self, the more mindful you can be to your parenting style. Making parenting a more conscious process, instead of just going with the flow, requires awareness of your strengths, your weaknesses, your triggers, ways of responding, temperament, your mindset and mood states.

You need to work towards being more flexible in your parenting. As your child grows through various stages of life, your flexibility will ensure a healthy growth, both emotionally and psychologically.

It will give your child numerous opportunities to evolve her or his sense of self and confidence, instead of being overwhelmed and feeling bogged down by all that life has to offer.

HIGHLIGHTS

- There is much that goes into making you into the parent you are.
- Parenting styles are not fixed. You can be flexible in your parenting approach.
- Modifying your parenting style as your child grows will enhance their sense of self and confidence.
- Your personal characteristics like temperament, personality, ways of attaching, thinking and feeling, contribute to your parenting style.
- No two people, despite their innumerable similarities or experiences, can have the same parenting approach.

Section Two

THE GUIDE TO GOOD COMMUNICATION

8

THE ROLE OF YOUR NON-VERBALS

I mirror you
Your loving gaze, your sparkling smile,
your tickling touch, your cuddly hug.
I understand you
Your silent voice, your lost eyes,
your absent touch, your tender love.

Non-verbal communication lays the foundation for a healthy parent-child attachment. Your gaze, eye contact, smile, and speaking 'motherese' as you interact with your child, are all gestures that help in forming a strong connection between both of you.

Non-verbal communication is a two-way interaction process that also elucidates how verbal communication can be and is interpreted. Parental mirroring of the non-verbal forms of communication is a crucial starting point for the development of confidence in later years as it expresses acknowledgment and admiration.

CONNECTING BEYOND WORDS

Parents are naturally attuned to the needs and desires of their child, often not requiring words to understand. Your toddler may have pooped in the diaper, your pre-schooler may avoid meeting your gaze after a mischievous act, or your adolescent would walk straight into her or his room upon returning from school after scoring low grades—their expressions say it all. Within a split second your instinct tells you something is amiss and you now attempt to determine your next step.

Children too gauge parents' mood from their posture, facial expressions and their gaze. All you have to do is say, 'Come on in, I need to talk to you...,' and (s)he infers from your tone and body language that something is off and this may not be an easy conversation.

Children learn to articulate their emotions through non-verbal means of communication. A warm and loving gesture of a parent arouses positive emotions towards self and others, which makes the child feel secure; whereas, a frown or harsh tones evoke negative emotions like anger, fear or frustration. Helping your child learn the skill to interpret non-verbal gestures, while also attending to effective verbal communication, teaches your child social skills that help her or him form strong relations.

Let's look at the ways in which you can effectively connect with your child through non-verbal means.

1. *Engaging eye contact:* Eye contact plays a significant role in a child's normal development. Communication and connection improve when you speak with your child while maintaining good eye contact. A loving glance from you makes your child feel more closely connected and accepted. It mirrors a healthy self-image to the child and is a sign of encouragement, which acts as a positive reinforcement. Conversely, a stern gaze signals to the child to back off and stop doing what (s)he may be doing at the time.

   Making good eye contact by crouching down to your child's height, shows full attention and focus to the child. Take the example of your young pre-schooler who has been running around making a mess at home. Calling out and screaming several times may not stop her or him, but the moment you go closer, look into her or his eyes and say, 'Let's stop this right away and clear the mess!', (s)he shows an immediate shift in behaviour. As children grow older, listening becomes increasingly about hearing through your eyes and ears, and less about the words you use. An engaged eye contact certainly leads to an empathetic connection.

2. *Facial expressions:* It's your child's first day at school and you wait to see the expression on her or his face. Children too learn to decipher various emotions—sadness, happiness, frustration, confusion, fear, disappointment—through the expressions on the adult's face. Non-verbal cues become the primary mechanism for understanding and interpreting feelings. Communicating your thoughts and feelings to your child using the appropriate facial expressions, enhances relatability and social learning.

3. *Healing touch:* An unconditional hug is the most comforting way to express warmth and love for your child. A soft, soothing touch has the power to heal any emotional distress that the child may experience. A child who is upset can often evoke feelings of helplessness, anger and frustration, while you struggle to understand what is going on. You would want to avoid any form of touch in such a situation as you think it can make your child feel uneasy, restless or discomforted. However, as you gently stroke your child's back or head when such a situation arises, it can make your child feel calmer and secure. It is important to remember that parental touch grooms an empathetic self for the child.

4. *Welcoming body language:* Your body speaks louder than words. Much can be inferred from body language, and thus, we often utilize it to formulate our first impression of a person. Our posture represents how we feel about ourselves. An upright posture conveys an assertive and confident bearing, whereas a slouching posture accompanied by slow movements is often interpreted to represent lack of confidence.

Our body language changes based on what we are communicating to our child. Widely stretching your arms while bending forward slightly, shows willingness for closeness, whereas turning your back or turning sideways expresses discontent. While talking to young children, maintaining a posture that communicates closeness by leaning towards them is helpful. During their teen years, they look for space and an open interaction. Sitting adjacent to your child and using hand movements gives the right tonality to the conversation. Some of the most intimate and empathetic conversations can happen with your adolescent over a walk or while you play a game or sport.

HIGHLIGHTS

- Non-verbal communication is a core ingredient in communication.
- It enriches the quality of the parent-child interaction and forms the basis for connectedness.
- Children learn to mirror parental non-verbal cues which translates into how they relate to the social world.
- A good mix of eye contact, facial expressions, touch and body language makes for effective and empathetic communication with a child.
- Use of non-verbal aspects of communication by parents enhances learning of social skills and confident interactions in the social world.

9

PICK YOUR BATTLES— CHOOSE YOUR NOES!

The challenge of parenting lies in making the right choices. And often the choice is not about what you need to do but about what you want your child to not do.

Parenting involves making numerous, very complex decisions. Choosing what to tell your children, how to share information with them, deciding on what they need, when to agree with them and when to put your foot down is complicated. Parents often vacillate, going back and forth in their mind and in their interactions and responses to their children, as they struggle to make and stick to choices.

This can make it difficult to maintain an atmosphere of seriousness when you decide to say a 'no' or can potentially create a situation where your child determines ways to push you when (s)he sees you perplexed and in a quandary. These situations necessitate a need to pick your battles and effectively choose when you are going to say a no.

MAKING A CHOICE

The choices you have to make don't need to bear relation to the more difficult or, the so-called bigger things in life. Simple things like which clothes to dress your child in or which toys to purchase can also assume monumental proportions in a parent's life. Take for instance the time when you had to choose the first toy for your child. Besides the sheer number of options available there would have been many other considerations to evaluate—what is age appropriate, what is going to facilitate development, is it something that everyone purchases, should I be going beyond what I think everyone is purchasing?—these and many more questions would make this seemingly easy choice very difficult.

Despite your expertise and experience as an individual and a professional, you might feel that the choices and decisions that you face as a parent can unravel you. It is possible that people around you—friends, colleagues or family—who may or may not have been through the same phase, can find it difficult to relate to your experience. Nevertheless, this is important for you, as a seemingly simple decision can involve a complex thinking process that needs an intricate methodology for reaching your conclusions, as you don't want to err in any way as a parent.

Consistently having to make these choices can create confusion. Faced with these situations you can become vulnerable to going back and forth between what you think you should do and whether you should do it or not.

TOO MANY 'NOES'

Plagued by the continuous decisions that you need to make, and worried about making the wrong choices, you can become someone for whom 'no' is the most frequent response. The question is 'What is the impact frequently refusing things or permissions can have on your child?'

A young child is fairly tolerant of continued refusal. It seems to not necessarily bother her or him at first, eliciting no significant reaction. Your child is too young to have a say, or evaluate the refusals. However, as (s)he begins to talk and move around, this can become detrimental to development, as it impacts the space you give your child to do things, explore the environment, make their mistakes and learn from them.

The child, through her or his initiative, attempts to create novel ways in which (s)he can then do things or get what (s)he wants. The resultant situation is one that often involves outbursts, tantrums, nagging and pushing, banging doors, crying or sulking and complaining to others like your spouse or grandparents. As the child gets older, particularly in the adolescent years, (s)he can start making nasty comments, indicating towards feeling like you don't care or listen.

As an alternative, your child can also move towards the other end of the spectrum where (s)he becomes extremely quiet and withdrawn. (S)He, in this scenario, may not develop a robust personality, and hesitation can become a prominent aspect of who they are. There is an awkwardness and evident discomfort surrounding their persona. The end result is presence of weak self-concepts which impact the child's confidence and belief system.

LEARNING THROUGH OBSERVATIONS

As the child is moving through these diverse experiences with you and finding new ways of negotiating, (s)he is also continuously observing you. There is a vigilant eye directed towards determining an approach that leads to a favourable result.

When your child observes that a particular approach is working, it starts becoming a pattern. You might notice that when you refuse to buy your child a toy, (s)he runs to your spouse stating (s)he wants it. This happened because while you might have been delaying it for a while, from past experiences (s)he has realized that your spouse would give in more easily. And true to expectations, your spouse does turn around and tells you to buy the toy that (s)he wants. You are now stuck because you have a different thought process, but over the years your child has figured what method can get her or him what (s)he wants.

There are two aspects that get highlighted in this entire exchange. One element is the lack of concordance between you and your spouse. The other aspect is the delay and vacillation that was happening at your end. If your thought was to say a 'no', then a clear communication from your end the very first time, was the ideal response. Also, once you have said 'no', you would need to inform your spouse of the exchange so that (s)he would also maintain the same stance. Moreover, it is important to have your rationale in place and stick to your position despite all tactics your child may indulge in.

Saying a 'no' requires a clear thought process on the reason for your refusal, as well as sticking to your decision. If you were to change your stance, your child learns to persist in the same behaviour that led to a change in your decision the first time.

WRAPPING UP

Your worries as a parent are legitimate. Mistakes are important in shaping the way you engage in the parenting process. However, keeping a track of your worries to ensure that they do not overwhelm you or begin to restrain and restrict your child is integral to effective parenting. This has intricate linkages to the development of confidence in your child at a later stage, as (s)he learns to understand people, negotiate situations, manage disappointments and alter their needs and behaviour in accordance with the environment.

HIGHLIGHTS

- A flexible approach does not mean vacillating in your decision-making as a parent.
- Choose wisely when you want to say a no.
- Your partner and you should maintain the same stance when you refuse your child.
- Think through your decision to make sure you don't have to change your choice later.
- Children learn through observation; shifting your decision due to a behavioural infraction will create a faulty behavioural pattern.

10

CREATE SPACE FOR SELF-EXPRESSION

The key to success involves the ability to express.
The space for expression is created through your interactions.
Be attentive and find ways that will make your child share.

A key role played by a parent involves working on and enhancing your child's ability to express and share. You would hear of instances where a child beautifully expressed herself or himself while narrating what happened in school or telling a story, and it was such a proud moment for them. At such moments you might wonder, 'How do I ensure that my child is expressive and speaks and shares her or his experiences with me and others?'

The ability to express with ease is associated with the confidence a child possesses. We know such children to be self-assured, finding it easier to negotiate situations. They make choices and take decisions and often assume leadership roles in their play groups and at school. Such children are also attuned to their own feelings. It makes it easier for them to state what they may or may not like. The clarity they reflect is mirrored in their sense of self, and belief within themselves.

HOME—THE FIRST PLACE FOR SELF-EXPRESSION

Home is the first place where children can find their space for self-expression. Encouraged by your words, expressions, body language and presence around them, children learn to explore the environment, knowing that you are there to tackle a problem, and extend support, if the need arises. This exploration of the environment at home is the first step that your child takes towards building the skills for self-expression.

Experiencing your joyous and enthusiastic reactions each time your child shares something, verbalizes their actions, thoughts and feelings, prompts her or him to express more. It is seen that the creation and provision of unstructured time and space, where there are no rules, and anything can exist, works best for children. Supported by such an environment, your child is able to test the limits of the surroundings, of the self and those of others as well. This develops an understanding of what can and cannot be done or is acceptable in a situation.

As you sit down to play with your child surrounded by paper, colours, crayons and clay, let your child choose what (s)he wants to do. Try not to make suggestions or indicate towards which object to use. Smile when (s)he picks an object and encourage her or him to go ahead and do anything that comes to mind, saying, 'Do what you would like. It can be anything.' If (s)he draws a flower don't ask the name of the object or correct the use of colours, instead state, 'That looks wonderful. I really like how you are drawing here.'

Such simple exchanges between a parent and child are crucial to the development of self-expression and the ultimate development of self-belief and confidence.

THE ROLE OF REINFORCEMENT

Your child receives reinforcement from you in multiple forms. Imagine a situation where your child gets excited when (s)he sees a dog and interrupts you saying, 'Look there's a doggy there. I want to go and play.' You were talking to a neighbour, so you give a stern look. (S)He realizes something is wrong and hesitates to repeat the statement. However, when you have finished speaking with your neighbour, you approach your child and ask lovingly 'What was it? You know I was speaking with someone and we have talked about how it's not nice to interrupt when I am talking to someone, unless it's an emergency.' Now, (s)he learns that her or his expression has value and there is a space for it. More importantly, (s)he also learns that (s)he needs to time it and not override someone else when they are speaking.

Each time you respond with a positive affirmation, a nod or a smile, to your child's verbalization, (s)he learns to value it as well. Your inability to attend to your child's utterances can affect the frequency with which (s)he shares experiences and situations at a later point in time. This can also sow the seeds of a negative belief system in later years, where the child can feel that it is not okay to express thoughts or feelings or that their expressions are not valued. This can further contribute towards the erosion of your child's self-confidence.

It is important to keep in mind that a singular incident is never responsible for a large-scale positive or negative impact. The consistency in patterns of responding is responsible for the development of any type of belief system in a child.

THE CONTRIBUTION OF LANGUAGE

Language—its understanding, interpretation and utilization—plays a key role in enhancing self-expression. The more your child develops knowledge and understanding of both verbal and non-verbal language, the more effective (s)he becomes in self-expression. As a parent, you play a pivotal role in enabling the acquisition and growth of the linguistic and non-verbal skills of your child.

Reading to your child, which parents usually initiate when the child is an infant, enables the acquisition of language. As your child's vocabulary expands and (s)he begins to understand the meaning of what others say, (s)he also expands on the capacity for self-expression. As you read stories that involve animals and other characters you teach your child about feelings and emotions, managing situations, coping with difficulties and understanding others. Equipped with these skills children begin to understand intention and emotion that can be conveyed through the use of language. It enhances your child's understanding of how situations can be managed. Through your words and observing the pictures in books your child learns to express more.

In situations where you ask for more information, showing a genuine interest in what your child is saying, (s)he expresses more. You reach the bus stop to pick your child. (S)He climbs off the bus and comes running to you. You start your walk back home and ask, 'How was your day today?' (S)he promptly turns around and excitedly tells you about how the teacher asked her or him to erase the blackboard today. A seemingly small event, but it has your child all excited. You play along and share the enthusiasm. You excitedly ask further 'Did you manage to reach the top of the blackboard?' Your genuine interest in what (s)he is sharing encourages her or him further and (s)he goes on to say, 'I could not reach the top. So miss had to get out a chair. I stood on the chair. And then I rubbed the blackboard!'

Role-playing, and modelling appropriate ways of responding, allow your young child to understand how to handle different situations which (s)he may find difficult, and also enhance her or his self-expression.

As children grow older, their expanding vocabulary facilitates the sharing of more complex ideas, feelings and thoughts, often reflecting an understanding of others. The reciprocity that gets built into language, enables the development of sensitivity and empathy, a key skill in your child's development which is crucial for confidence.

SHAPING OF CONFIDENCE THROUGH SELF-EXPRESSION

The impact that a child's expressions can have on confidence is enormous. As is evident, there is an intricate link and reciprocity between your child's expressiveness and your responsiveness. Both need to move hand-in-hand for the development and maintenance of confidence. Finding multiple avenues through which your child can express experiences, thoughts and feelings can at times be a challenge. Consistent effort from you to find mediums to stay engaged and provide praise, appreciation and reinforcement when your child is expressive is helpful in the development of confidence as well.

HIGHLIGHTS

- Confidence is intricately linked to your child's ability to express and share.
- You play an enormous role in shaping how much and how well your child can be expressive.
- The home is the first place where a child can be expressive. Provide unstructured, free space for your child to express.
- Praise, appreciation and reinforcement of the instances when your child shares and expresses encourages her or him to be more expressive.
- Self-expression creates the space for understanding self and others and building of empathy as well.

11

HONE YOUR LISTENING SKILLS

I hear you when I see you.
I feel you when I think of you.
You remain in the deepest space within me.
Always present even when you're not around me.

Listening is an exhaustive exercise. It can drain you of your energy and leave you feeling fatigued. At the end of a hectic work day, you may not want to hear anyone speak. Yet, you need to find the energy to sit down and listen as soon as you get home and your child comes running towards you, excited to see you and eager to share the day with you.

Being a parent is not easy and one of the biggest challenges you will face is to stay connected with your child, utilizing and applying your listening skills, as (s)he moves through the different stages of life. Through your attentive and involved listening, you can create a caring relationship which communicates to your child that you are there and available to support, while you provide the space to be her or his true self so (s)he can grow to be responsible, resilient and confident in the future.

LISTENING IS A SKILL

It might come as a surprise to most parents, but listening is a skill that needs to be nurtured and developed. People are usually habituated to and have a strong need for expressing themselves and sharing what they think and feel. This is not always complemented by a corresponding desire to be a listener who is keenly interested in knowing what is going on with another person.

Listening requires a vastly different skill set to be proficient at it. It is important to know and understand that if you are a good listener in your parenting role, you can possess the power to influence and shape your child's life, her or his performance at school, in social situations, the relationships with peers, belief in the self, attitude towards others, resilience as well as confidence. These key skills which are critical to success in later years are harnessed in large part by the carefully curated and applied attentiveness and listening that you accord to the conversations your child has with you.

Imagine a situation where you are watching the news. An anchor you closely follow is discussing and debating with experts on a topic of great interest to you. At a crucial point in the debate, your child walks up to you and starts talking about the clay animal (s)he just made. (S)He wants to tell you all about what (s)he has made, what it can do and how (s)he plans to play with it. You have the option to stay distracted while you partially try to keep an eye on what is going on in the debate or you could entirely shift your attention to your child.

Many such choices face you as a parent time and again as you strive to strike a balance between what you may want and what your child may like to do. In such situations the behaviour and listening skills that you model are going to shape the way in which your child is going to inculcate them as well. If you want your child to be a good listener, paying heed to what is being shared and communicated, you too need to be a good listener and demonstrate effectively important listening skills through your actions and interactions.

KEY INGREDIENTS TO BE A GOOD LISTENER

Many critical elements combined with each other make you a good listener. It requires you to be mindful of a few things that are important to the development of confidence and self-belief in your child.

1. *Listening is more than just hearing:* For listening to be an effective tool it requires that you process what is being said and be responsive towards it. If your child is talking to you and you are simply nodding while it is evident that you are distracted by a thought, if not an activity, it is not helpful. Listening effectively necessitates that you be actually present during the course of the conversation, which is possible by observation of your non-verbal behaviour and reactions besides how you respond verbally to the conversation.
2. *The eye contact you maintain matters:* A key component of what makes someone a good listener is their ability to maintain eye contact. This allows you to observe the changes your child is experiencing in their feelings and reactions to what (s)he is speaking about. It enables better inference of feelings and emotions, and communicates to your child that it matters to you that (s)he is choosing to share something, regardless of how trivial it may seem in the larger scheme of things.
3. *Get down to the level of your child:* It helps if you consciously make an effort to bend down to the level of your child. Having a similar height to operate from enables the maintaining of eye contact and lets your child know that you are listening and being attentive.
4. *Don't interrupt when your child is narrating an incident:* As you listen to your child narrate a situation and the exchanges that took place as a part of it, you may feel like you need to correct something or seek more information. Interrupting your child does not help. It is instead prudent to share your assessment and make queries once you see your child is done with sharing the story.
5. *Do not rush your child to end the story quickly:* Be patient and let it reflect in your body language as well. Your child should not feel that you are uninterested or in a rush when you are attempting to listen to what (s)he is saying. Instead it is better to defer the conversation to a later time, specifically stating when you would speak, and ensuring that you do reach out at that time for the conversation.

6. *Be reflective during the conversation:* Accurately reflecting the emotion that your child is displaying helps the child feel comforted about her or his feelings. Simultaneously, it is helpful to share what you thought about the conversation, reflecting and taking one step further to help elaborate on what your child might be thinking or feeling at the moment. This helps build your child's understanding of the self while also providing an opportunity to grow emotionally and cognitively.

IT TAKES WORK

Actively listening and being reflective in your interactions requires a conscious effort from your side. Consistency in following this approach permits your child to feel valued, heard and understood, all of which are stepping stones towards the development of confidence. Working on being an active listener can be difficult and you need to be empathetic towards your own struggles as you try to achieve this end. Be patient and don't judge yourself if you struggle to bring in a consistent approach to listening to your child.

HIGHLIGHTS

- Active listening is a skill that can be acquired and developed.
- Be reflective as you listen to your child to develop emotional and cognitive skills.
- Maintain eye contact and get down to your child's level as you speak.
- Do not interrupt as your child narrates experiences. Keep questions for the end.
- Model listening skills so your child acquires them by observing you.

12

MAINTAIN EYE CONTACT DURING CONVERSATIONS

How people connect is often reflected in the way they look at each other. The eye contact they make with another, shapes the understanding and experience of interactions. This is true for your conversations with your child too.

A child can be shy, hesitating to make eye contact. This hesitation can affect the responses to both adults and same-aged peers. The child does not understand why it is important to make eye contact. Knowledge and information about the manner in which it can impact interactions, relationships and self-concepts is unavailable to her or him. (S)He is too young to infer these aspects. However, as an adult in the equation and being the parent, you can play a vital role in understanding and shaping how (s)he initiates and maintains eye contact.

Let's take an example.

Each time you reach out and crouch on the ground to say a 'Hi', your friend's child hides behind her mum. You wonder how long it may be before (s)he is comfortable meeting you. After all, (s)he is your best friend's child. Even when (s)he responds to you (s)he doesn't look at you. (S)He squirms and twirls as (s)he keeps looking up at mum or down at the ground.

An experience like this can leave you feeling worried since you know that even a simple eye contact can have implications on confidence and relationships in the future.

THE VALUE OF EYE CONTACT

When you look at someone in the eye during a conversation you get to know and understand the other person better and also your own communication style. You can determine how interested the person is in your conversation. It allows you to predict whether the person is able to follow and process what you are expressing. The glint of recognition and understanding in the other persons' eyes can be invaluable in shaping how the conversation progresses.

This finds it's applicability with children as well. As they speak with you or with their peers, the eye contact they make helps them shape their conversations, and determine the course they would like the interaction to take. They gain information about whether they are being heard and really understood. They can utilize this information to decide how they are being perceived in the interaction.

When they see others paying attention to them, looking into their eyes and nodding in assent or expressing their disagreement, it enhances their understanding and application of communication skills. They learn to operate in relationships and become knowledgeable about reciprocity in conversations. It becomes apparent to them that as you or others continue to listen, their words have value and their stories are of significance. They feel acknowledged and cherished and this contributes to their developing self-concepts.

The process of shaping self-concepts is intricately linked to the development of confidence. This process impacts and has the ability to bring about a change in the existing levels of confidence a child displays.

YOUR ROLE IN ENHANCING EYE CONTACT

Parents play a significant role in helping children build eye contact that is warranted across situations and in conversations. This process starts in infancy as you bend down to look at your child or when you pick her or him up and look straight into the eyes.

This continues even as the child grows older and you can utilize varied means to reinforce this important element.

1. Observation of what you do contributes to how your child behaves as well. The eye contact you make is one of the first things that critically influences the eye contact your child makes. Seeing you ensure that you meet your child's gaze each time you speak to her or him conveys that it is important to engage in it. As you call out your child's name to draw her or his attention by saying, 'Look at me. I have something to share with you,' you reinforce that making eye contact is an essential part of conversations with people.
2. When your child is playing with her or his toys in your room where you are resting, (s)he says, while looking at them, 'I really like playing with my toys.' You can choose to encourage her or him to meet your gaze by saying, 'Sorry I couldn't entirely make out what you said since you weren't looking at me. Could you please look at me and tell me what it was that you said?' This acts as a gentle reminder to her or him to engage with people by making eye contact. It reinforces the concept that interactions are facilitated by the eye contact that is made during a conversation.
3. In social situations where your child may be hesitant in approaching others or looking at them when they speak, you can gently prod without being forceful to remind your child that it would be nice to look at the person who is speaking to her or him. Repeatedly pointing out something like this in public spaces where others can observe or hear is best avoided. It is usually recommended that you mention it a couple of times, at most, as a situation occurs, and then, speak about it in private using stories or role plays at home.
4. You can utilize situations that have previously occurred as well, by saying, 'Hey! It would be nice that next time when we meet Neeta Aunty you look at her when she is speaking to you. You don't always have to say something. You can also just smile at her.' You can end the conversation by asking your child, 'Tell

me how you feel about it? Do you think we could do this?' Checking in with your child encourages her or him to share if doing something like this seems difficult. It provides you the opportunity to be able to bust myths and build confidence. Simultaneously checking if 'we' could do this makes your child feel supported as (s)he feels that you would be there through the process.

THE NEXT STEPS

A number of things contribute to the development of confidence in children. We are often not aware of the simple things that can be a big influence. As a result, it is important to reinforce even a simplistic sounding thing like eye contact. As minuscule as it may seem, good eye contact is a stepping stone to your approach directed at building your child's confidence.

HIGHLIGHTS

- Eye contact has great influence, and is a sign of confidence.
- The way you maintain eye contact influences your child's utilization of it.
- Reinforcing the need to make eye contact is important to help your child utilize it.
- Encourage your child to meet your gaze when (s)he speaks with you.
- Find opportunities to remind your child how maintaining eye contact helps build communication in relationships.

13

CHOOSE YOUR WORDS WISELY

A word once spoken cannot be retracted. A sharp, harsh word is akin to an arrow that has left the bow, which causes fatal injury when it hits the target.
Be careful with what you say.
It has the ability to cause grave injury.

The words parents choose in their interactions with children have the ability to shape the thoughts and worldview of the child. A simple expression can be overloaded with meaning and much can be inferred from what you say. This influences the development of your child's personality. The words you use to raise, discipline and teach your child are invaluable for her or his self-concepts—their internal belief system, self-worth, self-esteem and confidence.

Often, unknowingly, a parent can say something or use words which can negatively impact the child. Commonly used expressions and phrases can also be perceived as such by your child. Something as simple as telling your child 'Just stop!', at the playground, when others are also present, or when they are offered a sweet by someone, 'Say, "Thank you",' too can have an effect on your child increasing her or his hesitation or feeling of embarrassment. This is particularly true for children who are shy, struggle with low self-esteem or tend to be anxious. In this context, the value of what you say and how you say it is particularly important and one-on-one interactions conducted in a polite, reflective manner in a closed space are very valuable.

YOUR CHILD IS LIKE A SPONGE

Parents do not approach their children with ill-intentions in their interactions. They want the best for their child and attempt to do everything possible which they deem is important for the child. However, over the course of experiences and situations that parents negotiate in their daily lives, many words become a part of their vocabulary which have the potential to negatively influence and impact the child.

Let's take a look at a situation. In a casual conversation over the phone with your friend, while your child is playing somewhat further away from you, you instinctively say, 'Oh damn! This is just so stupid!' You momentarily forgot about your child's presence in the room. You did not realize that your child might absorb those two words 'damn' and 'stupid.' Now, (s)he uses it the next time there is a conversation with you in which (s)he is feeling frustrated or unhappy with your response.

Children are like sponges. They absorb most of what they see and hear. They mimic their parents and emulate them. In their mind 'Mummy and Daddy are the best!' At this stage when a young child idolizes the parent, anything that you say and do is observed, absorbed and integrated into the child's repertoire of thinking and behaving.

Cognizance of this aspect can help you shape your interactions in a manner that facilitates a positive effect on your child's sense of self and confidence.

IT'S NOT JUST ABOUT THE WORDS

What you express and desire to share is communicated by the words you use. In addition to what you say, how you say it has great significance. Much about the intent, purpose and feelings relating to your communication is conveyed through your intonation, the expressions, posture, gait and eye contact. We discussed the relevance of these in regard to building your child's confidence in previous chapters.

Responsible parenting necessitates you to be aware of the tones and expressions that accompany the words you use to communicate with your child. Anything you need to communicate, be it pleasure, assent, unhappiness, disappointment or anger, you need to be mindful of the tonality of the conversation. This enhances your ability to respond to the emotions your child may display and also modify the approach you are taking if required.

Always remember that your child subconsciously processes these largely intangible elements of your communication and makes mental notes, which also influence her or his future interactions with you and with others around.

BE MINDFUL

Mindfulness is a key ingredient in determining what you say to your child and how you say it. Being mindful requires that you be present in the conversations with your child. You may recall situations where your child was saying something and you either did not hear it or responded to it without thinking it through. It may result in your child either feeling unwanted and uninvolved with you or (s)he may internalize these reactions, which may not be desirable.

Situations where you unintentionally react in a harsh manner as (s)he tries to attract your attention, can have a detrimental impact on your child. The usage of harsh language and tonality has the potential to negatively affect your child's self-esteem. Children who have been exposed to regular and frequent verbal degradation can have high levels of anxiety or worry, can experience low moods, and have difficulty in forming and maintaining relationships. These children can be extremely guilt-ridden and be overly sensitive to the feedback they receive from others.

Additionally, the approach you take to discipline your child needs to be attuned to the age, sensitivities and developmental level of your child. Being mindful in this aspect too is a must, as your words and actions create an impact as well.

FINAL WORDS

Language and its usage are of great import for your relationship with your child. It communicates your love, care and respect. Take the vocabulary away and you struggle to share what you think and feel with your child. So, be mindful of the words you use with your child. Is it communicating what you really want to say? Or is it sending the wrong message? Become aware of your own patterns of communication and use this knowledge to keep reshaping what you are saying and how you are saying it to your child.

HIGHLIGHTS

- Language and words you use influence your child's personality and confidence.
- Children are like sponges, continuously absorbing what they see and hear.
- Be mindful of the words and intonation you use in conversations with your child.
- Ensure you are fully present when communicating with your child.
- Harsh words can destroy your child's confidence and impact mental health and well-being.

14

MAKE THE TIME YOU SPEND WITH YOUR CHILD COUNT

A reflective and responsive parent has the power to change the life of a child. The time you spend with your child, and how you use it, is critical in shaping your child's personality, temperament and self-confidence.

The rigmarole of daily life is exhausting. For an adult, coming from any segment of society, there are always things that need to be done, work that needs to go well, issues to be taken care of and people to be looked after. The modern-day lifestyle leaves little room for spending time with loved ones in a relaxed manner. There is a rush to get from point A to point B, from task X to task Y. This also encompasses the time that parents attempt to segregate from their routine to spend with their child.

TIME IS PRECIOUS

The realities of our existence are such that time is a commodity that is precious and rare. The challenge is exaggerated on account of the busy schedules that children also have. From play dates to activity classes, nursery school to regular school, watching television and going out to play, not much time is left in their routines for spending with family. Finding the right balance can be a tricky proposition.

Those who chose to be a parent nevertheless, recognize the need to spend adequate time with a child. Recent discourse around this aspect of parenting emphasizes the need for being a reflective parent who spends quality time without focusing on the quantity. Variable meanings are attached to what it means to spend quality time, and it will be helpful for you to be informed about how you can move forward in accomplishing this.

THE ROLE OF THE OFTEN ELUSIVE QUALITY TIME

The parenting figure is the primary source of nurturance, love and care which are crucial for a young child to develop and grow into an adolescent and then an adult who is self-assured, confident, has a good understanding of the self and can take feedback directed at self-growth. This fact in itself highlights the need for parents to spend time with their child as a routine activity.

The much talked of phenomenon of 'quality time' plays a prominent role in the development of self-concepts in your child. Like we discussed previously, simply being present around your child is not sufficient. Ensuring that you are engaged and actively involved in the interactions is important. In addition to being mindfully present in the interactions with your child, you now need to look at engaging in activities, play and conversations in which you are an initiator, a participant and a contributor. Children often point out to their parents with innocence, 'But you are not playing with me,' and you helplessly shrug and respond, 'But, I am right here doing what you asked me to do.'

As the exchange above demonstrates, being responsive to your child is exceptionally important. Interactions with you where you take the lead and shape the course of the activity, play a predominant role for your child to feel loved, to develop laterally, be creative, expand on the social, cognitive, emotional, problem-solving and decision-making skills. This is where quality time takes precedence to help you decide the direction you want your child's development to take.

CREATING MEMORABLE MOMENTS

'Quality time' sounds like a difficult task to many parents. It has assumed a complicated status given the multiple conversations that continue to happen around it. Put simplistically, the essence of spending quality time lies in creating memorable moments with your child. A simple laugh, an exchange of a joke, doing a chore together, walking together, playing with a toy, pretending to be an animal—all of these create many memorable moments for you and your child.

Instead of grand gestures and big plans, small pleasures and a good time together are sufficient to create memorable moments that your child will recall in later years. Mrs Khanna is 53 years today and always recounts the time she spent with her family at the dinner table. She often says, 'The simple things made me so happy. Having the time to chat with Mummy or Papa was invaluable. When we would gather around the dinner table and each of us would speak about our day, it would make us feel so connected. It was as though everything that seemed difficult could be worked upon. We children would often speak of fights we had at school or a teacher having scolded us, and even in those moments our parents would find something that would make us laugh while teaching us how to negotiate those situations and to learn from them.'

As your child transitions to the later years you have an increasing number of conversations—about school, friends, experiences, cartoons and shows—and you create more moments which your child would later reflect on and recall. 'My mum said this to me when I was 6 years old.' When your child reaches the adolescent years and you have created a strong bond through multiple memorable moments and interactions you have had over the years, there is space for her or him to be open, to frankly speak and discuss varied topics with you. It creates the foundation for your adolescent to develop a healthy personality and a stable temperament which facilitates a confident approach throughout life.

SPENDING TIME EFFECTIVELY

Let's try to define what would constitute as effective usage of time spent with your child. There are certain activities which if used are more helpful in establishing a strong relationship and enhancing your child's skills.

- *Solve together*: Besides fun and play it is important to help your child develop the skills needed to negotiate difficult situations. You can do this not just by talking with your child but also playing games, solving puzzles, working through mysteries and mazes and also discussing real-life challenges.
- *Play their game*: Make a conscious effort to play the games your child likes. Crouch down on the ground and ask, 'What would you like to play today?' and see the excitement reflect in the broad smile and twinkle in the eyes.
- *Eat together*: 'A family that eats together stays together' is an advice passed down across generations. Eating together is not just an activity. It is a time to talk, share, laugh and be happy together.
- *Create your unique ritual*: Rituals that are unique to you and your child are very helpful in making your child feel special. (S)He will often say, 'Mummy or Daddy and I always do this. It is our thing!' This simple act creates a strong bond, a moment cherished for life.
- *Appreciate often*: Don't forget to appreciate your child in all that (s)he does. Even when your child goes wrong, there may be something which is correct or good. It could be the intent or thought which was really nice. Recognizing the good part, you can further discuss and help reformulate what went wrong so it doesn't recur in the future.
- *Have fun*: It is always important to have fun and joyous moments together. Do the things that make you and your child laugh and enjoy—those can be of her or his preference or even yours.
- *Switch off those gadgets*: Ensure that during the time you spend with your child you switch off your gadgets. Give your child your complete attention. Be focused on what you are doing together, even if it is watching something without having much conversation at the time.
- *Do trips together*: Spend good times with your child by travelling

together. Short trips or long trips, everything is a good idea while you expose your child to the world out there and help her or him curate experiences that will help throughout life.
- *Make sure you have their activities pencilled into your schedule*: Whether you are present when your child has some activity planned or not, knowing about it is important. Make a note of it in your schedule so you can talk about it before you leave for work or once you get back home. It conveys to your child that you are consistently attuned to all that goes on in your child's life.

THERE ARE NO FIXED MECHANISMS

Spending quality time is like art. It can be created in many ways and interpreted in an even larger number of ways. Find your unique style and go beyond your own boundaries to spend time with your child. You will no doubt do a fabulous job with the time you are spending with your child if you make it a priority for yourself.

HIGHLIGHTS

- Create memorable moments during the time you spend with your child.
- Be a creator and initiator of activities to spend quality time with your child.
- Remember, no one rule applies to how you can spend quality time.
- Remember to switch off those gadgets when you are spending time with your child.
- Remember to enjoy, have fun and do things your child likes and also those that you like.

Section Three

BUILD EMOTIONAL WELL-BEING

15

IDENTIFY YOUR CHILD'S EMOTIONS

*Emotions make us human and they make
a relationship humane.
It is the emotions that bind the parent-child
relationship, making it unique with its characteristic
unconditional love and support.*

A baby is born, but instead of crying, (s)he only coos in one tone. The baby also does not demonstrate a social smile. Only facial reflexes exist. When you imagine this how do you think it looks and sounds like? Momentarily you may think that no crying is a good thing. But the second thought that comes to your mind would be a worried one. You would wonder 'Why is the baby not crying? Is something wrong?'

Babies communicate, connect and feel life through their cooing and crying. They convey their feelings of discomfort and content when they cry or smile. It helps them fulfil their existential needs as they learn to associate a correlation between their physiological and emotional drives. As a toddler, the child's emotional states expand, elaborate and become well-defined when they begin to share their desires and express their innermost states of being.

Supplemental to the experiences children have, emotions play a key role in the development of language. Parents play an enormous role in influencing the nature and range of a child's emotional expressions. They affect this by accurately identifying the child's feelings, and responding to them appropriately.

UNDERSTANDING EMOTIONAL DEVELOPMENT

A child's emotional functioning acts as a means to fulfil adaptive and self-efficacious goals. For example, the most basic expression to reflect an emotional state, used by an infant, is crying. It indicates hunger, discomfort, need for maternal attachment and physiological processes. Through the fulfilment of these needs (s)he continues to build a self-regulatory soothing process that allows the child to learn to tolerate distress.

A child's inherent temperament does define the characteristics of emotional expressions—some infants cry louder and react immediately while others may be relatively calm. Your ability to sense and attend to the infant's needs forms the base for the development of secure attachment and a supportive environment. A child's perception of the outside world as trustworthy or not, also develops based on how stably and consistently you respond to the emotional needs. As the child grows, self-awareness of the emotional response also emerges—they understand if they are expressing anxiety, happiness, excitement or fear towards different people and begin to verbalize their feelings.

During the pre-school years, the need to attain autonomy gains more prominence giving rise to difficult behaviour termed as temper tantrums. Taming of the tantrums is an important milestone in the parent-child interaction process. Tantrums are not merely an aggressive outburst but also an expression of disdain and anger on constraints put by parents. The child sees these as a threat to her or his autonomy. The tantrum can arise from a feeling of shame as well. While some tantrums subside on a prompt response by parents, soothing or creating a distraction, others can become worse and go out of hand, often leading to emotionally frustrating and helpless feelings for both parties. Your ability to manage, respond and take control of these outbreaks can push the child in the direction of positive growth.

During the teen years, emotional experiences become more complex, and adolescents have mixed feeling towards self and others. New relationships form and refined emotional expressions moderate the relationship dynamics. Adolescents are able to mask their innermost feelings by expressing alternate or contrary emotions. If your child had a bad day at school, (s)he may pretend like all is fine, making it difficult for you to decipher the true emotion. (S)He may hide her or his feelings of guilt, remorse or sadness when caught lying or engaging in unpleasant or unacceptable behaviour. When feelings of shame or guilt mix with an adolescents' struggling self-esteem it sets the stage for challenges in the development of personality and self-constellation. Despite the roller coaster ride that you and your adolescent may go through, the initial emotional bond lays the foundation for an easier path ahead.

At each stage of developmental transition, emotional challenges faced by you and your child bring a unique flavour and learning to the relationship. Both of you need to determine the skills needed to adapt to the transitions. Your role is to provide your child/adolescent the right skills to recognize and deal with emotions. Simultaneously, you need to equip yourself with the ability to identify and connect with your child emotionally.

SENSING AND NURTURING AN EMOTIONAL COMMUNICATION

The onus for developing emotional maturity and expressiveness, the parent-child bond and the emotional temperament of the child falls on the parent. Parents and children operate on an asymmetrical platform. Nevertheless, moments of happiness, acceptance and emotional comfort can be built and experienced by being self-aware and conscious of the child's emotional needs.

1. *Enquire about your child's feelings*: Give your child the space to talk about the day, school, friends and more. Enquire about how (s)he felt to understand the true emotions. You can inquire with, 'Okay, so how did you feel when (s)he said that?' One child may be able to express freely while another may struggle. Or you may notice that in some situations your child is able to state their feelings, and not in others. Help your child to identify

the feelings, as it is also linked to enhanced problem-solving. You can always support your child during the conversation by suggesting words that (s)he may find helpful, like, 'So, did that make you angry or sad?'

2. *Know where your feelings start*: An important step in building an emotionally healthy relationship with your child is being aware of what you are feeling in a given situation towards yourself or your child. You may notice that in some situations you may be projecting your own feelings of fear or embarrassment towards your child. This can act as a barrier for you to understand what your child may be experiencing, while also creating confusion within her or him. This may happen when you say to your child, 'I am sure you are feeling angry with your friend for the other day, I would feel the same'. The suggestion here involves an implicit assumption while also communicating what you would have felt. This can be perceived by your child as an expectation or the right way to feel. Inadvertently, in this case, you reject your child's feelings which impacts the developing self of the child.

3. *Connect through role plays and games*: It helps to flip things around and change the roles and positions across situations, through games and role plays, to understand what the other side feels. Role plays help enhance your child's ability for understanding the other person's perspective, by getting into someone else's shoes. With younger children, this can be easily done through the use of dolls, animal figures and puppets, exchanging simple responsibilities with your child or creating hypothetical situations.

4. *Be emotionally sensitive to change and transitions*: Children can show behavioural changes when they struggle with adjusting or adapting to transitions, like shifting to a different location, change of school, loss of a friendship or even changes at home. They can become aggressive, irritable, silent or more resistant. You need to make an active effort to engage, listen and validate your child's feelings when you recognize the struggle (s)he is experiencing. Refrain from reacting adversely to the behaviour.

Instead, be sensitive and empathetic while addressing your child's emotional needs.

THE ULTIMATE FEELING OF BEING UNDERSTOOD

Your ability to connect to your child's emotional state and experiences helps her or him feel understood. Through the use of words, gestures and expressions, you create an environment of support, acceptance and comfort for your child. This makes her or him feel confident about feelings and emotions. It translates into validation and assurance of what (s)he is experiencing and results in developing healthy self-esteem. Concurrently, it is imperative for the child to learn how (s)he can identify feelings, both for her or his own self and that of others. We explore how parents can help children identify their emotions in the next chapter.

HIGHLIGHTS

- Emotions are the basic blocks which characterize humans and their relationships.
- Understand children's emotional development for age appropriate emotional grooming of your child.
- Be cognizant of the fine line between what constitutes your emotions and your child's emotions.
- Find new ways like role plays or fun games to identify what your child is feeling.
- The feeling of being understood is a building block for a child to feel self-assured and confident.

16

HELP YOUR CHILD IDENTIFY EMOTIONS

The tone of life gets set in the emotions.
The rhythmic experiences provide the foundation.
And children revel in the music of their true selves.

Your child's success is strongly linked with emotional growth and maturity. The ability to understand and handle emotions enhances emotional competence, problem-solving skills and interpersonal relations. Children who express and share their feelings freely are seen to have greater confidence and better social skills. Some children can and do find it hard to understand what they are feeling. Nurturing the emotional needs of your child, and expressions of their feelings, is perhaps the most important task for a parent.

EMOTIONAL COACHING IMPROVES LEARNING AND CONTRIBUTES TO PSYCHOLOGICAL GROWTH

Learning facts, reading scientific material, watching informative shows and studying subjects well at school are some of the key elements considered important for academic success. However, the impact of the emotions a child experiences and understands, also influences learning. This fact is not usually attributed significance.

Having greater emotional literacy makes a child feel self-assured and confident about what (s)he understands, experiences and wants to communicate. As the child assumes a more self-aware stance, it contributes to better understanding of what (s)he wants, likes, has an interest in and is likely to respond to. A child who is more emotionally attuned to herself or himself is able to engage actively with new experiences, can assume a learning attitude more easily, is responsive to those around her or him and can also shape the environment to better suit her or his needs. This lays the foundation for the development of a more conducive learning environment and provides the scaffolding for the child to grow psychologically.

When children stumble and struggle to find words to express themselves, it can result in frustration, anger, disappointment and irritability. Others may struggle to know what is going on, and thus, are unable to provide the child what (s)he needs in that moment to feel settled. This can further lead to undesired behaviour or being isolated by others. In such a scenario often parents shift their focus to the resulting behaviour and attempt to rectify them them, instead of looking at aspects relating to the child which are growth oriented. This, in turn, impacts the child's self-esteem and academic results.

The emotional maturity of the child plays a role in the development of enduring and positive relationships, not just during the younger years, but in adulthood as well. Thus, determining ways to make your child emotionally skilled and competent becomes a prime responsibility, in addition to providing the means to be academically proficient, and helping to create a positive sense of self.

BUILD YOUR CHILD'S EMOTIONAL UNDERSTANDING

At each stage of life, your child will often experience and struggle with emotional conflicts. The skills involved in identifying, understanding and processing situations, both rationally and emotionally, makes an individual resilient. Let's look at the ways in which you can nurture a child's emotions effectively from an early age to strengthen the self system.

1. *Choose which emotion to mirror*: Children do not understand the differences between various emotions at an early age. They also do not understand their functions. They learn to

identify emotions by observing your expressions, your tone and the gestures you use. This is supplemented by what they observe in others, on television, in cartoons, games they play, and the books you read with them. To help your child build her or his repertoire of emotions, and to understand them better, it is important to spend time, speak face-to-face and express that which you want your child to inculcate. Ensure that the emotion you express in response to a situation is concordant to what you want your child to take away from it. For example, you are having a bad headache and your child is asking questions about a new toy. You are feeling irritated but you also want your child to maintain her or his inquisitiveness and curiosity. You can choose to snap, or, you can make an effort to smile despite your irritability, as you want your child to feel encouraged to express and ask questions.

2. *Name the emotions in your conversations*: Name the feelings while talking to children. You need to do this in a situation where you are sharing your own experience. Also, help your child identify and understand what (s)he may be feeling in a situation by asking about the emotion. This helps children to create associations between emotions and situations. You can say, 'Mummy is going on a work trip for three days. How do you feel about it?' Or you can ask an additional question, 'Are you feeling sad about it?' You may ask your child about a playdate the previous evening by saying, 'Were you happy to have Maira over last evening? How did you feel when you shared your toys with her?'

3. *Use visual aids*: You can use emotion stickers or clay faces to teach children about the various kinds of emotions. These act as a visual aid to facilitate learning, and allow children to develop the ability to identify socio-emotional cues. Read storybooks where characters show varied expressions, to help children form connections between feelings and expressions. They learn to connect the dots when you state, 'Look at the tiger! He looks so angry!' 'Does the rabbit seem scared to you?' As children grow older, you can switch to checking with

them before giving them the word to see how they interpret expressions. 'How do you think the bear might be feeling?' This also helps in building perspectives about others, which eventually transforms into empathy.

4. *Build connections between behaviour and thoughts with emotions*: Stating a behaviour you observe, or sharing your thoughts about it alone, does not translate into your child developing the skills for taking the right emotional perspective. For children to have an empathetic perspective towards their own self and others, parents need to verbalize the emotions behind an action. They need to help link the emotion and the thought with the action. This helps a child understand why they acted the way they did, or why there was a specific reaction to their action. For example, instead of an angry retort stating, 'Why did you push your friend? It's wrong! You must say sorry,' you can word it to say, 'Pushing your friend can make her or him feel sad. (S)He may think that you don't like her or him. Let's go and say sorry.'

5. *Emotional vocabulary is not inbuilt*: Often, people, both children and adults, find it difficult to give a name to what they are feeling. They may just say that they are feeling 'blah' or that they just don't know how to explain it, like, 'You know, it's like I feel blah when that happens!' A difficulty in identifying the emotion an individual is experiencing interferes with problem-solving. It is important as parents to work with your child to build this vocabulary at every stage of their life. This enables better communication and enhanced problem-solving. Once you know what is happening, you can help your child work through the emotional experience as well as the situation. You may say, 'Let's see what can be done to make you feel better. We can then resolve what happened. What do you think about that?'

EMOTIONAL GROOMING—THE PATH TO SUCCESS

Conscious and collective effort to nurture and develop your child's emotional skills is critical for her or his success later in life. The sense of deep connection and assurance that is felt by being close to your own feelings, contributes to the development of positive self-esteem. It gives a child the confidence to take decisions, solve problems, work through situations and sustain relationships which are key challenges that one encounters as one grows and rises through hierarchies. As we move further, we would talk about empathy, which is the most valued social and emotional skill.

HIGHLIGHTS

- Emotional competence leads to overall psychological growth of a child.
- Give your child the skills to identify feelings by using visual aids, as well as by connecting behaviour and thoughts to emotions.
- You need to build you child's vocabulary of emotional words by sharing and discussing more about them.
- Help your child identify what (s)he feels by asking questions and providing prompts.
- Emotional competence leads to enhanced self-confidence and prosocial behaviour.

17

EMPATHY FOR BETTER CONNECTEDNESS

Cultivate and nurture the seed of empathy in your child.
Compassion, care and concern is what the world needs.

All parents work towards inculcating the right value system and laying the foundation for children to be sensitive and compassionate adults. Being generous, loving and caring are virtues that are valued across all cultures. These can be cultivated in your child by building and teaching her or him to be empathetic.

Empathy gives the power to connect lovingly and with care, with your own self and with others. Building empathy involves building a safe, secure and sensitive world. Today's changing times necessitate a focus on building empathy in children. Given the increasing incidences of aggression and violence, we need to reconstruct the basic foundation on which society operates.

UNDERSTANDING EMPATHY

We feel bad for the person who finds herself or himself in a challenging or untenable situation. This feeling 'bad' for another, comes from a place of pity and sympathy. Sympathy places an individual at a point where they know that a person is struggling, but do not have a personal understanding of it. While one may be able to acknowledge that, 'I do understand this must be difficult for you,' it does not connect with the person. It is then difficult to make them feel that you truly know how it feels to be in that particular circumstance.

Empathy, in contrast, comes from a place of personally being able to understand what it may be like for another person to go through the situation they are coping with. This can come from having gone through similar experiences yourself, or simply from being able to place yourself in the shoes of the other person, such that you can experience their feelings.

Empathy allows for a deeper and meaningful connect, allowing for greater communication between two individuals, and serving to improve the relationships people have.

EMPATHY IS A KEY LIFE SKILL FOR YOUR CHILD

Empathy is a critical life skill for children. Transitioning into adulthood can be a challenging process. Success during the adult years comes from the individual's cognitive abilities, as well as the emotional capacities. Forging relationships requires that one understand others and their experiences. Being able to respond sensitively to what another person may think or feel, sets the stage for more conversations and for being seen as a reliable and trustworthy person.

Empathy begins with compassion. It involves the ability to understand and accept others for who they are. It allows a child to see their own self being reflected in the other person each time they connect with the experience of another. It involves feeling what the other person is feeling and not just what they are able to express verbally.

During school years, the ability to be empathetic enables a child to understand the experiences of another and what it may feel like to be that other person. For instance, your child may narrate an instance where another child was laughed at or excluded from a conversation. If your child was narrating this experience in jest, it may have worried you. But if your child shared it with a tinge of concern and feeling bad for the other child, you would have had a good feeling inside. Regardless of the two states, you would have further wanted to help your child understand what it would be like for the other child in that situation. And even before that, you would need to explain to your child that all children come from different homes and settings, and it does not make anyone lesser than the other. Both these aspects together contribute to the development of empathy, of being able to know and feel what it could be like to be this other child in the class or in the bus or at the playground.

This also demonstrates that empathy can be taught and inculcated in a child. Children can be sensitive but the ability to truly know and feel what it can be to go through what another goes through—to be empathetic—can be harnessed through your interactions. Let's look at the ways in which you can be empathetic, in order to breed empathy.

EMPATHY BREEDS EMPATHY

To foster empathy in your child, you must equip yourself with the skills to be empathetic in your parenting and other roles. This learning and communication transforms into the empathetic character building of your child.

1. *Model empathy*: You must act and behave empathetically with and around children. Knowingly or unknowingly, through the course of stressful lives, an adult can lose the patience to understand the other person or the circumstances they are in. For example, while interacting with the help, drivers, shopkeepers or call centres, one can use language and words which are disrespectful and insensitive. Empathy represents respect and dignity for the other person. When you see your child distressed, saying, 'You seem upset and angry. How can I help you?' is more empathetic than saying, 'Why are you so angry? Cool yourself first then we will talk.' You can demonstrate through your words how children can act empathetically—'Let's take turns playing this game with your friend. May I show you how you can take turns?'
2. *Use teaching moments to connect*: As a parent, you may get preachy or nagging especially when you decide to teach your child about life. You may make statements like, 'Oh no! You are

not behaving kindly. Show me how to be kind. You must act kind towards others. How can you not be kind? Do you know when I was young...' Our fears grip us in such moments and we become too persistent when we see a problem. Instead, it may be more helpful to utilize these as teaching moments. So, while watching the news, a movie or referring to an incident at school, you can ask, 'How do you feel about what happened? What do you think that person might be feeling in the given scenario?' With younger children it helps to use stories and tales. Playtime with pets, animals or with their friends is also a good time.

3. *Embrace the child's empathetic self and not just the behaviour*: When the child shows good, kind and generous behaviour, parents praise by saying, 'Good job! That was great!' In some situations you may choose to use an extrinsic reinforcer to motivate your child by saying, 'I will buy you another big toy if you share this one with your sibling.' This does not translate into an inbuilt system of understanding and caring. You can instead encourage your child by saying, 'You are doing great by being a kind person.' This encourages your child to maintain the behaviour and also recognize the inherent value of being understanding and kind towards others.

4. *Remember to ask, 'How would you feel if it were you?'*: This simple question can compel your child to look into her or his own actions. This is especially important for children who struggle with sensing another person's feelings. Encouraging your child to relate to the experiences of another, helps not only to open the window to the person's world, but also prevents them from rationalizing non-empathetic behaviour.

I AM AN EMPATHETIC INDIVIDUAL

Empathy plays the role of a double-edged sword. At an emotional level it extends the ability to understand another person's feelings. At a cognitive level it makes an individual act rationally. Working towards being empathetically aware of ones' feelings and those of others, helps increase the quotient of concern and sensitivity. You can process situations, take perspectives, move a step back or forward and act accordingly. Building empathy helps your child to develop social, emotional and critical-thinking skills. Children who show empathy are able to form strong and secure relations, are more tolerant and accepting of others and are able to maintain social harmony. Empathy also promotes psychological well-being as it enhances acknowledging, embracing and accepting of feelings. It makes you an emotionally aware parent and augments states of happiness at home by reducing the general stress levels. Empathy also predicts greater success for your child since an empathetic leader is better able to connect, guide and lead people.

HIGHLIGHTS

- Empathy allows for the development of deep bonds and connections.
- An empathetic conversation shows respect for your child's feelings.
- Empathy makes children compassionate, warm and caring towards their own self and others.
- Lead by example and use teaching moments to foster empathetic understanding.
- Breeding an empathetic self is a step towards building a moral character.

18

CREATE SPACE FOR EMOTIONAL CONVERSATIONS

A conversation that
Sees,
Hears,
Feels,
Speaks emotions,
Is a healing conversation

Conversations are not just about conveying information. They allow people to know a person's thoughts and feelings in addition to knowing her or his situations. However, when asked to share their feelings, most individuals feel uncomfortable and struggle to express themselves. Besides the challenge of finding the right words, simply focusing on 'what I felt in a situation' is not emphasized in interactions. Often, adults recollect being asked to put their emotions aside, and to approach a situation in a pragmatic manner. Even when you were upset as a child, you were perhaps told, 'Don't be upset. Tell me what happened and let's find a solution' or, 'What's there to be upset about? These things happen. Get used to it. You need to have a thick skin.'

Sometimes, it is important to put the emotions aside and look at the situation for what it is. A solution-focused approach can be more helpful in working through and resolving problems, instead of an emotion-focused approach. But the flip side of this is the negation of the emotions that you may have felt. This need to discard feelings can be problematic as it prevents a person from being able to understand themselves and others, to form relationships, and to respond with sensitivity and empathy.

Effective parenting involves maintaining a space to talk about emotions and emotional experiences and yet allow for a problem-solving approach to be cultivated in children.

THE NEED FOR THE RIGHT SPACE TO EXPRESS

Creating the space to share and express emotions, serves an important purpose—to better understand your child, know what (s)he may be going through, how (s)he perceives and interprets situations and interactions, and the meanings that are derived about the self and the world. Conversations that involve your child's emotional experiences allow you to help tweak, harness and nurture them to evolve, become robust and to have a more comprehensive understanding of others and the world. You can utilize these interactions to further elaborate upon your child's thought process and help her or him to expand on existing world views.

Concurrently, having a space for your child implies having a space for your own self to share experiences and understanding with your child. You can utilize the existing space to help your child learn from you, to understand that people can think and feel differently, that there can be other perspectives which deserve importance and it is okay to have these different spaces and perspectives. This helps make your child tolerant, sensitive, empathetic and responsive towards the needs of other people.

The conversations and emotional expressions that characterize the interactions between your child and you, form the basis of your relationship with each other. The more comfortable your child feels in expressing and sharing feelings, the better your relationship with each other. This scenario facilitates listening to each other, which is a key skill needed to work alongside others and in relationships.

CREATING A SAFE SPACE FOR EMOTIONAL CONVERSATIONS

As your child grows there will be multiple opportunities where (s)he will test the waters, raise questions, want to know and understand different experiences that may be complex and confusing. For your child to have these conversations it is imperative that you consistently create a safe space for such interactions. Let's take a look at some of the things that are critical to building this safe space for emotional conversations.

- *Allocate a physical space or location*: It helps to have a designated place where serious or emotionally challenging conversations are engaged in, within or outside your home. It should be a quiet place where people don't come in and go out constantly.
- *Encourage your child to share when (s)he wants to have a conversation*: Tell your child, 'Come talk to me whenever you want to share something. Be it a story, something that happened, your thoughts or your feelings, everything is important. Let's keep talking about these.'
- *Create time for emotional conversations*: Ensure that when you need to have a conversation about emotions and emotional experiences you have ample time on hand. Even if it means halting your child for a bit before launching into a conversation so you can ensure there is no distraction, you should do so.
- *Be emotionally present, hold the space*: We spoke about being mindful and present in conversations previously. To create an emotionally safe space, it is not only necessary to be present, but to also to let your child know that you can handle and manage any emotions, thoughts and actions that (s)he has. This knowledge is important for your child to share freely and without inhibitions.
- *Tolerate the silence*: Your child may take her or his own time opening up. Sometimes, (s)he may be quick to share what's going on and at other times (s)he may find it more difficult to do so. There may also be intermittent silences. Be patient. Don't

be in a rush to pry, know more or do something. Take your time and give your child her or his own time to speak and share.

EMOTIONS EMBRACE YOUR TRUE SELF

By embracing your child's emotions, you shape their developing sense of self as well. The emotions a child displays across situations become a reflection of who (s)he is as a person. It is important that these emotions be seen, heard and felt as they shape your child's self-esteem. Being heard and validated for experiencing the emotions that your child feels, allows them to become confident in talking about their thoughts and feelings. In our next chapter, we explore how to build an environment of acceptance for these emotions.

HIGHLIGHTS

- Make space for emotions in conversations by showing interest through active listening.
- Accept the emotional experiences your child has. Don't reject them.
- Create a safe space for emotional conversations by allocating a space and time. Be present and tolerant of your child's expressions.
- Acknowledge, reflect and validate the emotions your child shares and expresses.
- Use the space you have created to also share your perspective. Help your child broaden her or his worldview.

19

ACCEPT YOUR CHILD'S SELF-EXPRESSIONS

Acceptance is a bigger virtue than change.
Build acceptance for yourself and your child.
Cherish the moments you have together.
The question 'what if it were...' can create distress.

How do you make your child learn? What is the way to teach a child to be good, do good and to learn the right values and methods of living? What is it that will make your child stand apart from the crowd, making her or him happy, confident, content and successful in life?

Many believe it is the continuous, consistent process of guiding, correcting and shaping behaviour that will lead to the aforementioned, much desired, outcomes. In this context, parents' thoughts and ideas become infested with many 'must's', 'should's' and 'have to be's'. Parents might feel pressurized to behave in a certain manner or to follow a prescribed process that is preordained for success. A parallel idea of letting your child make decisions also remains afloat. Intuitively, this might seem correct but it also creates anxiety as you worry about your child hitting roadblocks, experiencing disappointments or even going down the 'wrong path.'

More often than not, a parent feels compelled to warn or direct the child in order to prevent a future mishap. Within seconds, all probable negative and unhealthy consequences rush through your mind, and you respond to control it, believing it is for the good of your child. One forgets that this slowly chips away the child's ability to live in the moment. It also takes away the confidence to make decisions and learn from mistakes.

The choice you have is paradoxical and seemingly counter-intuitive. But you must remember that it helps to let your child make mistakes and go through her or his own learning curve. And, this also means being mentally prepared to take some risks—for both, you and your child.

START WITH ACCEPTING YOURSELF

Acceptance means seeing yourself in the moment as is, without any judgement. Perceive with full openness, acknowledge both positive and negative emotions and embrace your inner experiences. When applied to parenting, it implies that you learn the art of acceptance towards yourself, recognize the difficult emotions you experience in situations with your child, be aware of your strengths and limitations as a parent and embrace these. Mindfully watch the thoughts that flash through your mind when you are with your child, be aware of the physical sensations and notice your feelings—your heart rate may rise when angry, there may be tightness in the muscles and an urge to shout loudly. Similarly, when you experience love or warmth, the body feels relaxed and open, compelling you to express physical proximity through a hug, kiss or a touch. The idea is to accept both positive and negative emotions and not judge yourself as you move through these experiences.

When your child goes through a difficult experience or is struggling in academics, social relations, shows behavioural problems or low self-confidence, you may blame either yourself or the child. In most instances the blame is mutual. It evokes feelings of shame, anger and guilt which are difficult to bear within. You get angry and lash out saying, 'I told you to skip your activity class. You needed to focus extra on maths, now look at the results!' Then you turn around and think, 'I should have taken an off from work, I didn't take it too seriously. If I would have been there, things would have been different.' Both thought processes reflect emotions of shame, disappointment and guilt which turn into anger that is directed inwards and outwards. This anger can affect your child's confidence.

In contrast, awareness and acknowledgement of your feelings, identifying them, and simultaneous acknowledgment of your child's feelings would help in building acceptance of the situation. This creates the space for change. When you discuss with your child about her or his performance, and ask, 'How do you feel about your results? Well, I am disappointed too. Do you think you have been able to determine where you went wrong or what you could change? Okay, so do you think you can bring that change the next time? I'll be happy to work with you and help you in implementing this alternate approach.' Having a conversation like this requires you to look within, acknowledge your emotions, validate them as normal and then empathize with both yourself and your child. Such mindful acceptance creates space for a non-judgemental and unbiased conversation. This sets the stage for change in the future.

ACCEPTANCE–A BUILDING BLOCK TOWARDS CHANGE

In attempting to shape or change your child's personality, traits, actions, decisions or choices, some may tend to give in to disapproval and criticism. You may react and say things like, 'What kind of music is this?', 'Who wears something like that?', 'Why would you read that book?', or 'No, you are not going to watch that. I will put on something else for you.' Such interactions can cause some children to lose their confidence to make their own choices. Some others may become more resistant and negative towards their parents. There are five key ways in which you can work to build acceptance towards your child's expressions which will help build and maintain her or his confidence.

1. *Look beyond your expectations*: The first step towards acceptance is letting go a little, of how you want or expect your child to behave. Giving your child the space to explore and expand upon how (s)he may like to do things, can help you gain insight into how (s)he thinks and feels.
2. *Communicate mindfully*: Be attentive and compassionate while communicating with your child. Avoid controlling the situation to meet your needs. Instead, you can gently guide, without

being too persistent, nagging or insistent, on doing things your way. Be mindful of the situation, the emotions it evokes in you and your child, and communicating more with her or him.

3. *Experience the moment*: Be completely involved in the moments with your child. Help your child build her or his self by accepting who (s)he is now. Staying connected to the present moment is far more critical than focusing on the possibilities of what can be tomorrow.
4. *Identify your triggers*: Know what can trigger a reaction within you in order to take control in situations where your child can try to determine her or his own way of negotiating through them. This will help you build self-control, be mindful of your communication and also let your child have the space to explore and develop life skills.
5. *Respect individuality*: It is important to identify and embrace your child's individuality which is the best way of showing acceptance for who (s)he is. This also shapes and aids in the development of strong self-concepts in your child. This true acceptance automatically creates willingness to explore, discover and bring about positive changes in your child.

HIGHLIGHTS

- Acceptance of self and your child increases moments of happiness and joy.
- Redefine parenting by living in the present and making most of the moments with your child.
- Focus and embrace your child's self-expression in the here and now.
- Build greater acceptance for yourself as a parent by being aware of your thoughts, feelings and sensations.
- Respect each other's feelings and establish trust and connection by communicating emotions. This creates opportunities for self-growth and change for your child.

20

MODEL SELF-REGULATION OF EMOTIONS

*Do and be who you want to be and
who you want your child to be.
Before teaching your child the right mannerisms
and attitudes, engage in a process of self-regulation
of emotions and behaviour.*

Your child's emotional reaction at a marketplace or a friend's house, a fight to switch off the TV, to wear a certain dress, at dinner time to eat the greens, in the morning before going to school and other small infractions can often push you to the edge of losing your temper. You feel anger, frustration, embarrassment, pain and rarely do you laugh on such occasions. You find yourself having to make a choice between giving in, giving up or reacting angrily in the moment. Before you know it, you have already reacted in a manner which later makes you unhappy and induces guilt or even shame.

Modelling the right ways of responding and regulating your emotions is not easy. The multiple roles you play as a parent, a wife or a husband, an employer or employee, a citizen driving on the roads, can often make the worst in you magically appear. You vent the anger and frustration that you experience in the moment and later regret it. You experience 'emotional hijacking' where your mind freezes and does not let you respond rationally to the situation as the emotions have taken control.

The impact that these situations have on your child can be enormous. Besides your child learning and internalizing emotional dysregulation, (s)he can either become fearfully submissive towards authority figures or externalize aggressive behaviour when faced with challenging situations. In both these circumstances your child's self-confidence and self-esteem can get a nasty jolt.

BACK TO THE BASICS—CHILDREN LEARN THROUGH OBSERVATION

Take a leaf from all that we have looked at. Recognize that children learn by observing adults around them. A child learns through imitation, learning the mannerisms and attitudes of a parent. Your child's small, sudden act of innocent imitation, like putting on make-up in front of the mirror, calling you by your name in the tone, as her or his father, pretending to be you and feeding a toy, may take you by surprise and make you laugh many a times. It does not imply that everything, without any exclusion, is learnt and imitated. Learning is dependent on whether you provided positive or negative reinforcement for the behaviour.

Concurrently, a child subconsciously absorbs what goes around her or him. The manner in which you think, react and respond to situations is silently observed, and aspects of interactions are internalized. These varied interactions include your running out of the house in haste on a particularly stressful work day, unhappy and angry with the help for not having things organized, and then snapping angrily when you get a call from a salesperson. Your child is having breakfast and is silently observing and processing what's going on. The next time you talk in an irritated tone with the help, the behaviour gets subliminally reinforced and the child, over a period of time, derives the understanding that it may be okay to react and speak with the help in the house disrespectfully. The next week you witness a scene at home where (s)he shouts at the help for not getting her or him a glass of water immediately when (s)he asked for it.

Many such situations occur without parents being consciously aware and attuned to what may have happened. You may later recognize that you could have handled the situation differently, but the fast pace of daily life does not always leave time for reflection. It then becomes rather critical that you learn the skills of self-regulation, to model the right and effective ways of regulating emotions in front of your child.

EQUIP YOURSELF WITH EMOTION REGULATION SKILLS

To raise an emotionally healthy child, it is important to work on your inner emotional experiences as a parent. To model the right emotion regulation skills, you need to first develop the skills yourself and then ensure that you effectively apply them. Let's look at how you can equip yourself with the right skill set to regulate your emotions across different situations.

1. *Observe your emotions while in the situation*: It is important to learn the art of identifying and being mindful of what you are experiencing emotionally in a given situation. Experiencing anger, shame or guilt, may make you judge yourself negatively. Work on building regulation skills by acknowledging and accepting complex and difficult emotions. Create a sense of comfort around them. Instead of reacting, attempt to sense the physiological changes in your body like tightness in the chest, lump in the throat or restlessness in the body.
2. *Engage in slow-paced breathing*: As challenging as it may sound, it helps to breathe slowly and calmly when you go through difficult circumstances. It will help you rescue yourself from the complex plethora of emotions you are experiencing in the situation. When you observe your emotions surging, take a step back and focus on your breathing immediately till the time you feel you are calm enough to handle the situation.
3. *Identify your triggers*: Identify the things that act as a trigger for you in your daily routine as well as across specific contexts. Making yourself aware of the triggers will create mental preparedness to watch out for those signs in the future. It also enables you to reflect on and choose the situations where you can let go and the ones that you would like to intervene in.

4. *Reassess the situation after the day has passed*: Though you identified your triggers you may still find yourself in a situation where you reacted despite your better judgement. Step back and take another look at the situation. Try to determine by taking a pragmatic approach, what is it about the situation that made you react despite your trying to be calmer. Understand the more subtle aspects that may be contributing to your continued reaction so you can work on these subsequently.
5. *Keep up the attempts to model emotional control*: It is important to keep trying to model emotional control, particularly when your child is around you. You may still falter and miss but don't stop in your efforts to maintain a calm demeanour around your child. Your relaxed, emotionally low-key response will help build an internal self-soothing system in the child.

ALWAYS LEAD BY EXAMPLE

Children need the right models in their lives to become responsible, empathetic individuals of society. To accomplish this, adults need to lead by example—show mastery over emotions, respond empathetically and build compassion towards self and others. These skills that you demonstrate around your child will be internalized consciously and unconsciously by her or him, and shape personality, temperament and attitudes.

HIGHLIGHTS

- Children learn behaviour through observational learning.
- Emotion regulation needs to be inculcated in parents to nurture emotional resilience in your child.
- Work on building awareness of emotions, accept their presence and control the urge to respond to negative emotional states immediately.
- Create self-regulatory strategies by engaging in activities that calm you, like gardening, reading, or deep breathing.
- Be aware of the physiological changes you experience which can act as a signal to control your urge to react impulsively.

21

WALK WITH ME

From holding a finger, grasping the palm tightly to having their hands in the pocket, parenting is about walking together with your child...always.

As you interact with your child—see her or him respond, do things, solve problems, make choices—you wish and hope dearly that (s)he would do what you would do in the given situation. Parents want their children to be able to imbibe those strategies and ways of doing and behaving that make them more like their own selves.

You want your child to grow into being her or his own person who is aware of and understands the self-system, is independent, can think for her or his own self, and can make her or his own decisions.

But there is usually a corresponding part of you which also wishes for parity in how both of you think and do things. A part of the reason is that it reduces chances of conflict. Another reason is that it makes you feel more comfortable and confident since you have an existing trust in how you think and do things. Finally, it allows you to be, in some way, incharge of things while your child explores the world and develops unique measures of negotiating the way through it.

This is not an easy process. It is not always a smooth process to get children to cooperate, to see the same perspective and do things in your way. It's a beautiful thought to have—It would be amazing if my child would listen to me, understand what I'm saying, where I'm coming from and do things the way I request her or him to.

But we all know and realize that it may not be a thought that is always realized. Nevertheless, there are ways in which you can create a path and work with your child to move along it together.

This path involves developing a participative approach to parenting. Making shifts in how you parent—from the dependency your child has to striving for independence in the adolescent years—your availability and presence through the journey will be instrumental in shaping confidence and belief systems.

CREATE SPACE FOR CONSTRUCTIVE DIALOGUES

Giving your child the confidence to have a say in decision-making and making independent choices contributes positively to the development of self-concepts. Creating space for your child to voice concerns in matters of importance to her or him and respecting the views of the world, builds a sense of agency. Your child comes to view herself or himself as an important and integral member of the family and community and is motivated to contribute actively to society.

Giving your child absolute freedom to think and act in a manner that is self-determined can appear to be radical. The idea is not to do this from day one, but to gradually move in the direction of supporting your child in developing greater belief, choice and self-determination in the things (s)he does and how (s)he does them. This gradual process necessitates that there be greater scope for constructive dialogues which nudge your child in this direction.

What this also does for your child is to cultivate a sense of responsibility for the decisions and choices that are made. It exposes your child to the diverse challenges that life can pose, while simultaneously helping in the attainment of new skills. Being an active and involved participant instills a sense of belonging and connection, influencing the relationships a child forms and the manner in which they are maintained.

BUILDING ACTIVE PARTICIPATION

A child's active participation can be built into the family dynamics during the early years through simple acts like encouragement to perform small chores together, putting toys back with mom or dad, singing along together, etc. These give your child a sense of recognition and identity within the family constellation. Active participation, as you help your child walk alongside, has many benefits which support your child's developing personality in the long run.

1. *Hear your child as an individual with a viewpoint*: Refrain from cutting off your child during a conversation. Don't negate your child's perspective by making comments like 'You are a child, you wouldn't understand it' or, 'Kids are not supposed to say anything in this matter.' Instead you can consider, gently stating, 'I know you have thoughts and feelings about this. How about you tell me what you feel and let's see if there is another way to look at it. Also remember, sometimes things can be complicated and you may not always understand them. But it's good that you speak and share with me.' The idea is to not undermine the child's self-expression or curtail speaking freely. Hear your child's opinion, maintaining her or his respect during the conversation, and address it with a response that is age appropriate. Verbally prod by using statements like, 'Yes sure, please go ahead and share what you feel about it' or 'So you think we must first plan the itinerary of the trip and then plan the rest. That seems like a good thought. Let's explore this.'

2. *Channelize your child's potential through active participation*: Willingness to perform increases with encouragement to participate and to keep trying. You can utilize this willfulness to help your child reach her or his potential. As an example, you can ask your child 'Do you think you can categorize this list?' When your child says, 'Yes I would like to try my hands at this' you can further support her or him by saying, 'This

looks great! How about you try this one too?' The feeling of accomplishment builds motivation to perform and explore more.
3. *Use a creative and reflective communication process*: Your conversations should have a welcoming tone for your child to feel encouraged and comfortable in responding. An inviting dialogue creates a space for engaging conversations that has the capability to unravel multiple possibilities. As an example, take a look at the following exchange. 'Well, I believe this piece of the puzzle must be put here, what do you think?' 'I think it should come below this.' 'Okay let me try it out. Yes, I believe you may be right on that and do you think we can put some more of those pieces here?' 'Sure, we can try them there.' This interactional style of parenting and participation has the potential to create a transformative change in your child at an emotional and cognitive level.
4. *Work towards enhancing social skills*: Participative and engaged parenting allows you to work on the social skills that your child already possesses. To negotiate their way through interpersonal situations, your child needs to discover the real self through interactions with you, understand strengths and weaknesses, learn different ways of working with people and also develop a cohesive understanding of what works and what does not, across different situations. As you engage in discussions, solve problems, and help your child develop a thought process and way of working, it augments her or his ability to comprehend the social environment and act with agility, which is critical to overall success and well-being.

THE FINAL STEP

For active participation and to build a harmonious environment at home, it is important for parents to model equal respect for each other's feelings and the opinions which are shared in conversations. Conversations that are heard, address questions, support inner experiences, develop the bond and companionship between a child and parent. Finally, it provides the opportunity to help your child look beyond pre-existing notions and re-interpret shared experiences, creating positive outcomes directed towards the development of your child's self-confidence and identity.

HIGHLIGHTS

- Shape the way your child thinks and responds by walking the path of her or his experiences.
- Create the space for engaging dialogues to discuss and reflect on shared experiences.
- Help your child achieve her or his true potential by being encouraging and discussing outcomes.
- Be creative and flexible in your conversational approach. Remember to recognize and validate, instead of being critical in interactions.
- A participative approach to parenting enhances self-confidence in children, builds healthy self-esteem, social skills and cognitive abilities.

22

ACKNOWLEDGE YOUR CHILD'S ABILITIES

Harness your children's abilities and talents,
Not for them to fit into the world but for
the world to fit around.

A budding artist, a good orator, a potential player, a beautiful singer, a strong leader—your child may possess the quality and potential to be one of these or someone else. Each child is born with a set of natural abilities and inherent qualities. If harnessed in the right way, these can become a part for your child's identity as an adult. Recognizing your child's ability in an area where there is potential, enables the child to work on a pre-existing foundation. This enhances your child's confidence to utilize these abilities across situations. These then begin to define your child's developing self, adding positive experiences that buttress your child's self-concepts.

To understand the areas where your child has a potential, it helps to know where the interest lies. In the early years, children like to explore. As they grow older this exploration turns into a more well-defined area of interest. Children typically show inclination towards many diverse areas. (S)He may be keen to paint, join a swim club, try the piano or solve puzzles. Each area of interest indicates a potential talent or a skill. As you provide the opportunities to develop these interests by identifying these early signs, your child can determine whether these should be pursued over the long run.

However, a word of caution. Don't go overboard by burdening your child with a packed day full of activities which take away the fun and joy. It is crucial to understand that for any potential talent to flourish, it needs a balanced environment. The right learning opportunity, support and ability to enjoy it are the key elements required for your child's skills to blossom.

MAINTAIN A DISCERNING EYE

A child has many opportunities to explore and develop her or his interest. (S)He may not possess similar talents as you, but something unique to her or his own self. As parents, it is important to maintain a keen eye to discern your child's abilities. Art, music, sports, academic pursuits, drama are some of the overt interests that are easily tapped by parents and pursued by children. However, it is also possible that despite the opportunities to explore and engage, your child may struggle to identify her or his area of interest. Frequently changing activities, without keenly focusing on any one, can frustrate you given the time, energy and cost involved in it. It is at such times that the right guidance from you can help your child identify an area that best suits her or him.

An interest can grow and develop over time, becoming a skill or a character strength. For example, your child might be a quick problem-solver—shown by the ability to solve puzzles or come up with quick solutions to simple problems. Or, (s)he may be a creative thinker, coming up with good endings for stories or showing empathetic understanding and sensitivity towards others. You need to be on the lookout to identify these strengths.

Covert abilities like skills of persuasion, problem-solving skills, craftsmanship, social skills, etc., can be helpful during a child's day-to-day living, allowing her or him to better work with people and also take care of the self. Acknowledging these skills strengthens your child's innate character. This further enhances self-esteem by providing an internal locus of control.

HARNESS YOUR CHILD'S CAPABILITIES

Parents want their children to shine. In recent times, there has been a surge to find varied avenues through which children can explore different activities. There is enhanced cognizance towards new ways of enriching your child's abilities. With both schools and community bringing in different concepts that capture a child's interest and capabilities, the challenge can shift, and you may ask yourself, 'How do I help my child choose the right interest?'

1. *Let the initial activities be playful*: Your child engages in various activities at school and at home. In the early years, children like to play with multiple objects like using a box of paint and enjoying playing with colours, spending time in the park swinging from a rod, or reciting a poem just learnt in school. Each of these playful activities may or may not develop into an interest later. The focus should be to encourage your child to enjoy different activities and see which of these persists over a long period of time. The ones that continue to engage your child for a longer duration are the ones that may later become abilities and skilled areas.

2. *Club the enjoyment with exposure*: The playfulness you observe can be further enhanced by giving your child multiple options to explore it further. For example, if your child likes colouring, (s)he can be exposed to different forms of art, taken to galleries, encouraged to use different mediums and maybe join a class. If your child enjoys watching science shows you can organize trips to museums and science centres, do mini projects together and watch more videos to further enhance the interest. When you preserve the joyfulness of doing something and club it with increased exposure, the child is able to understand how much an area interests her or him. Your child may be enjoying swinging from a pole as a playful activity in the park but may not necessarily like to be a gymnast. True potential can be reached if your child experiences the joy of doing it. Feeling the pressure and stress more than the fun of doing something can affect your child's performance.

3. *Be a facilitator*: Let your child choose her or his dreams. Act as a facilitator of learning by creating the right settings for enhanced exposure that allows her or him to imbibe the

right skills and hone talents. But refrain from imposing your own desires while helping your child choose a path. Your child is like wet clay that has immense flexibility and can be shaped by being given the balanced touch of your hands. Give your child a safe space and a supportive environment to grow interests.

As a young child, Shivaan, who is currently 25 years old, always enjoyed playing with colours. He used to throw colours on paper and tilt and turn it to create beautiful abstract shapes with the colours. His parents kept providing him with opportunities and avenues to nurture his art. They would let him participate in workshops, go for competitions, learn from teachers and discuss with those more informed about art. As he grew older he used art as a means to express his thoughts and emotions. He exhibited his work in school and was quite popular for his artistic skills. He always dreamt of being an artist. During XI and XII grades, Shivaan realized he was also keenly interested in political science. To everyone's surprise, he was so enchanted by the field that he decided to pursue it in college and eventually as a career. Shivaan's parents played a supportive role and, despite their apprehensions, stood by him in his decision to pursue political science. Though he had great artistic flare and a creative bent of mind, his inclination towards political science was stronger. He felt happy even though he had changed his larger goal.

4. *Cultivate practice and perseverance*: For any interest or hobby to transform into a talent, your child needs to learn to commit and persevere with it. It is the consistency of engaging with an area of interest that creates a platform for practising it, becoming skilled at it and doing well in it. As a parent, encourage your child to practise, be dedicated and persevere to finish what (s)he starts.

YOUR TRUE WORDS OF ENCOURAGEMENT CAN MAKE A DIFFERENCE

One child may have wings to fly and another may have fins to swim. Identifying, acknowledgment and encouragement by a parent plays a critical role in shaping a child's abilities. The difference lies in the degree of emotional nurturance that each child requires. So continue to be flexible and adaptive in your approach in parenting your child.

HIGHLIGHTS

- Identify your child's strengths and abilities by focusing on areas of interests.
- Emphasize the joy and playfulness of engaging in activities that are of interest.
- Create an environment that helps your child to build her or his interests, skills and character.
- Provide your child the emotional nurturance to blossom into their true self.
- Let your child make choices to build and maintain intrinsic motivation and commitment.

Section Four

BUILD CONFIDENCE THROUGH PROBLEM-SOLVING

23

SOLVING PROBLEMS WITH YOUR CHILD

The fun is in sharing,
When you show you're caring.
As you solve problems with your child,
Life skills you will provide.

Throughout people's lives, they are primed to know that they will cross paths with problems and that they should be prepared. This, in turn, also makes people determine ways to solve them. When you hear someone significant in your life narrate a problem, your mind may automatically try to find solutions—you start thinking about different things that can be potentially done so the situation is better managed. Whether the other person seeks a solution from you or not, your mind is churning and processing, attempting to find answers that can be helpful.

You are tempted to follow the same paradigmatic approach with your child as well. A part of it stems from the innateness of the tendency to solve things for a loved one. Another part is from the need to ensure your child does well and is fine. You don't want her or him to struggle, face difficulties or be stuck in unresolvable situations. So you do what you think is best—protect and take it onto yourself to solve the problem.

This tendency to solve things for your child can hinder the growth of your child's self-confidence. It creates a dependency and prompts your child to look for immediate help outside rather than exploring solutions by himself or herself. It is important to ignite your child's critical-thinking skills and help her or him develop a better perceptual understanding of the world. This can be done when you work with your child through problems together.

THE IMPORTANCE OF PROBLEM-SOLVING ABILITIES

Problem-solving typically starts appearing by the second year of birth, with a few primitive applications becoming evident in the child's first year. On seeing a toy car with a string, an infant crawls swiftly towards it. However, the next time, the child pulls the string to get the toy car. Through exploration and play, the child fine-tunes problem-solving skills with age.

As a child grows older, (s)he faces problems in her or his day-to-day life. Making new friends, achieving academic goals, conflicts with peers, pressure to perform, can all become different challenges they have to learn to juggle. While some children take the problems head on and work their way through them, others may struggle to do so. These then make a child feel vulnerable as well. The child may either withdraw from the situation or engage in externalizing behaviour patterns like screaming, yelling, or defying. Parents often respond to such situations by imposing a solution they think will be effective or just giving in to the tantrum. However, these are moments when your child needs a calming response and steady hand to work on the problem together.

By developing the skill of problem-solving in your child, you also accelerate processing skills and expand on perceptual skills. As a parent, your role is to help your child independently seek solutions to problems. Engage with your child in games like puzzles, sudoku, crossword, chess or other board games to enhance problem-solving skills. Taking on challenges and finding probable solutions helps build self-confidence in children. This further motivates them to take steps to achieve their goals.

PROBLEM-SOLVING IS A SKILL

Problem-solving involves a complex interplay of diverse yet

interrelated skill sets. It is not, in fact, about merely understanding what a problem entails and thinking of the best way to solve it. When problem-solving is looked at as a skill, it also implies that it can be nurtured in your child and (s)he can be helped to learn the techniques that represent good problem-solving.

Problem-solving involves being able to understand what the problem is—analytical skills. This requires a deep analysis and not a superficial understanding of the perceived problem. Determining what contributes to the problem, what maintains it, the different factors which influence it and how it affects others around, require the child to do an in-depth analysis.

Solving a problem requires your child to develop good creative skills to look for novel ways of solving it. This subset of skills allows your child to go beyond conventional ways of looking at the problem to create distinctive solutions, which focus on the unique aspects of the situation. Creativity allows your child to believe in herself or himself—this reinforces confidence in her or his abilities to do things in the long run.

In the course of problem-solving, an integral aspect that presents itself is decision-making. This key skill is instrumental in learning to make a choice between the available options. Understanding and analysing the pros and cons of making a choice form the crux of this aspect. It implies having prospective thinking abilities to envision the potential consequences that can result from making a choice.

WORK WITH YOUR CHILD TO DEVELOP PROBLEM-SOLVING SKILLS

You are the first person with whom your child develops engaging interactions over a long period of time. These can be utilized to teach and develop problem-solving skills in your child. Given the early dependency your child has on you, the numerous situations the child experiences with you, the differing problems you each encounter individually and together, as well as the role model you are for your child, particularly in the early years, you can effect a significant influence on the development of these skills in your child.

There are some concrete steps and measures that you can inculcate in your overall approach to parenting. These support the continued development of problem-solving skills in your child, to a great extent. Let's take a look at them.

1. *Help your child define the problem*: When the child is very young, it can be difficult to verbalize the problem. You can help identify and define problems by stating them yourself and help your child develop the vocabulary for it. For instance, when you see your child angry and struggling to state what (s)he is feeling, you can guide by asking, 'It looks like you are angry. Are you feeling angry because you didn't get candy from your teacher at school?' For an older child, you can be less instructional and encourage your child to think more about a perceived problem. For instance, you may ask your child in a given situation 'Where do you think the problem is?' Your child may answer, 'I don't know.' You can further prod and say, 'Let's try to think of three things that might be bothering you. Let me come up with one and then you could come up with the remaining two.'

2. *Help your child understand the multiple facets of a situation*: Through the numerous situations that you come across with your child when you observe her or him or when you are playing and spending time together, there can be challenges that present themselves. Utilize these moments to help your child develop a well-rounded, holistic understanding of the problem. Point out the different aspects that appear to be potentially associated with the situation. This helps your child develop the understanding that there can be more to a situation than what meets the eye.

3. *Encourage your child using guiding questions*: The aim is to ensure your child develops better abilities to think through problems. This can be facilitated by brainstorming and encouraging your child to think more about the different

situations (s)he encounters. This need not always be done when (s)he is in the midst of a situation but can also be done as a post-facto analysis. It helps if you ask your child questions like, 'What more do you think it could be when you look at this situation?', 'Do you think there could be another way to look at this?', 'Is it possible your friend may also be upset and so she got angry because she wasn't being able to explain things to you?' Gently guiding your child can help her or him reach the answers which can be helpful in ensuring that the approach gets internalized within your child.

4. *Use stories and the media you watch together to teach problem-solving skills*: When you read books to your child or watch cartoons and other media together, use the situations that are projected in the narrations to help your child determine ways in which (s)he could potentially solve the presenting problem. You can stop before the solution is revealed and brainstorm together to generate multiple solutions and think through the possibilities together. Post that, you could read further or watch the show together to see what the characters actually did. You can take this approach a step further by asking your child to further think through if (s)he agrees with what was suggested.

5. *Collaborate on a plan*: In situations that you can foresee, take a proactive approach to support your child to decide steps to be taken to achieve the end goal. Collaborate with your child to work out a strategy while identifying potential challenges and ways to handle them. In the process, take care to not jump in with the solutions yourself. Let your child define the strategy and support when (s)he may stumble. For instance, when your child is trying to figure a way in which the teacher may appreciate her or him, you can support the idea by saying, 'Okay I hear you. You think if you read well, the teacher may give you a candy. That sounds good. Will you try it out tomorrow and let me know how it went?' Or when your child is trying to make her or his study schedule, you can support by saying, 'So you are saying you would first finish your urgent assignments

by day after tomorrow, and then, you will work out a timetable. Okay, works fine. How about you make a tentative plan for the next two days to ensure you get your assignments done? I'm here in case you need my help.'

6. *Reinforce the need to evaluate*: Define a timeline to test a strategy mutually, and check for its effectiveness. Then, evaluate the success and points of failure with your child. In the evaluation process, refrain from reacting negatively or blaming your child. Focus your discussion on points where the strategy needs to be reworked or replaced. For instance, when your child achieves the goal you can say, 'I am glad to hear that you got a candy for reading well.' In contrast, when your child is unable to apply the strategy, you can say, 'You could finish all assignments, except one. I know you feel disappointed but let's appreciate what you have accomplished. We should also try to figure where you went wrong in your planning so we can prevent this from happening in the future. What do you think you could have done differently?'

TRANSFER THE POWER TO NEGOTIATE IN THE REAL WORLD

Your primary role is to transfer the power of problem-solving and facing situations, to your child. You want your child to develop the ability to think beyond what is easily evident and develop a more nuanced approach to problem-solving. This is a process that takes time. Engaging in conversations and having a discussion-oriented style that fosters thinking, creativity and uniqueness is most helpful. This helps create a stable self-structure with greater belief and confidence.

HIGHLIGHTS

- Problem-solving can be fostered within your child.
- Problem-solving involves the interplay of connected subsets of skills like thinking, analysis, creativity, decision-making and negotiation.
- Help your child understand the multiple aspects of each presenting problem.
- Work with your child using stories, cartoons and real-life situations to brainstorm together and solve problems.
- Support your child instead of providing solutions. Do so by asking guiding questions and encouraging your child to share thoughts and solutions.

24

PERSISTENT CORRECTIONS CAN BREED SELF-DOUBT

*Children must learn to walk their own path,
steer in their own direction.
Each wrong turn teaches far more than the right ones.*

Parents do their best to foster the right values, a good character and self-discipline in their children so they can grow to be bright and dignified adults. They focus on teaching children the difference between right and wrong, what is appropriate and inappropriate, and make them aware of appreciated and accepted behaviour in different contexts. These efforts start when the child is at a young age. You may often point out, 'Don't shout when you are at someone's house', 'You must eat without spilling', or 'Greet your aunt properly'—consistently finding things to correct in your child.

The need to invoke corrective action persistently is largely attributable to the parents' belief that their children should put their best foot forward in situations and not cause hurt or harm to themselves or others. Additionally, parents dread that the undesired behaviour may become a part of the children's personalities unless they are checked. Finally, parents often believe that children should benefit from the parents' life-learnings, and listen to what they have to state. There is a hope that children will acknowledge and bend towards the choice of parents. However, this can also work contrary to the expectation of the parents, and cause children to feel resentment and be unhappy.

For children to build an understanding of different perspectives and dwell upon possibilities other than their own, parents need to help develop consequential thinking. A child who is able to relate actions to outcomes grows to be an effective and confident problem-solver.

UNDERSTAND THE MASKING EFFECT OF PERPETUAL RIGHTING

Parents are often plagued by what is known as the righting reflex—non-maligned, intentional or unintentional corrective responses to the child's behaviour. For generations, such approaches have been strongly embedded into existing parenting styles. Without much thought, parents tell the children, 'You have to colour between the lines', 'You are not eating right. At your age, you must eat all this', 'Forty-five minutes is not good, you should study for at least an hour.' However, as a parent reflects on these, it can be determined that such comments occur as reflexive responses to the child. Parents don't even recognize the negativity associated with this constant correction. At times, these corrective measures even involve an emotional component—like when you state, 'You are going to go with us. The world can't revolve around you.'

A child may develop a mental block due to the overbearing requests to follow the parents' advice. Consequently, (s)he may feel less equipped to manage her or his needs and choices. This can contribute to the development of self-doubt. The child may either develop stubborn behaviour or be overly dependent on others, seeking external feedback to make internal corrections. Rather than becoming a confident adult, the child may grow up to be a dependent, seemingly helpless adult.

However, this is not intended to state that the intervention of parents by correcting the child and providing guidance is going to have a negative impact alone. Parental intervention is very meaningful if done thoughtfully and at the right time. If parents respond in a manner that provides the space to cultivate and develop the child's thought process and encourages the child to take ownership and responsibility of actions towards the self and others, it can be rather fruitful. This can eventually result in the development of positive self-concepts in the child.

EFFECTIVE WAYS TO CORRECT YOUR CHILD

Most often, parents are aware of where their children need to shift their thought process or change how they do things. There are ways in which a child can be provided with the right environment and support to be able to bring about the desired changes. How this shift can be brought about needs careful consideration as one does not want the child to feel burdened, resentful, unhappy, ridiculed, pushed or berated. We want the child to be a part of the process and engage in a way that helps her or him to rethink the way things are being done.

1. *Choose and precisely define what to correct*: Choosing what to change is very important. You cannot go overboard nor can you keep brushing things under the carpet. Be precise in defining what you feel needs to be modified. Giving a very broad-based feedback can be confusing for your child. Instead narrowly focus on what specific aspect you think needs to be altered and only point that part out to your child.
2. *Be calm and respectful while making corrections*: Your child should not be made to feel embarrassed or shameful when you are correcting her or him. Rather than saying something like, 'How could you take such a foolish step?' rephrase it and state, 'This does not seem to have worked out very well. It helps to try and think about the consequences of your actions before enacting them. Next time, you can try and use this strategy.' While the first statement can make the child freeze in the moment due to shame and anger, the second one is a solution and a feedback on how things need to be done, without it making the child feel guilty or ashamed.
3. *Think of a code word*: Devise a code word along with your child that can communicate when there is an inappropriate behaviour. Be specific and use this for only one type of

behaviour at a time. This ensures that you are not consistently nitpicking or having negative interactions with your child. Alternatively, your child can use a word to share with you when (s)he feels that you are being too nagging. For example, your child may use the word headgear or take cover when you are persistently bringing up the topic of studies even though (s)he may feel that (s)he is doing what is needed to be done at the time based upon the conversations (s)he has had with you recently.

4. *One parent at a time*: It's a lot of teamwork! Rather than both parents lecturing the child on the same issue at the same time or at different times, it is better to bifurcate who speaks on what. This ensures that the child always has access to another adult within the house who (s)he can reach out to in case something needs to be discussed which (s)he finds difficult to bring up with the parent who is discussing the topic. At the same time, it allows for a channel of normal communication to be open at all times between the child and the parents. It is also important that if your partner is discussing an aspect with your child that you refrain from commenting on it. Your approach should always be to tell your child, 'I'll speak with Mummy or Daddy about it and see how to take this forward with you.' This ensures that your child realizes that both parents are on the same page.

5. *Mutually decide upon alternative strategies and wait to see the change*: Involve your child in the process of coming up with creative alternative solutions to a problem. For example, you and your child may come up with the idea of leaving post-its on the table for things-to-do for your child to go through once (s)he is back from school. You can also tell your child that you would observe this system for a week, and if it works well, you would continue with the same strategy. If not, the two of you can brainstorm and come up with more solutions together.

A FINAL WORD

Children look for parental guidance, especially at a young age. They naturally seek support and help when they are stuck, and parents act as their first point of contact. Each time they reach out, if the nature of communication involves a problem-solving attitude and a reflective thought process accompanied by warmth, acceptance and understanding, it makes your child feel more comfortable in continuing to have such conversations. This builds the right analytical climate that is self-driven and not externally imposed by you or any other adult. A process that is driven by the child is crucial as it preserves the core of the self-system, and it does not get influenced by any emotional threat, allowing for the development of healthy self-concepts.

HIGHLIGHTS

- Persistent negative interactions can adversely impact the child's self-concepts.
- Do not impose your choices on the child. Instead, create an environment that allows your child to learn how to make those choices.
- Be conscious of not engaging in the righting reflex—take a step back, think, let go or act.
- Choose your battles with your child and avoid nitpicking.
- Mutually create ways that act as reminders, and sustain change by using code words and post-its.

25

NEGOTIATE TO PERSUADE INSTEAD OF BEING COERCIVE

*It is a skill to be able to persuade without
getting angry and frustrated.
Find the willpower to disengage from
coercive means of persuading.
Instead, focus on using skills of negotiation
to maintain harmony at home.*

'Pleaassseeeee…may I have one more candy?'
'Can I take another half an hour to finish my game?'
'I really really want to go to that party today with my friends!'

Small wishes can become demands in a short span of time, leading to the child throwing a tantrum. You can find yourself in a big tug-of-war over a minor issue. It becomes frustrating as you watch your child unable to take no for an answer. It worries you as well, since this behaviour worsens with each demand. An assertive 'no' from you gets an aggressive outburst, a huge tantrum, or your child walks away slamming the doors.

Such struggles happen in many homes. Parents consciously work towards setting boundaries to contain and shape the behaviour displayed by their children. Sometimes, no one takes a step to listen patiently to each other's points of view and what ensues is forcible enforcement of rules. In the heat of the moment, neither does agreeing to mutually acceptable choices happen, nor is the point which led to such a large disagreement looked at.

It is often forgotten that successful resolution of these situations happens only when both parent and child resolve the conflict through collective effort and cooperation.

To this end, rules and regulations are pertinent to the smooth functioning of a home. They create the space to know and understand the boundaries for the self and others. Within this context, negotiation plays a crucial role to define the functionality of the said rules and regulations.

THE ART OF NEGOTIATION

Negotiation is a necessary life skill for children and adults. Learning to negotiate is a great learning tool for your child. It is a skill that a parent can foster through the medium of daily interactions. Negotiation involves coming to an agreement or finding a middle ground through discussion without the use of coercion.

Through negotiation, children learn to accommodate the perspectives of others and find ways to create a path for themselves instead of feeling stuck. It fosters creativity and channelizes the child's ability to think through a problem. It teaches the child how to work through and resolve conflicts in a constructive manner. At the same time, it helps your child understand when (s)he needs to stop trying to push an agenda in a conversation.

Using a contingency agreement that involves either an incentive for doing or a penalty for not doing a certain thing is something that works well when negotiating with your child. For example, your child insists on staying at a friend's house while you have guests coming over to your place. You then tell your child, 'We need to leave now as we have some guests coming over today.' Your child replies, 'I don't want to go right now. I haven't finished my game.' You reply, 'I am sorry. I understand you want to stay longer but we have guests coming over. How about you either spend half an hour more the next time when you are here, or we can stay for another fifteen minutes but you help me with the preparations once we get back?' This lowers the risk of non-compliance, as your child is able to see the benefit of either scenario and makes the choice.

While some children are able to negotiate and adhere to the contracts, others may be resistant to any kind of trade-off. They may go around in circles to persuade you with their demands. Instead of picking either option, the child may keep countering your offer. For example, you refuse your teen the permission to go to a party and (s)he continues to argue with you. When you point out, 'I can't allow you to go for this party as I will not be able to pick you up later tonight. I have a meeting tomorrow and Dad is also out of town. You could go for the next one.' (S)he replies to you, 'But you told me the last time that I can go for two parties in a month. If you cannot pick me up, I will ask my friend to drop me.' You remind her, 'Like we have decided, at night it is going to be either your Dad or me who would pick you up. You can't get dropped by anyone else. You can go to the next party that comes up in your group. I promise.' (S)He retorts angrily, 'I decide which party to go based on your availability?' You get frustrated and after repeated back-and-forth dialogue, you finally respond by saying, 'We cannot have arguments on everything I say a no to. Fine! Go for this one but do not hound me soon for another party.' In this situation, you have given in to your teen's demand who has managed to persuade you by being pushy and coercive instead of reaching an understanding with you through negotiation.

Negotiating with your child can be challenging. It is important to develop a better understanding of how you can do so. Giving your child the space to negotiate on small decisions like choosing clothes, picking a household chore or favourite food, empowers her or him to have a voice that is heard and respected. This enhances a child's self-esteem and confidence in making choices and to be who (s)he wants to be.

NEGOTIATING THE RIGHT WAY

Negotiation helps bridge the gap between demands that have the potential to create a conflict. As a parent, it is important to model these skills the right way in your day-to-day interactions in front of your child for her or him to internalize the same. Let us take a look at the essential principles that allow for better negotiation.

1. *Understand the other point of view and come up with probable solutions*: The first rule for negotiation is to hear out the differing opinions. Actively listen to your child to understand the problem at hand. Share your perspective with your child in a direct, simple way. Break the problem down into parts, think about it in a focused manner and generate solutions. While listening to her or him, try to think of alternatives that can be traded in for the demand. Encourage your child to also think of creative ways of resolving the problem.
2. *Clearly define the rules at home*: It is important to clearly define what is negotiable and what is non-negotiable at home. This leads to an understanding of expectations in terms of behaviour and demands. You must also ensure that the rules are followed consistently by every member in the house for the internalization of family norms and expectations. This leads to the inculcation of values and self-discipline. Your child is also able to understand the culture of the family.
3. *Think before entering the negotiation situation*: You must think about the reason for saying no to your child's wish or demand. Sometimes, when strapped for time, a parent may end up refusing without giving due consideration to the reasons for saying a no, only to later realize that they could have agreed on the same. This also creates a situation where you might reverse or retract your decision, where your child might think (s)he could try and push to see if you would relent each time you say no.
4. *Discuss the contingency contract in advance*: It is important to enter the contingency contract with your child in advance and discuss the rewards and punishments to achieve the desired results. If you feel it is appropriate, you can involve your child in the process of choosing the rewards or penalties as children feel more motivated to follow through if they establish the rules themselves. They are more likely to comply and tend to

cooperate better with the terms of the contract.

5. *Be open to more conversations*: Sometimes, it can be hard to conclude a particular contract, given that neither your child nor you are entirely satisfied with the conclusion. Be open to rethink the matter and come back to discuss it further, instead of giving in or giving up. It is important to stay on the matter and keep working on it. Be ready to reassess your beliefs and give your child the time and space to rethink and renegotiate as well.

NEGOTIATION IS A LIFELONG JOURNEY

Negotiating one's needs and demands and understanding other people and their perspectives is a lifelong process. It teaches children the ability to accommodate the needs and desires of oneself and others with respect and dignity, and it generates empathy. Children learn to communicate and assert better when they understand the application of negotiation. They can cope with difficult situations across the various transitions in life better with confidence, resilience and a stable sense of self.

HIGHLIGHTS

- Negotiation is a critical life skill for children.
- Negotiating situations will help your child and you resolve conflicts by finding the middle ground amicably and by listening to each other.
- Engage in the creation of a thoughtful contingency contract with rewards and penalties mutually decided to increase cooperation.
- Negotiation helps children to be considerate, accommodating and compromising, by understanding the perspectives and needs of others.
- Negotiation skills empower your child to voice and assert opinions confidently.

26

WORK TO NURTURE SELF-AWARENESS

The awareness of the self...of thoughts, emotions, traits and temperament...is critical to success in later years. Nurture and adequately equip the developing self of your children with the right abilities to give them a chance at happiness for life.

Self-awareness, in simple terms, is the child's cognitive ability to be attuned to her or his body, thoughts, feelings, traits, temperament and personality. Understanding one's own needs, desires, likes and dislikes, and using language and mobility to fulfil these needs and desires, shows early evidence of self-awareness in a young child. This self-awareness is used to make sense of the world and of those around the child, to determine relationships, to find ways forward, and to know where one may struggle and where one will be successful.

The ability to develop a deeper understanding of and operate within the interpersonal and intrapersonal aspects of social context makes self-awareness a very critical skill to learn and nurture. Self-awareness makes space for self-reflection that helps in creating meaningful relationships with others. This awareness of the self is integral to the child's self-concepts. As the awareness expands, it helps in defining who the child is in relation to the world.

As the child gains greater knowledge of her or his own ability to think and act in a certain situation, it helps optimize learning such that it contributes to self-growth. Awareness of the mental, emotional and physical self makes children confident individuals who are able to gain mastery over their inner mechanisms in a given situation, thus being able to move past that which can be self-limiting.

SELF-AWARENESS OPTIMIZES LEARNING AND BUILDS SELF-CONFIDENCE

Technology often overtakes our lives in today's fast-paced times. We forget to look at what is in front of us. We become oblivious towards the most obvious things in our surroundings. Nurturing self-awareness in such times is essential. It is important to direct attention towards building self-reflection and introspection, which can help your child feel more connected to experiences.

Encourage your child to go beyond simple observation to extract and weave meaning into experiences. This can be done through the process of reflecting upon the role played by the self, others and the surroundings. For example, when a classmate is getting bullied, the child is not merely a witness to the incident. (S)He experiences fear or anger that can either prevent or push your child to take action. Understanding and tuning in to internal feelings and thoughts enables your child to know what drives her or him to act or not act in situations. This enhanced knowledge contributes to building confidence in your child as (s)he becomes more aware of the self.

Self-awareness is vital for academic success and learning too. A child with greater awareness of strengths and limitations can utilize the understanding to her or his benefit. This knowledge empowers the child to know where to put more effort and the reasons why something may or may not fall into place. Simultaneously, the child is able to focus on working on limitations or utilize the strengths to be able to optimize performance. The process of self-reflection lets the child edit existing ways of working.

Self-aware children are able to employ this skill as a tool to monitor, process and control feelings and behaviour, and adapt their beliefs in relation to the self and the world. They learn to share by accommodating their needs with those of others—developing perspective-taking abilities. For example, from stating, 'I want to play with my toys because I like it,' they move forward to accommodate a friend by saying, 'You can take some of my toys and let us play a game with them.' This awareness extends itself from 'self' to the 'other'.

Being able to use the information gained through introspection allows the child to feel in control of the self. This, in turn, increases confidence. The process of being self-reflective and adaptive increases the brain's flexibility to accommodate and assimilate various experiences and promotes further learning. This also cultivates positive self-esteem and generates happiness.

CULTIVATE AND PRACTISE SELF-AWARENESS WITH YOUR CHILD

Cultivating self-awareness promotes self-care in your child—awareness of their mind, body, sensations and emotions pushes children to look at their social, emotional and physical health. Parents can play a crucial role in instilling and reinforcing the process of self-reflection by creating space for it in their conversations, talking about the importance of shutting out the constant chatter of the world and becoming in tune with oneself. By following these simple and effective steps, you can foster self-awareness in your child.

1. *Create moments of self-awareness*: The initial step to nurture self-awareness in your child is to build self-aware moments. When you are with your child, tune into your child's experience. Focus on your child's play, stories and activities and make more in-depth conversations about the experience. Ask questions like, 'What do you think of it? How do you feel about it?' When the child speaks about emotions, talk about what (s)he felt in the body, the sensations and thoughts that rushed through the mind. These simple conversations can help build self-awareness.

2. *Stimulate a self-reflective process*: It is important to challenge your child's assumptions and perceptions of experiences, to stimulate deeper thinking about actions and choices. Remember to ask your child, 'What do you think made you so upset?', 'What makes you believe this is your weakness? or 'How would

you react in the same situation if I replace your emotion of anger with sadness?' Posing self-reflective questions to children nudges them to redefine the meanings derived from their experiences, and expand upon their existing mental, emotional and behavioural processes. It also instills greater responsibility for the feelings, thoughts and actions harboured by the child as (s)he becomes aware of their impact on others.
3. *Validate your child's emotions and thoughts*: Your child needs a framework within which (s)he can engage in the process of self-reflection. This is usually provided through the validating statements and affirmations you use to encourage or caution your child. As you validate the child's thoughts and emotions by being non-judgemental and accepting of experiences, the child is made aware of the correctness or appropriateness of what (s)he is saying and doing. Validation is an important aspect of self-awareness as it is important for the child to feel acknowledged for her or his experiences and responses.
4. *Cultivate opportunities to further knowledge of the self*: For your child to move forward on the path of increased self-awareness, (s)he would need a growing framework within which to operate. This would mean providing your child with more opportunities to learn and grow, explore the surroundings, have novel experiences, test skills and engage with others. Such rich experiences allow your child to expand on the understanding of the self and build on comfort and confidence across a broad range of situations.

NURTURING SELF-AWARENESS IS A PROCESS

Self-awareness, to a large extent, expands depending upon how well it is groomed and nurtured during the early years of a child's life. Listening mindfully to your child's experiences, and providing affirmation and validation contribute towards the development of self-awareness in your child. As (s)he learns the skill of being self-aware, (s)he develops a stronger yet flexible sense of self that is resilient and positive.

HIGHLIGHTS

○ Self-awareness involves helping the child to be attuned to feelings, bodily sensations and thoughts.
○ Nurturing self-awareness optimizes learning and self-growth in your child.
○ With increased self-awareness, children become better learners and gain more confidence to assert their choices.
○ The process of self-reflection and introspection enhances cognitive skills and builds flexibility and adaptability in situations.
○ Foster self-awareness in your child by creating mindful experiences through open-ended, self-reflective and validating conversations.

27

REINFORCE THE EFFORTS

Reinforce and acknowledge the child's efforts.
Success will automatically find its way.

Children seek the acknowledgement of their parents when they try something new, accomplish a task on their own or outperform their own personal best. A simple, positive, encouraging statement like 'Great going!' can make your child happy and it motivates them to do more. Recognizing the efforts with positive feedback helps your child understand the value you place on the energy invested on her or his task. This also contributes towards building a sense of control and mastery over actions, and creates a strong internal drive to attain goals.

Through reinforcement, you provide your child the validation for the way (s)he thinks and acts. As your toddler climbs up the stairs or down the bed and you encourage using words like 'Wonderful, my baby', you provide a sense of security to the child to explore further. As children grow older, they direct their learning towards honing their skills to solve problems. Some experiences can be frustrating, and your child may feel demotivated to engage with the task. However, encouraged by you—as you extend a helping hand and gently prod her or him—you create the environment to motivate and enhance complex learning.

By supporting and encouraging your child to attain the goals (s)he sets for the self, you help build self-determination and confidence. Your positive strokes can go a long way in generating and sustaining self-motivation to take on challenges, thereby building self-sufficiency to achieve outcomes. Children who have confidence in their ability to achieve goals possess good problem-solving skills and demonstrate greater resilience in the face of difficult circumstances.

ACKNOWLEDGING EFFORTS IS INCREMENTAL TO POSITIVE SELF-BELIEF

Positive acknowledgement of the child and/or accomplishments through statements like, 'This drawing looks beautiful', 'Your score is fantastic', or 'You are a good player' enhances self-confidence and performance. However, the use of such statements in the context of accomplishments alone does not allow them to be translated into a system of positive self-beliefs. To reinforce the child's motivation to perform well and sustain continuity, the benefits of emphasizing and acknowledging the child's efforts need to be stressed.

The efforts the child directs to accomplish goals should not go unnoticed or unappreciated. This helps build a significantly better awareness of the process that the child utilizes, and helps in understanding that the way something is done is rather important. Specific feedback is effective in creating greater knowledge of the steps taken by the child in the process of achieving a goal. This helps her or him to build the knowledge base for utilization across similar situations in the future, increasing the probability for better problem-solving and outcomes.

Remember to be specific. Use statements like, 'I really like the way you thought of looking at the edges to fix those pieces to complete your puzzle', 'The shades and strokes that you have used are so beautiful in the painting', 'You dribble the ball so fast and swiftly', or 'You finished your lunch and homework on time. You did such a great job today.' When you break down the process for the child, reinforcing the specific skills used and pair it with the end result, (s)he is able to correlate the skills and the effort with the outcome. This leads to progression in the development and application of skills. The subsequent reinforcement of the skill transforms into a strong and positive self-belief.

EVERY TIME IS NOT A PREREQUISITE

You may wonder how often and how much should you reinforce the efforts by your child. There is no hard-and-fast rule that can be generally applied. However, it is not necessary to reinforce every time without fail when you notice your child making an effort. Even if you miss some opportunities to appreciate the effort being put to work on a problem or situation, it is alright. Be mindful about providing appreciation in a balanced manner, and do not overdo it as it can then lose its meaning and effectiveness.

Simultaneously, you do not want your child to be over-dependent, constantly seeking external approval and appreciation for what (s)he is doing. Balancing the reinforcing act can be a mysterious phenomenon. A mindful parent, attuned to the needs of the child, is able to assess when and how much to support.

You need to make your independent judgement in deciding how much you think your child needs reinforcement for her or his efforts. Some children are good problem-solvers and temperamentally more driven to achieve their goals. In such a scenario, a slight approval by the parent is enough motivation for the child. Other children can need more cajoling and support through the process initially, which can later be tapered and reduced. But in extreme cases, there can be children who do need consistent prodding and encouragement by the parent for a longer duration.

BE EFFECTIVE IN REINFORCING THE EFFORTS

The significant efforts of your child need to be reinforced, but making these choices can be tricky at times. There are many aspects you need to be cognizant of which can aid you in reinforcing the right efforts and actions displayed by your child. Let's take a look at these.

1. *Your acknowledgement should not express an evaluation of the child but recognize the abilities*: It is common practice to show approval to the child about her or his achievements or desired

behaviour by associating it with who the child is such as when you say, 'You are a good dancer.' These statements, in part, convey an evaluation or judgement about the child and not the ability per se. If you support these reinforcing statements with what makes you think (s)he is a good dancer or runner, the child feels recognized for the abilities and the effort that has been extended. For instance, you can say instead, 'Your moves have become precise and clear, and your expressions have evolved too. You surely are becoming a good dancer.' This allows the child to understand that being a 'good dancer' is not independent of the various elements that contribute towards making one a good dancer. The next time the child does not perform well, (s)he does not automatically think, 'I am a bad dancer' but identifies and assesses what was done differently that led to a decline in the performance.

2. *Help the child have a view of the progress in the efforts*: Take note of the details of the efforts put in by your child in terms of the strategies and skills used. Have a good understanding of how (s)he has progressed over time to achieve the results today. When you speak with your child, pointing out the shifts made by her or him, use elaborative statements like, 'When you started playing basketball, you found it difficult to dribble the ball and chase it around the other player. With consistent practice, you were able to improve these skills and the ability to score points for your team. From not being able to score when you started, you are now able to make the basket in your matches.' Seeing the transformation in the skills, the child is able to feel greater control and mastery over her or his game. It also contributes to the developing identity of the child and contributes to building confidence.

3. *Assess the efforts to open channels of communication for future problem-solving*: When discussing the efforts expended at length and reviewing details, your child attains clarity about what needs to be done further. It provides opportunities to determine where problems are and find ways to circumvent them, thus engaging in problem-solving. (S)He is able to

judge where changes need to be implemented in the current strategies. Thus, reflecting on the efforts helps your child think from a problem-solving standpoint to augment performance.

4. *Begin your feedback with a positive statement to make it constructive*: When assessing your child's performance, start your conversations acknowledging the efforts. This gives your child a secure platform to review things further. Kicking off a discussion about subpar performance and lagging skills can make your child feel unsure—this prevents the internalization of feedback. The child either becomes defensive or may shut down, feeling ashamed, embarrassed, disappointed or angry with herself or himself. Use statements like, 'Your initial planning was good with everyday goals to study two subjects, but where we lagged was in the implementation of this strategy.'

5. *Encourage your child to give herself or himself a pat on the back for the efforts*: When you praise a child for her or his efforts, (s)he develops a natural tendency to seek external feedback. Help your child internalize positive external feedback to develop the process of self-validation by asking her or him to reward herself or himself verbally.

THE FINAL STEP TOWARDS SUCCESS

A child who is able to place efforts in the right direction smoothly progresses towards successful outcomes. The understanding of the direction comes from the adults around—parents, teachers, older siblings or any other adults. Children who lack the ability to understand the importance of the efforts and how they lead to the desired outcome, struggle in the long run as they focus on factors that may not be in their control. Acknowledging and assessing the efforts your child displays during the early years and later in adolescence builds the ability to introspect and develops a reservoir of skills that your child can put to use effectively.

HIGHLIGHTS

- Reinforce your child's efforts and the process used to reach goals.
- Be specific in providing feedback about the child's efforts.
- Acknowledge your child's efforts and encourage your child to develop a self-modulated mechanism of acknowledging them.
- Review your child's efforts and skills to create opportunities for reflection and problem-solving in the future.
- Be mindful of evaluating the efforts, and not the child, in your conversations to develop strong self-concepts.

28

SUPPORT YOUR CHILD THROUGH FAILURES

*Biggest learnings in life come through failure.
Imbue the belief 'I still can' in the face of setbacks.
Not by shielding but supporting.*

A child's failure in any domain of life can be a painful and devastating experience for both the child and the parent. While some failures may be short-lived, others may last longer—leaving a scarring impact on the child's self-esteem and confidence. The resultant emotional setback can be disturbing and challenging for the family—triggering an automatic reaction from the parents to prevent and, sometimes, even overly protect the child.

A parent, at times, might even begin to shield the child from stumbling or performing below average by means of recurrent conversations about good academic results, starring performances in sports, music or other extra-curricular activities. But these can communicate an overarching message about success, creating a perception that the child has very little room for her or his failures being accepted. Even thinking of failure might evoke fear and anxiety in you and your child. As a result, you either rescue your child and yourself prior to a potential failure by overt parenting deeds, or feel helpless and compelled to use negative reinforcement.

Failures and obstacles are faced by everyone. The manner in which you communicate with your children about failures influences their ability to perceive and approach them. It shapes their beliefs about failure and success.

FAILURES ARE IMPORTANT STEPPING STONES IN YOUR CHILD'S LIFE

Failures are inevitable. What is seen as a failure by a child is relative to her or his developmental stage. For a toddler, the inability to make a tower with Lego can evoke a response of loud screams; a pre-schooler may find losing a game with playmates absolutely disheartening making her or him cry incessantly; during the teen years, peer rejection, poor grades or lack of parental approval become moments that make your child feel dejected. While a toddler is able to let go quickly and bounces back to re-engage with the play and exploration, a teen cannot. As children grow, the fear of failing rises and the desire to succeed without failing becomes a need. This realignment in thinking is often defined by the narrow standards set by us as parents for what constitutes success.

An A grade on a test or winning a competition is connoted as success. Stories of success revolve around the final outcome rather than the challenging struggle behind them. With this changing culture of success in the society, both adults and children feel the pressure to outperform and work towards the prevention of failure. This, in the real sense, is walking backwards rather than moving forward—as failure teaches a child to look beyond the present. When a child fails, (s)he thinks of various possibilities to rise again and find success. Failure instigates problem-solving, whereas a one-stop pre-tested solution to avoid failure blocks critical and creative-thinking abilities.

Undoubtedly, it will be difficult for you to see your child fail. Your instinctive response will be to jump and save your child from the aftermath of the debacle. Yet it is important to, at times, pull back and allow your child to go through the experiences of failing to build character and develop a better sense of self.

For children to learn from failures, parents and adults need to change the narrative of success. Failures need to be celebrated as opportunities to learn and success should be seen as a collective outcome of both past failures and present efforts. Acknowledging and accepting failures gives your child a space to embrace the self with all the limitations and mistakes (s)he may possess. It builds a robust internal system and resilience in the face of setbacks, enhancing the confidence to manage them.

SUPPORTING YOUR CHILD THROUGH FAILURES AND SETBACKS

Children who are unable to deal with failures often find themselves being excessively vulnerable to stress and anxiety. They can experience frustration and distress when they are unable to accomplish their goals. Staying besides your child through such times, giving her or him the space to talk about failures, normalizing the experience and empathizing emotionally, promotes mental well-being. However, other effective ways can be utilized to support your child through failures.

1. *Be cognizant of how you respond to failures*: What is most impactful and stays with a child for life is how you deal with situations in which (s)he failed. Children maintain a vigilant eye on the responses of parents as they get their cues from you. They learn from whether you get angry, frustrated, dejected, avoid the problem or acknowledge it, calm yourself down, think of a solution and bounce back from your setbacks. Your child learns to adopt a similar approach when (s)he experiences setbacks. If you communicate your disappointment about your child's inability to do a task by saying, 'It is so simple. I don't understand how you cannot learn it till now,' it can make her or him feel dejected. Instead, a calm response like, 'We have done it together multiple times, why don't you try it first yourself and I will come in if you need my support,' can enhance your child's willingness to try.
2. *Talk to your child about failures openly*: Give your child a free and open space to talk about failures. If your child is worried about facing failures or experiencing a breakdown, it is important to talk about their feelings and fears. Sometimes, talking about the worst and saying it out loud can aid in releasing the mental

burden the child may be carrying. Acknowledging the most feared consequence that your child may be harbouring can help normalize the thought process, providing you with the opportunity to alter or dispute it. While comforting your child, refrain from using phrases like, 'It is not such a big thing. It's all going to be fine.' Instead validate by saying, 'I understand your concern. Failures are a part of one's life. What do you think is the worst that may happen here? And if it happens, what do you think you could learn from it? Is there something we can do to make you feel more comfortable? You know we will find a way to manage the situation, whatever it may turn out to be.' Help your child associate the logic with fear and express the failure as a lesson from which much can be learnt.

3. *Refrain from portraying yourself as an overachieving parent*: There are times when your child comes to you excitedly to show you her or his attempt at creating a painting, solving a difficult problem, writing a poem or any other task. You might then respond by suggesting changes that can make it better. You may say, 'Oh, you did great! But I suppose you could have used this colour and changed this part of the figure it would look nicer!' This is you being an overachieving parent. The message that is communicated to the child is that what (s)he does is not good enough. This translates into a belief system where the child does not see herself or himself as being good enough. It is prudent to be appreciative and engage your child in a self-reflective process to evaluate how (s)he has done instead. Use an open-ended statement like, 'Well, this looks lovely! I like the way you have coloured the mountains and made the water appear like it's flowing. What do you feel about your painting? Can you think of any improvisations?' This nudges the child to think of possibilities to improve and improvise the work in a self-driven manner.

4. *Identify signs of self-criticism in your child*: Some children take failures too harshly upon themselves. They engage in patterns of self-blame and criticism that can affect self-esteem and motivation to perform well. These children also find it difficult

to bounce back easily as each failure is perceived as a failure of the self. It is important to talk to your child and separate the developing systems of self-beliefs from experiences in which there is failure. Help your child view failure as an element encountered within the natural course of life. Simultaneously, break down the situation by recognizing your child's efforts and acknowledging the external factors that can be implicated in the process of failing while allowing your child to focus on what (s)he could potentially control to ensure the same outcomes are not encountered in the future.

5. *Share stories of your own failures*: Lead your child by example by sharing your stories of failure. Rather than feeling embarrassed or shameful to share your own experiences, talk openly about them. It allows your child to view failures as a normal part of life. It also gives her or him a sense of hope that failures are temporary and they provide the opportunity to learn and grow. Perseverance and resilience in the face of a failure is the key to a successful path.

FAILING IS NOT AN ENDPOINT

Failure is just the beginning. It is the beginning of learning—about the self, others, world, what works, what does not, being adaptive, reflective, flexible and perseverant. Failures do not indicate an end. They do not put a stop to the process of growth. Instead they act as indicators of the areas where growth is possible and efforts need to be directed.

HIGHLIGHTS

- Help your child understand that failures are inevitable experiences of life.
- Talk about failures as learning blocks that create opportunities to grow.
- Beware of how you approach setbacks as a parent.
- Have open conversations about failures by understanding your child's fears, sharing your stories and turning them into moments of problem-solving.
- Re-align success stories by talking about the importance of losing.

29

CREATE INTERNAL DRIVE THROUGH GOAL SETTING

*You want your child to be self-driven,
motivated to achieve and do more.
Support this desire by helping your child set goals,
and master the skill of motivating the self.*

Goals are a quintessential feature of an individual's life, driving her or him to work towards achieving something or reaching a mythical endpoint. Having a family, raising children, earning finances, achieving dreams, being a successful professional, and other personal and professional goals drive people to keep moving forward. Without a purpose in life, you would not be motivated to do things.

Having a goal encourages you to put your best efforts in whatever work you may be doing. Fulfilling the goals that are vested in your multiple roles give you happiness, satisfaction and contentment. Not having a goal in life makes you worry, feel listless and rudderless. You may find it challenging to sustain tasks for long if you are not able to see their purpose.

This is applicable to children as well. When you find your child lacking focus or not showing the zeal to perform, there is a possibility that it is happening on account of not having a goal. Goals give your child a direction to follow, place efforts and redeem benefits. Achieving goals acts as a positive reinforcement to do more, set new targets, challenge the self and continue to invest energies in that direction.

To be able to define goals, the child needs to understand and determine what is essential. Goal setting does not come easily to a child—(s)he learns it by observing and internalizing an adult's ways of communicating, setting expectations and providing targets. For example, when you tell your child, 'You need to perform well in your final exams this year,' you are giving a larger goal, but you also need to work on providing your child the ability to break it down into small concrete steps which act as short-term goals. Over time, it creates the internal drive and self-discipline in your child to stay motivated to complete tasks and find more to do.

GOAL SETTING INDUCES INTRINSIC MOTIVATION

Each child has areas of strengths, abilities and talents. For your child to be able to reach her or his true potential and actualize the talents that (s)he possesses, a direction and a path are needed. Your child needs to know exactly where energies and efforts need to be focused. For young children, this reflects in not wanting to do daily chores and tasks, consistently pointing out that they feel bored and being restless a lot of the time. When your child reaches teenage and still does not have a sense of purpose, (s)he can slip into a state of inertia characterized by aimlessly watching TV, spending more time with friends and other leisure activities. But if you try to understand what is going on, you would recognize that underneath the short-lived enjoyment lies a sense of purposelessness in life and the feeling of being lost.

Lack of focus and purpose in a child's life evokes anxieties in a parent as well. It is a matter of grave concern for a parent to see their child not have purpose and aimlessly engage in undesirable actions. When faced with this situation, you may be tempted to offer rewards or use fear-inducing statements to motivate your child. Making rewards contingent upon the accomplishment of a goal can act as a positive reinforcement in the short term. However, it does not result in the generation of persistent motivation to perform in the long run. Concurrently, the child learns to expect rewards and it is difficult to sustain this for long. When the rewards are withdrawn eventually, it leads to angry outbursts and a systemic collapse where the child may refuse to do anything that (s)he is being asked. This makes it even more important that parents work towards creating an internal drive within the child to set goals and achieve targets.

Understanding the value of accomplishing a goal is integral to the creation of an internal drive. The purpose behind the action attaches meaning to the task making the child feel self-driven to reach the target. It leads to persistent efforts from the child to keep moving in the decided direction, ensuring re-engagement with future goals. This leads to enhanced feelings of competence and self-confidence. As a token of appreciation, you can reward the child using acknowledgement and appreciation for the efforts being put. Using rewards discretionarily augments the self-esteem of the child and makes the child feel recognized.

FOSTERING GOAL-SETTING SKILLS IN YOUR CHILD

Setting goals is a skill that a child can develop through a clear understanding of how to define goals and to set strategies to achieve them. First and foremost, your child must be able to decide on a goal. You play a crucial role in the initial years in helping your child formulate the strategies for reaching these goals. Helping her or him evaluate possibilities, decide upon what is important and of an interest, where one would like to direct efforts over a long period of time is important.

If your child is a good singer and can potentially be a musician, (s)he must have a clear understanding of whether (s)he would like to pursue it as a career or a hobby. The decision to be a singer would require the setting of multiple short-term goals that lead to the eventual outcome. Concurrently, (s)he would have to plan daily practice rituals, improvise on learning and engage in other exercises would help enhance performance. This strategic planning with you on a daily basis would be crucial in helping her or him reach the target and developing an understanding of how (s)he needs to do it for herself or himself in the future.

Goal setting also teaches time management, as setting timelines to achieve both short-term and long-term goals is important. Setting timeframes keeps your child focused. It creates self-discipline as it encourages the child to assume responsibility of her or his efforts.

Inevitably, major or minor obstacles come in the way of reaching goals. The child's ability to face these challenges enhances resilience. It requires cognitive flexibility to redefine aspects of goal planning as (s)he moves forward. Assisting your child to assess and realign certain processes is important. For instance, while your child is preparing for exams, you both might realize that the time and practice required for mathematics would be more than what was expected initially. Then, redefining goals or the strategies become necessary.

Goal setting requires that an array of skills be learnt and implemented. As this skill is mastered, it also enhances a child's self-awareness and psychological growth.

TEACH YOUR CHILD TO MASTER GOAL ACCOMPLISHMENT

You are your child's first mentor on how to achieve goals. Children master basic skills through observing the parent, imbibing what is taught through persistent efforts. During the early developmental years, children see a goal through your eyes, understand them through your words and gestures and move towards accomplishing them using your encouragement and support. To make goal setting a constructive exercise and goal accomplishment a consistent feature, you can teach your child some effective strategies.

1. *Help your child set realistic goals:* Work through the process of setting realistic goals both for the short and long term. Your child may either choose something too big or outside of her or his ability to achieve. If your child wants to be an artist, have a long discussion to help her or him have an understanding of what artistic abilities and skills (s)he possesses. Provide a reality check about how far one can achieve the goal and the intense, arduous process of reaching it. The idea is not to discourage your child from pursuing a goal that may be too challenging. However, it is important to be gentle in your approach and

make your child think by asking the right questions that make her or him reflect upon the choices being made and goals being set.
2. *Facilitate by helping your child create specific goals:* It is important to have specific goals that provide a precise indication of what is to be achieved. A child's generalized goal like, 'I want to be a good student' or a parent's verbalization of a goal like, 'I want you to perform well this year,' are expectations that lack precise direction. Specificity would teach your child how to plan in detail and with precision for the goals. Helping your child answer questions like what, how, when and where, all aid in making goals more specific.
3. *Measure the progress:* Help your child measure the progress that is being made over a period of time. Once the child follows the specific and relevant goal plan, (s)he can evaluate her or his own performance at multiple points, and measure the progress by creating benchmarks for further improvisation. This lets the child have clarity and control over where (s)he stands, how good the performance is and what changes are required to improvise and hasten the movement to achieve the goal.
4. *Guide your child to create achievable timeframes:* Having a timeline helps give a definite focus and commitment to finish the stipulated goal. You can help your child decide a timeframe, which is neither too rigid and stringent nor too lax. Help your child maintain some amount of flexibility and take into account other contingencies which can act as a barrier to the achievement of the goals.

THE ART OF GOAL SETTING

Goal setting is an art that requires you to help your child maintain an intricate balance between what (s)he would like to do, what (s)he has an interest in, and the basic abilities (s)he possesses. Being present to monitor how your child is progressing towards achieving goals is important while ensuring you are not nagging. The ultimate goal is to pass on these skills to your child by encouraging her or him to discuss, and plan steps and goals with you. This helps your child feel confident in making choices about where to invest her or his energies.

HIGHLIGHTS

- Goal setting is a skill that can be fostered in your child.
- Goal setting evokes an intrinsic desire to pursue and achieve goals.
- It teaches the child self-discipline, responsibility for one's own efforts and resilience to overcome obstacles in the path to reach the goal.
- Be a facilitator in helping your child set realistic and attainable goals within a specified timeframe.
- A clear process with specific details about how to achieve the final goal creates precision, focus and commitment to accomplish it.

30

ENCOURAGE PERSEVERANCE

*Encourage your child not to work
hard but persevere to work hard.
It develops true grit to rise after each fall.*

Dealing with daily challenges, minor setbacks, overcoming major obstacles or surviving worst circumstances is made possible on account of the individual's perseverance. The ability to be resilient and persevere enables you to live through pain, take risks, explore new experiences, bounce back from failures and re-engage with new goals and challenges. Perseverance maintains hope and allows one to keep moving steadily through problems.

Fostering perseverance in your child from an early age is critical to developing a positive belief system about the self and the abilities the child possesses to be able to overcome difficulties. Some children possess perseverance as a character trait, and you will find them working on an activity till they reach the end. A child who has recently learned to button the shirt struggles to do so but continues to work on it diligently, refusing to take help. Patience and endurance required to finish the task are innate in such children. Other children may give up easily or feel emotionally challenged in being able to engage with difficult tasks. You may find them frequently giving up too soon or getting upset on age-appropriate challenges or leaving them mid-way due to loss of interest.

Perseverance is a skill that can be taught to children. It is a skill that not only aids in reaching the end-goal, but also prepares children to deal with larger adversities in life. It nurtures resilience and strength in your child's personality.

PERSEVERANCE KEEPS YOUR CHILD STEADY IN LIFE

The wide range of options available in today's world makes it easy to find comfortable means to reach targets or make ends meet. On evaluating the effort and time a task demands, it is a natural tendency to choose the easy option from the myriad possibilities that are available. Easier alternatives can replace a burdensome task. Acquiring objects is just a click away with the use of technology. Staying connected with people at distant places or pursuing your dreams has become more accessible through the use of social media. With the easy availability of comforts, the need to inculcate the value of perseverance in children has become ever more critical.

Perseverance teaches self-determination to a child, helping the child to successfully conclude a task. Your child may possess talents and potential, but success cannot be achieved without diligence. A dose of perseverance is what your child needs to manage and cope with challenges at school, in interpersonal relationships or extracurricular activities. For example, when a rigorous exercise is being taught at school your child may be tempted to skip it as it requires physical endurance, or when (s)he has to present a project in class but is unwilling to put in the effort and contemplates skipping school. Even when the child knows something has to be done and requires the best effort be put in, (s)he can try to find the easy way out especially when it is not of interest or seems like a difficult task.

Perseverance equips your child to move past challenges. It is important to let your child experience failures and keep encouraging her or him to try once, twice and even multiple times till (s)he finally reaches the goal. This helps the child let go of resistance or fear and builds acceptance towards the upcoming challenges in life. As a result, your child learns the value of giving the best shot and putting an effort instead of being solely focused on the end result. It also helps your child to understand that (s)he may not achieve the goals every time but the very act of perseverance makes her or him a better learner in life. It keeps the yearning to learn, grow and achieve intact. This gives a sense of pride and enhances self-confidence.

WAYS IN WHICH YOU CAN BUILD PERSEVERANCE IN YOUR CHILD

Bringing up a child is in itself an act of perseverance. In playing your role of a parent, you strive to make your child happy, ready to travel miles to protect, secure and provide the best for her or him. You may sometimes feel that you failed on a particular day to gather yourself and re-engage with your child. You wipe your tears to put up a smile and hide your pain to walk with them. For your child to learn this perseverance, it is important to create the balance and withdraw yourself from playing the protective role each time. By using various means, you can develop the skills of perseverance in your child. Let's take a look at some of these.

1. *Be observant of your child's perseverant acts and reinforce them:* Children show signs of determination or will to pursue when the activity is of their interest. Be observant of such actions and reinforce those moments where your child engages in an act with diligence. For example, when your child's tall tower made using blocks falls once, and (s)he tries again, you can encourage her or him by saying, 'I like how you want to try that again. Trying hard is very good and playing this game is fun! And you did even better this time!' By focusing on the act of trying, you build courage in your child to take up the challenge. The child also begins to relate to perseverance as being fun and enjoyable rather than burdensome and difficult.
2. *Play games and activities that pose a challenge:* Introduce your child to games like Jenga and Scrabble, or puzzles and any sport that pushes the child to take up a challenge. For example, make a bicycle ride into a fun challenging game by putting obstacles on the way and raising the difficulty level at an age-appropriate level. Explain to your child how you are increasing the levels so your child is informed and this acts as a learning

experience on how to persevere.

3. *Use stories and folktales:* Life's most valuable lessons can be taught to children using stories and folktales. Stories give children a medium to explore their thoughts and feelings. Listening to a story helps children develop perspectives as an observer and are one of the best tools to inculcate life skills in a non-preachy way. There are examples of stories such as in *The Panchatantra* that share the value of perseverance. Similar stories are also seen in books from other cultures. Such stories with characters depicting failure and resilience help children understand both the process and meaning of success in life.

4. *Encourage your child to see challenges as an experience to be enjoyed:* How you approach a challenge sets the stage for how your child views them as well. If you view a challenge as a problem that is stressful or as something that can be enjoyed, your child will also imbibe a similar perception and approach towards managing it. Every new challenge brings with it an array of difficulties and stress, so it is important to emphasize the need to not resist or run away but find a fun way to experience and work with it.

5. *Make your child practise more:* Children often tend to compare themselves with others, and feel discouraged to engage in the activity if they think others are better than them. Help your child understand the need for practice to gain confidence and expertise in any activity. Persistent efforts play a crucial role in accomplishing life goals.

6. *Help a perseverant child build perspective:* Some children who are perseverant about their needs and demands, should be encouraged to build perspective. They may find it difficult to find their way with other children while at play or in group work as they can rigidly stick to their own ideas. Encourage them to explore alternatives and find mutual resolutions to problems.

BE OPEN TO PUSHBACKS

You put a lot of effort and energy to motivate your child and make her or him persevere with the objectives (s)he has undertaken. In such moments, your child is likely to push back. (S)He can have a unique independent viewpoint that needs to find space in the interactions with you. It is imperative that the road to building perseverance is two-way, where there are engaging conversations and space for each of your perspectives.

HIGHLIGHTS

- Perseverance is a life skill that teaches children the importance of persistent efforts.
- It motivates children to take on challenges with enthusiasm and diligence.
- As a parent observe your child's small acts of being perseverant and reinforce them.
- Perseverance decreases a child's resistance towards difficult tasks and establishes determination to accomplish them.
- Use various means like stories, games and activities to inculcate perseverance in your child.

Section Five

WATCH OUT FOR THESE PARENTING SYNDROMES

31

PARENTS, WATCH YOUR REACTIONS!

Knowingly, and more often unknowingly, you see, say and react to things without thinking through the impact it has. Not just the words you use but your overall reaction is crucial. Be mindful as your child is always observing you.

The responsibility of being a parent is enormous. It is one thing to want to have a child and another thing to take care of your child and create the right environment that facilitates your child's growth and development. Many factors impinge upon your daily existence. These cause you to react and respond as you cannot be a passive observer of what goes on around you. What you believe influences and impacts you.

Often you may not realize that your child is watching you during the course of these daily interactions with your environment. And, each thing your child is seeing is shaping her or his belief systems, attitudes and behaviour. Finally, and perhaps most importantly, what is lost is the awareness that your child is deriving understanding about how life is and how the world can be. Let's look at these aspects more closely.

YOUR RESPONSE STRUCTURES YOUR CHILD'S BELIEF SYSTEMS AND BEHAVIOUR

A growing child is working hard to develop her or his own understanding of people and the world. The expanding worldview is integrating many belief systems. These belief systems are often derived from seeing parents respond to different people and situations. What you end up doing, ultimately becomes responsible for the developing expectations and beliefs that your child holds.

As your child sees you respond to people around, (s)he develops an understanding and belief about how people can be looked at and treated. Their perceptions about relationships and relatedness with others develop on the basis of the manner in which they see you working within your relationships. If they hear you constantly bickering or getting angry with other adults in your life, your child derives the belief that it is okay to be angry and show your temper to adults. If you snap at the help or at people on the road, your child derives the belief that it is okay to be rude with others.

The more adverse your response is to situations, the more anxious it can potentially make your child. It can make her or him feel that the world is not a nice place or that it can even be scary. This causes your child to become timid and sometimes withdrawn. Often such children can be unsure of how people may respond to them. They feel a sense of threat from the environment and struggle to take calls and make decisions. They can be wavering in their self-beliefs and unsure of how they can be effective within the environment they function in. For a child to be creative and to explore the environment freely, trust is an important element. But when a child operates from a space of anxiety this basic trust goes amiss, which inadvertently also influences the confidence your child possesses.

This same attribute of responding adversely to situations within you can also work in the opposite direction, making your child angry and aggressive. If what your child is observing is constant outbursts, it is possible that the same behaviour gets internalized by her or him. Your child imitates your expressions, verbal responses, demeanour and repertoire of behavioural characteristics. This becomes the reality of your child's life which is replicated in her or his reactions in diverse situations. This negatively influences interpersonal relationships. At the same time, it changes your child's self-constellation, making her or him aggressively over-confident and also unmindful, insensitive and mostly non-empathetic towards others.

MOVE FROM REACTING TO RESPONDING

The challenge is to make a move from being reactive—which implies not being in control of your reactions—to being someone who responds to the situations—which implies a conscious understanding and controlled reaction. This is a tough task, as often adults have a tendency to respond instinctively without necessarily putting much thought to what they are doing.

The move from reacting to responding can nevertheless be done by being cognizant of the following aspects:

1. *Know what you want to achieve:* To shift your strategy of doing something new and different, you need to have a goal to remain motivated to the new method. Keep in mind how it would help you to be more mindful of the way in which you respond to people and situations. With your reasons in place you will find it easier to stay focused on being non-reactive. Remember the benefits you accrue from your parenting for your child by being mindful of how you respond.
2. *Maintain your understanding of the current context:* The context of your interaction, as well as the situation, can help you to be mindful of your response within them. Frequently, current reactions are influenced by past experiences (not always from the distant past) which can create an excess of emotions being associated with the way one reacts. Cognizance of the current situation and reminders to dissociate it from the past helps prevent excessive and extreme adverse reactions.
3. *Take a step back to evaluate what you are doing in a situation:* It is helpful even when you are in the midst of an ongoing situation to take a step back. Consciously decide to move yourself mentally and sometimes even physically away from the situation that is unfolding in front of you. When you do so, you create distance in your thoughts, behaviour and the situation in front of you to be able to decide in a relatively calm manner about what you would like to do.
4. *Ask yourself, 'Do I want to react? Would it help me?':* Interjecting

your thought process before you react by asking yourself a simple question, also gives you that momentary timeframe to be able to reassess whether you would like to react. You push yourself to evaluate the manner in which you would like to behave and be perceived in a situation. This can help you decide how you would like to shape your response to the situation.

5. *Post-reaction assessment:* Often, people do not take the time to look back at situations where they reacted in an undesirable manner. This does not allow you to understand yourself in a better manner. A continued lack of understanding of your triggers, what makes you react, how your body felt, what thoughts and feelings ran within you, inhibits your ability to respond instead of react to situations.

IT TAKES TIME

The changes you attempt to incorporate, require some time to implement and show results. Changing yourself can be an arduous task—draining and taxing you to constantly redirect your energies. There will be moments when you will feel irritated and impatient with your own self and the need to engage in this process. However, this is a process which will reap you great dividends, not just in your role as a parent but also in your overall life as a professional, partner, friend and a child yourself.

HIGHLIGHTS

○ Make a move from reacting to responding to situations by generating greater self-control.
○ Always remember the reason you want to change your way of responding.
○ Answer the question 'Do I want to react? Will it help me?' to develop greater control over your way of responding.
○ Your reactivity can influence the personality, temperament, belief system and attitudes your child holds.
○ Go back to a situation where you reacted adversely to learn from it and prevent it.

32

DO NOT CRITICIZE THE BEHAVIOUR

What you see is not all there is to know.
Go beyond the behaviour.
Understand what lies beneath it, what guides and shapes it.
Remember a critical stance can mar growth.

Parents are often surprised when they learn that the biggest error they make is being overly critical with their children. Instead, they expect their over-indulgence and excessive protection of their child to be their greatest folly. The fact is that, in trying to ensure that your child does well, reaches full potential, has a good schooling and an even better career, great relationships and lots of success, a parent often points out too much that is wrong and becomes exceedingly nagging and critical.

The intent is not to hurt or harm your child. No one wishes for that. You want to protect and do the right thing. But inadvertently you may be doing the wrong thing. By the time parents do realize that something is going wrong, children may be already showing emotional challenges and behavioural issues which require in-depth interventions both with the child and the parents.

THE IMPACT OF CRITICISM

When you see a problem and you constantly point it out, you nag your child. The behaviour doesn't change and you talk about it even more. Often you feel like you are hitting your head against a wall and nothing you say or do has an effect. So you keep escalating the content of what you say and how you say it. You don't realize, but the negativity within conversations increases significantly and your child either withdraws into a shell or starts reacting to what you say aggressively. In either scenario you keep reaching a dead end while your child gets affected.

The biggest effect criticism can have on your child is in the views and beliefs (s)he holds about the self. Criticism is easily internalized and it starts becoming a part of your child's self-concepts. It turns into an internally held belief system where your child consistently thinks and feels that (s)he is not good, is bad, can't do things right and will never be good enough. The result is low self-esteem and self-worth and a corresponding negative perspective about the abilities your child holds.

Often children who have low self-concepts tend to be withdrawn and find it difficult to interact with others. Low self-belief and worthiness that the child experiences, adversely affects her or his confidence in social interactions and in the abilities that (s)he possesses. As a result, the child can often struggle to perform in other areas where (s)he may be skilled as well. In contrast a child can also swing towards the other end of the spectrum and become irritable and aggressive. In this scenario, the child feels increasingly frustrated with the negative feedback that is being directed towards her or him, and lashes out angrily when there is even a remote indication towards a criticism being directed towards them. As such these children can end up being bullied or become bullies themselves.

Criticism can have a huge impact on the parent-child relationship. The dyadic relationship that is shared between the parent and the child gets marred and negatively shaped. Mutual respect and regard goes amiss and negative interactions become a characteristic feature. This creates the foundation for a toxic relationship with many negative-interaction cycles.

In the long run, over-criticism on the part of a parent over a long period of time is also known to be associated with the development of mental health concerns in children. The child can become anxious, withdrawn, low or depressed. Besides this, it negatively shapes the developing personality of a child and impacts relationships in a big way.

NOT TALKING IS ALSO NOT A SOLUTION

Your role as a parent is to inform, shape and transform your child into an adult who is set to do well, be successful and be a good person. To achieve this you need to have multiple conversations and often these conversations need to point out where your child is going wrong. At times, you need to nudge and push your child to do a little more and sometimes a lot more.

There is a fine line between being a parent who is doing the above and the one who is becoming a nag or overly critical. The solution does not lie in not saying or not pointing out where your child is going wrong. Instead it is important to be cognizant of what to say, what to comment on, how much to say and when to say it. These four different elements are crucial to the success of your communication and can be instrumental in determining whether you are being negative and critical or positively shaping your child's thinking and behaviour.

- *What to comment on:* Not everything needs to be commented on. Picking your battles is important. If every instance in which your child errs becomes a contentious space of engagement, it will only increase the negativity quotient within your relationship. Instead pick on only two or three things at most to work on with your child.
- *What to say:* Your communication cannot be just about the problem. It is possible that after you have pointed it out once, your child may recognize the problematic behaviour the next time. What is crucial is your ability to point out a problematic behaviour while also providing a remedy to resolve it. These two, when provided together, can help your child incorporate a change. Additionally, reinforcing by acknowledging and praising a change in the displayed behaviour encourages your child to sustain the change.

- *How much to say:* Don't vent your day's frustration on the one display of inappropriate or unacceptable behaviour by your child. Parents can sometimes inadvertently unleash their pent up disappointments at their child. These may relate to their past experiences with the child as well. Instead, find a way to stick to the current situation alone and look at it independent of what may have happened previously. A calm demeanour has greater impact than a rant by a parent.
- *When to say:* Sharing your thoughts and feelings about what your child did or did not do doesn't always have to be done immediately. Sometimes it is more helpful to have a conversation after you are both in a calm and relaxed headspace. This can lead to a more productive outcome than a conversation had in the moment where emotions and tempers may be flaring.

MOTIVATE. DO NOT BERATE YOUR CHILD

Motivation is a key ingredient to create the right foundation for success for your child. Many believe that being bluntly honest about what is wrong can act as a motivator. However, this can be rather counterproductive. Instead, finding ways that gently shape and motivate a child is very important.

1. *Acknowledge, appreciate and praise:* Use the power of acknowledgement, appreciation and praise to motivate your child to inculcate the behaviour you intend. Each time you appreciate or acknowledge your child when they behave in a manner that you had previously encouraged, it helps your child internalize the same. Saying things like 'I really appreciate you doing this the way we discussed' or 'This is really great. I think you are doing a good job at keeping in mind what we talked about', can be encouraging for your child.
2. *Look at the silver lining:* Pointing out the things which your child does well and interspersing these with comments about how something can be done differently is usually a better approach of working with your child. This allows your child

to maintain the feeling of goodness about the self.
3. *You can't change everything—learn to let go:* Not every child can be good at everything. Sometimes you have to let go and accept that there would be areas in which your child may not be as good as another or the way you would like her or him to be. Ask yourself if consistently focusing on this aspect is really that important or life altering. If the answer is no then be ready to let go.
4. *Understand the reasons that may be hindering change:* It helps to try and analyse for yourself what may be preventing your child from changing her or his behaviour. Sometimes the answer may not be obvious. There may be more to why your child continues to respond in the way (s)he does despite your repeated interventions. Look within as well to recognize if there can be something you can change about yourself that may facilitate a change within your child.
5. *Focus on strengths:* It helps to focus on the strengths and enable your child to harness and develop these. While you may be letting go of some aspects which your child may not be good at, the areas of strengths can be focused on and made into skilled areas which would stand your child in good stead in the long run.
6. *Think of multiple solutions and ways of working:* Sometimes you may get stuck on solving a situation in the same way. This may not work or help with your child. It may be important for you to brainstorm and come up with alternate ways of working, which may be unique to your child and give the desired result. Your flexibility in this regard would go a long way.

THE CHANGE STARTS WITH YOU

Removing criticism, being positive or focusing on strengths, all sound very easy. However, these are difficult things to apply on a daily basis. They require practice and mindfulness. You need to be connected and present in your daily interactions, make conscious efforts to be cognizant of what is going on and also consistently work towards changing your own patterns of responding and interacting before you try to change your child. Remember it all starts with you!

HIGHLIGHTS

- Criticism lowers self-esteem and confidence.
- Effective problem-solving necessitates taking a constructive approach that focuses on strengths.
- Everything may not be amenable to change. You need to pick your battles.
- Problems can't always be fixed in the moment. Sometimes you need to let things go for a while and address them later.
- Always remember to acknowledge and appreciate what your child does and remember, the change always starts with you!

33

DON'T BANISH THE MISTAKES

You learn through experiences.
Mistakes too teach you a lot.
Your children need to go through their
own cycle to be able to learn the most.

A parent worries. A parent supports. A parent provides the right environment. A parent protects. The many roles a parent plays are directed towards ensuring the well-being of the child. Each parent hopes that through their actions and verbalizations, they provide the best for the child and also ensure that the child is always safe and taken care of—'No problem should befall my child and if there is one I shall be right there to protect.'

In doing so and by ensuring the protection of the child, parents can often lean in the direction of over-protection. This does not allow the child to make her or his own mistakes and derive their own unique, individualized learning from these experiences. It interferes with the development of the child's ability to think through situations, build coping skills, learn to manage emotions, take care of the self and find ways to solve problems.

Since olden times parents tell their children, 'You should learn from our mistakes. Save yourself the trouble of facing problems.' This would be an ideal situation where the child could learn from the experiences of another through observation. However, the reality is much different. Children learn most by making their own mistakes. What they need is the guidance and support to be able to internalize the right learning from the mistakes they make.

THE THINGS MISTAKES TEACH

One would believe that making mistakes would erode the confidence of the child and make her or him reassess the way they think about themselves. However, the result can be quite the opposite. Mistakes can be instrumental in shaping the character and temperament of your child, providing the opportunity to develop life skills which can have a significant influence on how they respond and move towards success later in life.

The most important thing that a child can learn is that mistakes can happen. It is okay if something goes wrong so long as the child is able and willing to take responsibility for the consequences of the actions they engage in. Taking onus of their experiences and actions is a big step which helps build her or his character. This is perhaps the most important learning that a child can derive. It develops the understanding that things may not always be perfect and can go wrong at times, but there can always be ways to fix them and take care of yourself through these situations. This can be furthered to help the child understand that making a mistake or something going wrong does not indicate a deficit in who the child is. It enables the development of healthy self-concepts which are grounded in abilities and not unduly influenced by negative self-evaluations.

The errors a child makes help her or him develop coping skills. They also build an ability to tolerate disappointments and frustrations. Learning that things don't always play out the way that you want them to and that these experiences need to be embraced and accepted allows the child to develop better distress tolerance. The key in such scenarios is to also help the child work through and find ways of redeeming themselves after mistakes have been made. This also allows for a better understanding of the various ways in which problems can be solved, thus helping the child to have the knowledge that a problematic situation can have multiple solutions. These situations can act as precursors to helping your child develop the skills to find multiple solutions and learn to choose the best way for a given situation.

Finally, the mistakes that your child makes can help her or him recognize the impact their verbalizations and actions can have on others. This provides you with multiple opportunities to help your child develop greater sensitivity towards others' experiences, build empathy and find ways to refrain from hurting others intentionally or unintentionally.

SIMPLE WAYS TO HELP YOUR CHILD FIND THEIR WAY THROUGH MISTAKES

Despite the positives that can be derived from making mistakes, the fact that one has made a mistake can nevertheless have a negative impact on a child. Parents play a crucial role in helping the child see the errors they make, especially at a young age, in the right light, which allows for learning. Parents need to take special care to avoid the creation of a negative self-image which can finally culminate in an attitude of saying, 'I don't care because I know I can't stop myself from making these mistakes.'

Here are a few things that you can say and do to help your child understand and integrate the mistakes they make.

1. *Be calm when your child makes a mistake:* The manner in which you react to your child's mistake shapes the way (s)he looks at it as well. If you react harshly, getting upset or angry, it conveys the message to the child that what happened was too big a thing and not redeemable. It can make your child feel guilty and cause her or him to engage in excessive self-blame. To prevent this from happening, having a calm demeanour and helping your child realize where the mistake was made is important.

2. *The small things too can have a big impact:* Even a small situation like putting things in the wrong place, dropping something, breaking something, interrupting you while you are speaking, etc., can affect your child if you have a very adverse reaction. Being mindful of these simplistic situations is also very important to ensure that your child does not develop a

negative belief system about her or his own self. It helps to keep explaining to your child while maintaining a calm exterior across these situations, till you see the change in the direction of the desired behaviour.

3. *It is not about doing it every time but a predominant number of times:* It is understandable that a parent cannot always demonstrate a patient and calm exterior. There are times when your patience can wear down and you may react negatively towards the behaviour displayed by your child. However, if this does not happen always and only happens as a one off situation it is okay. When you do react adversely it is important to go back and speak with your child about what happened so that (s)he does not engage in the negative loop of self-blame, guilt, anger and distress.

4. *Reassure your child that it is okay to make mistakes:* Speak to your child and share with her or him that it is normal to make a mistake. Emphasize that what the child does after a mistake has been made is more important. Discuss about the need to accept, take responsibility and make amends for the mistake that has been made. This helps build your child's character.

5. *Emphasize on the need to learn from a mistake to ensure it's not repeated:* Help your child learn that the most important aspect is to know why the mistake happened and understand how it can be prevented from occurring the next time. Work with your child to help her or him determine how (s)he can stay away from being in the same or a similar situation in the future. Brainstorm on this aspect so that your child can move past the experience and feels comfortable in the knowledge that (s)he has the information that will ensure (s)he is not in a similar situation again.

6. *Encourage your child to reach out to you always:* Your reaction to what your child does is critical in determining whether your child will approach you again for a similar situation or not. If you are following the above mentioned strategies the chances are that each time your child finds herself or himself in a tricky situation (s)he would reach out to you. At the same time, you

need to consistently encourage your child to come and speak with you, discuss the experiences (s)he has with you and solve problems with you.

THE KEY LIES IN CONSISTENCY

To achieve positive results in the long run, a consistent approach is mandated in the work you do to change your relationship with your child and help her or him be equipped to negotiate the way through situations. Often, consistency goes amiss in a parents' approach, which can be confusing for the child and does not allow her or him to feel settled with the approach. This causes the child to also vacillate in her or his behaviour, creating irritability and discontent for you as a parent as well.

HIGHLIGHTS

- Emphasize to your child that it is okay to make mistakes.
- Help your child learn from the mistakes to ensure they don't get repeated.
- Use the instances where mistakes are made to teach your child life skills.
- Enhance your child's coping skills by focusing on change and making amends, instead of being critical about what has happened.
- Be consistent in maintaining a calm demeanour when handling situations with your child.

34

NAGGING LEADS TO SHUTDOWN

*To hear your child you need your child to speak.
Don't diminish the verbalizations by your constant
worrying and nagging.*

Some children speak a lot and others don't. Parents often wonder about what causes these differences to exist. Apart from the biological factor which is implicated in the differences between people, there are elements related to the manner of parenting that further contributes to these differences. Sometimes it further pushes the child in the direction that is biologically determined and at other times it pushes the child in the opposite direction.

The question that comes to mind is 'What is the right approach?'—Allow the child to move in the direction that comes to her or him naturally or attempt to shape and change the direction in which the movement is happening? The reality of the matter is that there is no fixed, prescribed way of finding your answer to this question. What comes naturally to the child is of course the best. Yet, your role as a parent is to see how you can gently, but firmly, guide your child in a direction that is beneficial for her or him in the long run.

The corollary to this would be that, as parents, you also need to exert restraint to the amount of guiding and shaping you are attempting to do. Too many do's and don'ts, pushing and pulling, will no doubt influence your child negatively. There needs to be a balance in the way conversations happen with your child so that (s)he does not feel consistently nagged and pushed.

NAGGING MAKES YOUR CHILD FEEL UNHEARD

Children have a need to exert their own agency. They want to explore their surroundings, independently interact with others around, find ways to work with objects, and develop their own methods of doing things. This innate tendency helps the child develop a belief system about skills, abilities, self and others, which contributes to confidence and esteem in later years.

Concurrently, the child also seeks the parents presence and involvement in what (s)he is doing. (S)He looks to you for assurance on whether what is being done is okay or not. Your feedback—received through your verbal responses, gestures and expressions—further contributes to how your child feels about herself or himself. This can lead to the development of a stable, strong and assured sense of self. At the same time, it feeds into perceptions the child has about how others perceive her or him.

However, when there are situations in which the parents' feedback involves pushing the child, nudging her or him to do things in a particular way, or coaxing the child into being a certain way, it can be interpreted negatively and make the child feel that they aren't heard. The child can internalize the feeling that they are incapable of occupying space in conversations, or that their way of thinking is not good enough.

When the image the child is developing about the self is negative, (s)he can withdraw into a shell, often feeling low and sad. The withdrawal is propelled by the consistent feeling that (s)he is not good enough. It also creates potential grounds for your child to react harshly—being snappy and irritable and lashing out at you and others who tell her or him to do things differently. A vicious cycle can be put in place which exaggerates the disruptive behaviour and intensifies the emotion of the interactions.

This takes away from your child the ability to feel comfortable in conversations. A negative feeling begins to colour the exchanges. It can set the stage for difficulties in interpersonal relationships which can extend into the school, at extracurricular classes, with neighbours and with members of the extended family.

Overall, your child feels unheard—not having agency in making choices and taking decisions. (S)He also feels incompetent, which leads to negative self-evaluation.

KNOW THE REASON YOU MAY BE NAGGING

There are multiple reasons why parents can fall into this trap of nagging. A primary reason is the unavailability of time to spend with children. This causes parents to worry a lot about the things they may be missing out on. Thus, to ensure that nothing goes missing in their interactions towards the child, a parent can become over-involved, pushy and nagging.

Parents' anxieties and worries filter and percolate into their behaviour in the form of constant pushing to do things differently. This anxiety is then manifested as nagging, which can be rather bothersome for children. The child cannot understand that your worry is about the world being a difficult and competitive place which necessitates them to be on top of their game always.

Sometimes, the parents' expectations can be on the higher side, which also makes them push the child more than what is required or warranted. These expectations can inadvertently create too much pressure on their own selves to have their child be a certain way and do things differently. This gets transmitted to the child who then feels the parent is nagging.

Finally, parents also nag because they experienced it themselves when growing up. A parent may have learnt that this form of parenting can help contain and control elements that may otherwise be detrimental to success in the future. A corresponding belief that can coexist involves the parent feeling that 'If the approach worked for me, it would also work for my child.' This disallows a change in the approach till the child pushes back and causes the parent to reassess what (s)he is doing.

PUSH WITHOUT BEING A NAG

It is a fine balancing act to be able to push your child to keep moving in a direction that provides greater chances for success, and yet, not come across as a nagging parent. Often a parent can fail at this, not because of unwillingness to toe the line, but because the line can often get blurred and cause one to fall on the nagging side.

Nevertheless, there are some things, which if kept in mind, can help ensure that you are not perceived as a nagging parent.

1. *Don't have too many things on your agenda:* Often you can get perceived as a nag if there are too many things that you are trying to redefine and change in your child. Instead, look at working on only a limited number of things. Allow your child to see that not everything needs to be worked on and that there are areas in which the child is doing well.
2. *Emphasize on the positive:* Each time your child displays a positive behaviour, appreciate it. This maintains a balance for all the times that you end up pointing where (s)he made a mistake. Moreover, it gives the child the feeling that (s)he does do things well.
3. *You don't always need to warn:* Reminders are not always required for your child to toe the line. Point out an error only when your child does something incorrectly or forgets about something. You don't have to shout out a reminder or a warning beforehand. Don't pre-empt that your child will necessarily make a mistake. It will erode her or his confidence.
4. *Know what is causing you to nag:* If you can understand why you are nagging, you can gain control over it and change it. Not knowing your reasons will not help you gain control of it. Always try to identify and understand what about a particular situation may be making you behave the way you are. If you are angry, address it, and, if you are feeling frustrated, then discuss it.
5. *Have a plan and reassess if required:* If something is not changing, then instead of nagging, re-evaluate the approach to help your child change things. Brainstorm with her or him to determine an approach together, make the plan and stick to it. If the two of you are not able to figure it out, then involve

someone else to help both of you come up with a mechanism.
6. *If nothing works learn to let it go:* If nothing is working then ask yourself, 'Is this that important?' If the answer is no then let it go. Not everything can be changed and sometimes you have to make the hard choice of letting it go. If it is important, then seek someone else's inputs on it, since you are hitting a roadblock with the options you are exercising.

A LOT OF EFFORT AND SELF-DISCIPLINE IS REQUIRED

Preventing yourself from getting into the negative loop of nagging requires a lot of effort. Thoughts can get stuck in your mind and you may not find it easy to let go. Falling into a pattern of nagging and pointing out constantly what can or is going wrong, can be easy. It takes a lot of self-discipline and effort to keep pulling yourself away from getting into this pattern for long. The key is to keep checking yourself each time you do fall prey to the need to nag. Remember practice makes perfect!

HIGHLIGHTS

- Know the reason you tend to nag. Work on it to be able to break the pattern.
- Remember nagging makes your child feel unheard and incompetent.
- Instead of nagging, identify the problem areas and make a plan with your child.
- Don't keep extending warnings to your child. Instead, react when something happens.
- Let it go if something is not getting solved. Get someone else to intervene instead.

35

COMPARISON DEPLETES SELF-CONFIDENCE

You need your children to be their own true self.
Comparisons mar the process that
leads to realization of the true self.
Step away, reassess...don't compare.

Uniqueness is a much desired attribute in a child. Parents wish for their children to have traits and abilities that make them stand out in a crowd and that allow them to occupy positions that value the creativity and thinking that their child displays. In this endeavour, it is important that you nurture and harness the different ways in which your child thinks and does things. It necessitates that you encourage your child to think differently—more important, laterally—to look at things from multiple perspectives, and not get stuck with a typical way of seeing, knowing and understanding things.

The more you encourage, appreciate and accept the differences, the more confidence your child develops to share her or his unique perspectives. This does not mean that you allow your child to break rules, go against all norms and systems, or become an overly permissive parent. It actually means that instead of asking her or him to be like someone else, you find it within yourself to be able to value and cherish what your child is.

The fact is that comparisons create self-doubt, reduce confidence, deplete the feeling of worthiness and esteem, and get children stuck in cycles of negative thinking about the self, the world and themselves in the context of the world.

THE GOOD, THE BAD AND THE UGLY COEXIST

Each of us has different aspects that combine together to form our sense of self. There are parts that are good, those that are bad, and some that are ugly. All of these coexist and contribute towards making us into the people that we are. You would not be who you are without each of these parts coexisting within you. How you temper and shape the amount that the bad and the ugly influence you and impact your interactions and relationships, is instrumental in your success today.

This same is true and applicable to your child as well. (S)He will have multiple elements that form a part of her or his personality. Some of these would be good, endearing qualities that make you love her or him—cheerfulness, kindness, care and affection—and then there would be those that worry and upset you—like anger, irritability, tantrums and stubbornness. In parenting your child you need to find ways in which you can help them focus on and enhance the good while subduing the bad. You do this by making the child aware of the ways in which the bad and the ugly can manifest in speech, behaviour and responses to others. You work collaboratively to find ways in which these parts can be altered and fixed. You exert your influence and utilize the relationship you have with your child to keep consistently working in the direction of bringing about these changes.

While you work to help your child simmer the bad parts, you need to remain aware that your child cannot be perfect. Despite your best efforts, there will be multiple moments and instances in which your child will go back to the same, so-called bad ways of acting and behaving. This does not reflect a failure on your part to be able to impart the right skills and attitude to your child. It is a reflection of the tendency where, what comes naturally to your child, can and does find its way, despite all the measures that have been put in place to prevent it from occurring. The focus needs to be on supporting your child to identify the instances of transgression, finding reasons for why it happened and thinking of ways in which it can be prevented from happening later.

COMPARISONS ARE NOT ENCOURAGING

There are multiple faulty beliefs which parents can harbour. The way parents believe that children can learn from their own experiences and those of others, they also feel that when they point out another person's achievements to a child, it encourages the child. It is believed that it acts to motivate the child to do more and go beyond her or his current accomplishments. It is often forgotten that there are two sides to the coin. Yes, there is a part of the child which can learn from what you are sharing, can recognize that there is more that can be done and achieved or that there are other alternatives which can be explored. However, there is the other part which also begins to think and evaluate the self to ask, 'Why do I not look at things like this?' or, 'I never come up with such things. I am just not good enough to think of it.'

The intent of any parent is not to make the child question the self. However, the negative impact of constant comparisons can be rather grave. Besides the negative self-evaluations that it can lead to, there is the additional impact these can have on the relationship the child has with the person (s)he is compared to. Children are very sensitive and can easily get thrown off by comparisons. Not knowing how to process these comparisons, and the meaning that needs to be derived from them, children can develop an instinctive dislike towards the person they are compared to. They can harbour feelings of jealousy and envy and not want to associate much with the other person they are compared to. There can then be frequent fights and arguments as a result of the comparisons.

None of the above mentioned effects are consciously brought upon by the child. They come about insidiously, over a period of time, without the child recognizing that something like this is happening. It can be equally bewildering for the child to realize how their thought processes are becoming negative, which can cause further negative self-evaluations.

THERE IS A RIGHT WAY TO MOTIVATE

It is understandable that you want to motivate your child to do more and go beyond her or his own limitations, make weaknesses into strengths, and achieve all that (s)he wants to. Motivating your child needs to be done in a way that is positive and encouraging, and makes your child do more while feeling good about herself or himself. Let's look at the things you need to keep in mind while looking to motivate your child, without making comparisons and using others' experiences to push her or him.

1. *Be realistic in your expectations:* Each child is different and will have her or his own set of skills and abilities. Yes, there are some things you can inculcate in your child but not everything can be changed. Be realistic in your expectations to understand how much your child can actually change. Also assess your expectations in the context of whether it is actually needed or not.
2. *Focus on harnessing the skills:* Be sure to encourage your child to work on the areas in which (s)he is skilled and find more opportunities in which your child can utilize these skills. This will help build confidence and make her or him feel good about the self. This feeling of goodness can be utilized to then further work on other areas in which the child may not be as skilled.
3. *Create benchmarks instead of comparing children*: It helps to have a benchmark towards which your child can work, instead of comparing her or him to another child. This allows the child to realize that (s)he is working to enhance her or his own skill base, and not to offset someone else's accomplishments. This further contributes towards the child's ability to maintain positivity in the relationships that (s)he has.
4. *Shift your focus to the process instead of the end result*: It is helpful if you focus your attention on emphasizing the process that your child follows to achieve results. This helps the child develop essential life skills. Not focusing on the result helps remove the pressure that children can often feel in situations,

and allows them to take a more relaxed approach to situations.
5. *Avoid using rewards:* Rewards act as external reinforcers. It is, instead, helpful to build your child's intrinsic motivation by using more intangible rewards, like giving free time if the child accomplishes a task instead of giving a favourite food or toy. Celebrate the joy of completing a task or making a change. This then begins to act as a motivator, and encourages your child to give herself or himself a pat on the back.

HIGHLIGHTS

- Comparisons do not help to motivate. They erode confidence and self-belief.
- Emphasize the areas of skills your child has in addition to working on things that need to change.
- Create benchmarks for your child instead of engaging in comparisons.
- Remember to harness your child's uniqueness and creativity by shifting the focus to the process.
- Results don't always matter. It is important that your child learns and uses the right life skills to work through situations.

36

RESTRAIN PARENTAL EXPECTATIONS

Having expectations is natural.
Expecting those expectations to get fulfilled is fallacious.
Taming of expectations is a skill that parenting demands.

There are two predominant areas in which parents have expectations from their children—academic performance, and behaviour in personal and public spaces. These two areas encompass, by and large, the whole life of a child. This basically means that often, without realizing, parents can push and have expectations for too many things and across too many areas which can place undue pressure on the child.

Some amount of pressure from parents is helpful in motivating the child. However, too much pressure can make the child fearful of making mistakes. This can be very counterproductive, specifically when the aim is to encourage the child to explore and become independent in making choices, taking decisions, solving problems, building relationships and working on weaknesses.

A healthy understanding of their own competencies is essential for the child to do well in life. This can only happen if the child can maintain confidence in working on problems, instead of wanting to run away from them.

WE HAVE AN IMAGE OF HOW THINGS ARE SUPPOSED TO BE

Parents harbour within themselves an image of how things are supposed to be, not just for themselves but also for their child. This image is what causes a parent to have many expectations from the self and from the child as well. These expectations then translate into pushing and pulling in the parent-child relationship, making it conflict-ridden, tense and tenuous. It often causes a parent to be unnecessarily rigid and insistent on things being done in a certain way. The need for perfection can also raise its head in this circumstance, which makes the situation more critically poised.

Concurrently, a parent can forget that besides the image they have for the child's life, the child too possesses a corresponding image. The divergence between the images that the two have, can be detrimental to the relationship, as both the parent and child are motivated to work in different directions. The image each has in mind determines the goals, and the lack of concordance between these goals leads to different measures being adopted to achieve results.

THERE IS NO PLACE FOR SHOULD AND MUST

Unknowingly, a lot of times, a parents' thoughts can be ridden with 'should' and 'must' that are not grounded in the reality of what can be achieved and accomplished. These should's and must's make it rather difficult for the child to follow through on what the parent wants and demands, as there is no space for errors and mistakes. It makes the child tentative, nervous and anxious in doing what is being asked. At the same time, it can often lead to a negative thought process about the self, as the child consistently feels that (s)he is not good enough, especially when there are failures in achieving the goal that has been set by the parent. This can also make your child question her or his skills and abilities, which takes away from the self-confidence the child has.

LET GO OF THE URGENCY AND RIGIDITY

A core characteristic of expectations is the sense of urgency and rigidity that is associated with them. Often, expectations come with a belief that there is no alternative. This rigidity—not allowing her or him to be creative, preventing exploration of the environment, and also not allowing for an independent thought process to develop which is imperative for problem-solving and decision-making to develop as skills later in life—can be confusing for your child. Confidence goes amiss as the child does not believe that (s)he has the requisite skill sets in place that allow her or him to be able to determine solutions.

Furthering the problem is the sense of urgency that accompanies expectations. The message that is communicated to the child is, 'I know best and you need to trust me. Don't think for yourself as you don't have the ability to think for yourself.' This is most certainly not the message that you, as a parent, want filtering down to your child. Thus, removing the urgency from situations where you have expectations is crucial, so your child can understand that even if you have a thought process there is still space for her or him to think about things and try to determine her or his own alternatives.

SEE YOUR CHILD AS AN INDIVIDUAL

Parents see their children as an extension of their own selves. Unknowingly, they project on the child their own dreams and visions. They expect the child to be able to see the merit in these and be able to follow what the parent has in mind. The child, to a large extent, does internalize what the parent shares with her or him. However, with time, as the child is exposed to the world, makes friends, learns more, interacts with more people, and gets to know what all exists in the world, (s)he is tempted to look at and try things which the parent never had in mind.

Your child tries to, and often successfully, exerts her or his independence. In doing so your child changes the direction in which you envisioned things to be. To be prepared for this difference, it is imperative you see your child as an individual who will have her or his own unique way of looking at things and working on situations. This understanding, if integrated at an early stage into your thought process, would be helpful in ensuring that you are seen as an ally and support instead of as another person with whom the child needs to struggle to reach what (s)he wants.

PERSPECTIVES WILL BE DIFFERENT

Remember that there was a difference in how you saw the world and how your parents saw it. You wanted something that perhaps your parents could never think of. It shaped the way your relationship developed with your parents and made you feel closer or further away from them. It's no different for your child. Both your perspectives will be different and the influences that shape these perspectives too will be different.

To maintain a good, healthy relationship with your child acknowledging this difference is important. Giving it the importance it deserves is crucial for you to be able to side-step the negative influence it can have on your relatability and connect with your child. It is crucial for you to share and discuss what your experience has been and what you expect your child to take away from it. However, it is equally important for you to be able to support your child when (s)he decides to step away from what you expect and find her or his own path and goal.

THERE IS LIGHT AT THE END OF THE TUNNEL

Not all of a parent's expectations get ditched by the child. The fact is that by and large your child is going to follow in your footsteps and will derive a lot of what will shape her or his personality from you. But it will not be a hundred percent. You need to be prepared for having some things fall into place the way you would expect them to, and others to fall away, along the way. Be an ally and a confidante, gently suggesting, calmly approaching your child to do things a certain way, and solving problems together when your child wants to follow a different path. Collaboration is going to be a necessity, especially as your child grows older.

HIGHLIGHTS

- Don't expect all your expectations to be fulfilled by your child.
- Be an ally in helping your child determine her or his own goal for life.
- Your child too will have a vision for her or his own self. Facilitate the process of achieving it.
- See your child as an independent individual with her or his own needs and desires.
- Collaborate with your child to align to each others' expectations and reduce conflict.

37

REFRAIN FROM BODY-SHAMING

*Teach your children to feel good about themselves.
Be mindful of the situations in which you
may unintentionally body-shame them.
A healthy self-image incorporates a healthy
body-image as well.*

How a person feels is intricately linked to how they look. However much we may dislike this, it is the reality of the world we live in. This association has developed over a period of decades, where, how a person looks, dresses up and presents herself or himself has assumed significant importance. These ideas percolate into all segments of society and are largely shared through the media, through our social narratives and communications and conversations with others.

People strive to receive compliments like, 'You look good today' without realizing how much it is influenced by and influences the self-concepts that they hold. They put a lot of effort in getting the look right, having a particular body type and maintaining a certain image in the social spaces they operate in. Such statements can have a critical impact on the person's confidence and self-assurance.

These ideas also get transmitted to children and adolescents. Parents often do not realize the role they may have played in making children more conscious of how they look, the body type they have, the food they eat and the impression they make on others.

RECOGNIZE BODY-SHAMING

Your child is not equipped to recognize, understand or handle episodes of body-shaming. It is easier for you, as a parent, to determine if your child has been or is being body-shamed. This is a skill that needs to be exerted by you, not only with others but also with your own self. You need to refrain from body-shaming your child as well. It is also critical that you provide the buffer and support your child needs to stay protected from body-shaming.

1. *Don't make comments about your child's body type or size:* Be mindful about not making comments that relate to your child's body type and size. Sometimes, a parent can make statements like, 'Don't eat that. It'll make you go fat' or 'If you don't play, you'll become like a balloon' or, 'Who wears such clothes? You wear things which make you look bad. I'll help you choose from now on.' Despite not intending to hurt your child, such comments and questions can make them feel ashamed of how they look, and develop a negative self-image, eroding confidence and wellness.
2. *Don't comment or make fun of someone else's body in front of your child:* Even if you may not comment on your child, your child can extrapolate from what you may have said about someone else. Vicarious learning shapes the child's beliefs and attitudes. It also contributes towards developing an unhealthy thought process about how much looks and body types matter.
3. *If your child speaks about someone else's comments on body shapes and types, discuss it with her or him:* It is important to speak and discuss with your child about experiences they, or someone else, may have, that can impact their views about body types and shapes. To help your child develop a healthy body image, it is essential that you de-emphasize what they may hear others say about looks and body type.
4. *Focus on the abilities the child has:* Keep emphasizing on the importance of personality and skills as the defining factor for people. Looks and body types matter to the very limited extent

of being healthy. Make sure your child understands that looks and body type do not say anything about how a person is, and these should not be used to make any inferences about people.
5. *Correct the child if (s)he makes any comments, or body-shames the self or someone else:* Be vigilant and prompt in checking your child if (s)he makes a comment that is derogatory towards the self or another. It is important that you correct your child each time (s)he makes inferences about a person, or body-shames someone. This will ensure that your child is able to actively step away from such situations, develop a healthy self-image and is not judgemental of others either.
6. *Don't make conversations about food, which make body shape too big a thing:* Lay emphasis on encouraging your child to have a healthy lifestyle. This should include conversations about the need to eat right and be physically fit. However, it should not be associated with how it can help maintain a certain body shape or type. This allows your child to understand that maintaining health and well-being is important and not looking a certain way.

DEVELOP YOUR CHILD'S SKILLS TO HANDLE BODY-SHAMING

You cannot be present to protect your child from every episode where body-shaming may occur. You need to work actively to equip your child with the right skills to tackle situations where (s)he or someone else is body-shamed. This would mean not just helping your child understand when body-shaming is occurring but also knowing exactly what to do when (s)he does identify a situation.

1. *Help your child know when body-shaming is occurring:* A child cannot know on her or his own that body-shaming is occurring. You would need to precisely define what does and does not constitute body-shaming. Help clarify about whether (s)he or someone else has been body-shamed.
2. *Tell your child it's okay to disagree with someone who may be*

body-shaming: Enable your child by telling her or him that it is okay to tell someone who is body-shaming to not do so. Build an understanding of the need to speak one's mind, and further this understanding by providing your child with the skills to have such a conversation with another in a non-conflicting manner.
3. *Encourage your child to be patient, firm and respectful while communicating to someone about not engaging in body-shaming:* You need to point out to your child that a calm demeanour can accomplish just as much as conflict can. Demonstrate through role plays and brainstorming that it is not okay to body-shame, especially when situations occur in media or around you. Help your child understand the right way to speak and state.
4. *Let your child know that you, or some other adult like a teacher, are there if (s)he needs help:* It is important for your child to know that (s)he does not have to work through such situations on her or his own. (S)He should feel comfortable in reaching out to other adults like teachers, friends, siblings, other relatives and parents, if (s)he struggles to handle such a situation. It is important for your child to know that seeking support in this regard is not a sign of weakness. Instead it indicates regard for the self and the other.

MUCH IS GAINED FROM HAVING A HEALTHY BODY IMAGE

A healthy body image contributes towards your child having a confident and self-assured approach in life. Children, just like adults, extrapolate how they feel about themselves, in relation to their body image. A positive, healthy body image, which is disconnected from the body shape and type, is critical in ensuring that your child has a balanced viewpoint about the self.

HIGHLIGHTS

- Children learn about body image from you, the media and others around.
- Be mindful about how you speak about food, clothes, body type and size with your child.
- If your child witnesses an instance of body-shaming, discuss it immediately.
- Enable your child to develop a firm and assertive response if someone body-shames her or him.
- Encourage your child to support other victims of body-shaming.

38

BALANCE INSTRUCTIONS WITH REQUESTS

You may know more and you may know better.
But it is not wise to give guidance every time.
Exert control and tweak your approach.
It will enable much better learning.

Sharing information and knowledge is a common practice that all individuals engage in. People are naturally inclined to give inputs, provide explanations, share wisdom and instruct another, even when it may not be required. This arises out of multiple reasons. From wanting to share your own expertise, to feeling good about yourself when you explain something, or experiencing a sense of joy seeing another person feel relieved that you helped them solve a problem, people like to be able to give these multiple inputs.

For a parent, there are additional reasons that get added to this list of rationales. Preventing a problem, ensuring perfection, needing your child to do well and being protective, all compound and further contribute to this natural tendency to instruct. However, sharing an experience or providing general guidance is very different from consistently instructing your child, or, breaking down tasks into ever smaller bits and pieces that you believe would make things easier for her or him.

Everything has its pros and cons as does this need to explain and instruct. It is a double-edged sword which can be very helpful or create significant problems for you and your child. The ideal solution involves finding the right balance between instructing and requesting your child to do things.

KNOW WHAT YOU CAN ACHIEVE THROUGH YOUR INSTRUCTIONS

Children are not born knowing how to do things and manage situations. They undoubtedly need guidance and support in handling different people, situations and building experiences. This is usually done through the gentle yet firm guidance that you provide as a parent. It involves telling your child what to do and how to do it. This is in addition to all that your child learns by simply observing you and vicariously learning through the observations (s)he makes.

Your instructions serve to ensure that your child is able to know and understand what is okay and what is not. Through the instructions, you are able to provide your child a step-wise process for accomplishing tasks. Even something as simple as opening a bottle can require that you demonstrate and provide instructions for her or him the first time (s)he tries to do it on her or his own. This process finds application across a range of situations—from doing things, to being around people, to moving through different or new spaces.

The instructions you provide can find significant application in helping your child avoid unnecessary problems. For instance, each time you remind your child to stay away from the plug points or from hot things like the iron, it ensures the safety of your child. This becomes necessary also because a child wants to know and understand things better, and in doing so (s)he can end up ignoring the instructions you provide. Curiosity is a core trait in a growing child and this can lead to inadvertently getting exposed to problematic situations which can be warded off through your reminders and instructions.

ISSUE INSTRUCTIONS IN THE RIGHT WAY

There are some things you need to keep in mind when giving instructions to change or shape the way your child behaves. These include the following:

1. *Don't over-utilize instructions:* Anything which is overused tends to become ineffective. The same holds true for instructions. You give too many instructions and you will lose your child's attention. (S)He will not pay heed to what you are asking her or him to do. So think before you issue your next instruction. Ask, 'Is this really needed? Or can I let my child choose?'
2. *Ensure that you get your child's attention:* Getting your child's attention is very important if you want her or him to follow through with what you are saying. To get your child's attention, get down to her or his eye level, call to ensure (s)he is looking at you, be close enough, and then say what you have in mind.
3. *Be mindful of your tone:* Do not come across as nervous, anxious, fearful, angry or upset when issuing an instruction to your child. Be careful with the tone you adopt to communicate the instructions. You should come across as calm and firm. Also maintain a conversational tone that gives your child the space to be able to state what (s)he is thinking or feeling. You can then address any concerns.
4. *Be precise and clear about what you want*: Don't over-complicate the instructions by adding too many parts to them. Brevity is the key to ensuring that instructions are followed. Complex instructions are difficult for a child to process and apply.
5. *Incorporate an element of request into your instruction:* Use words and phrases like 'Please' or 'It would be great if you could'. These engage your child and make her or him feel a part of the decision-making process, even though you are giving instructions about what is to be done. It engages your child enough to want to cooperate with you.

BALANCE THE TWO—GIVING INSTRUCTIONS AND MAKING REQUESTS

Utilizing requests to get your child to do something or to alter the way they are approaching a situation, can be more effective in bringing about a change. Children do not respond well to consistently being told what to do. If too many instructions are used and a child is constantly being told to 'do this now' and 'do that now' it makes her or him feel frustrated. It increases irritability and at some point in time (s)he can react by saying, 'You keep telling me what to do all the time!' This is not a good situation for you and your child as it impacts the relationship you have with each other and develops in your child, a desire to rebel.

Instead, in order to let your child experience some amount of control over life and what (s)he is doing, it is helpful if you reduce the number of instructions you give. Devise an alternative approach for telling your children to do or not to do something. Use a strategy that gives your child options which (s)he can select from. This can be far more effective as an approach to get your child to engage in desirable behaviour. This also contributes towards satisfying the ever-growing need for independence that children have. It also strengthens your child's decision-making skills and teaches them how to negotiate their way through situations.

REMEMBER WHAT YOU WANT TO ACHIEVE

There is a twofold goal when using instructions with your child. One is to ensure your child walks on the right path. The other is to ensure that your child also internalizes the right skills to make choices herself or himself in the future. To accomplish this dual goal, it is necessary to continuously transition between telling your child what to do and letting her or him make choices. This can be difficult, but it is the right methodology to make your child confident and independent, and effective in resolving various situations.

HIGHLIGHTS

○ It is easy to fall into the trap of instructing your child on what to do and how to do it.
○ Instructions are crucial in helping your child know and understand the world.
○ Parents need to transition between instructing, providing alternatives and making requests.
○ Be clear, precise and brief in issuing instructions to your child.
○ To make your child confident and independent (s)he needs to make choices.

39

TONE DOWN THE EXCESSIVE PAMPERING

Among the many expressions that
love can find, pampering is one.
Beware of its evils as it can skew the
way you nurture your child's skills.

A child is born into a family surrounded by numerous aspirations that each member holds. Parents and other family members have their own independent ideas about what they would do, the things they would buy, and the manner in which they would indulge and pamper the child. It brings sheer joy and happiness into everyone's life to think of the ways in which life would change and everything would be so different with the arrival of the infant.

Taking care of the child and pampering her or him makes the child feel cared for and loved. The child develops a belief in the inherent goodness that (s)he possesses and formulates ideas about who (s)he is. These notions are further enhanced on the basis of the experiences the child has through the years of growing up. As the child continues to accumulate both positive and negative experiences, it contributes to her or his developing self-concepts. This builds the confidence the child has. Over a period of time, as the child gains knowledge and understanding from the adults around, it feeds into her or his beliefs about the abilities (s)he has.

There is, however, a possibility that the child can develop an inflated or false sense of self. This can happen when excessive positivity, which is not grounded in reality, is directed at the child.

When the child's needs and desires are consistently gratified it can lay the foundation for a difficult personality.

THE REASONS PARENTS PAMPER CHILDREN

Modern-day parents are limited by the paucity of time. To compensate for what they miss during the course of the day, while they are at work, parents can often over-indulge the child. Giving into what your child wants, ensuring that (s)he has the toy that is demanded, is given the food that is desired, is allowed to sleep late or even skip school, can become frequent situations that get played out at home.

Additionally, the need to be perfect parents, prevents drawing of any boundaries when it comes to providing things and experiences for the child. In being protective and ensuring that no harm gets directed at the child, the parent can engage in a pattern that does not allow the child to have her or his own experiences that are critical to the learning process. This over-protectiveness—pampering—is where adults may not provide corrective experiences to the child and refrain from saying anything when an inappropriate behaviour is displayed.

Not knowing any other way of showing love and affection, parents end up pampering as a means to demonstrate the same. Often, this is seen to exist in homes where similar patterns exist across generations. Parallel to this, parents often nestle within them the desire to provide the child with the best standards of living. This can also play a significant role towards the amount of pampering that is done with the child.

THE RESULT OF EXCESSIVE PAMPERING

When you expect too little and you give too much you are causing damage to your child's personality. It negatively influences the child's behaviour, the way (s)he thinks, the expectations (s)he has and the way (s)he responds to people. The child learns from being over-pampered that needs are always fulfilled. Critical skills for coping with disappointments and frustrations are not learnt by the child, which is something that children usually learn at a very early stage. Simple situations like trying to shift your child to taking feed from a bottle, or encouraging your 5-year-old to sleep in his room, can become instances through which the child is pampered.

As you continue to give in to the demands your child makes, (s)he moves from being a pampered child to a demanding child. From being someone who knew her or his needs will be met, the child begins to expect all their demands to be fulfilled. The child does not develop essential life skills which are critical for success. (S)He does not develop a good, robust understanding of the strengths and weaknesses (s)he has. In this situation the child is exposed to problematic experiences later in life, as (s)he is unable to tolerate frustration.

Children who are over-pampered have an inflated sense of self. They overestimate their skills and abilities and underestimate those of others. This takes away from how well they know and understand others. They are likely to make faulty assumptions and operate on the basis of these. Their understanding of the world and how it operates is also based on these faulty assumptions. This is particularly detrimental to the child's success and well-being.

As experiences later on shatter the false assumptions the child has harboured through life, it can be especially difficult to integrate them into the existing self-system, potentially leading to mental health problems later in life.

STEPPING AWAY FROM OVER-PAMPERING

Take steps towards creating a balance between how much you give and where you set boundaries. There are measures that can be put in place that ensures that your child is not over-pampered, and that (s)he acquires the right skills to lead a good life and achieve success.

1. *Privileges should not be understood as rights:* The conversations you have with your child need to communicate that the facilities

that are available are privileges that are acquired on account of the position and the hard work of others. It is essential that your child understands that these privileges are not rights, and what (s)he receives is also contingent upon the actions and the behaviour that (s)he enacts.

2. *Know what you want your child to learn from the exchange:* Have a precise understanding of exactly what you want to communicate to your child through the conversations you are having. Keep a check on how much meaning your child is actually deriving from your interactions, and maintain flexibility to adapt your approach if required.
3. *Understand the benefit of getting your child to do chores:* Recognize the importance of chores. These teach your child about hard work, taking responsibility, being involved with others, supporting and caring for people. Be sure to involve your child in doing small things around the house from an early age. Even simple things like putting the plates in the sink or dishwasher, putting out the garbage, setting laundry, etc., can be very helpful.
4. *Set firm limits:* Make sure that you set firm limits on what is acceptable. It is also important that you stick to these limits. Do not vacillate after you have told your child a 'no' for something. Think through the situation and be certain about your decision to say a 'no' before you communicate it to your child.
5. *Remember to start early:* Starting early is important. It makes it easier for your child to internalize ways of thinking, understanding and behaving at an earlier stage. The older a child grows, the more set (s)he becomes in the ways of doing things, making it difficult for you to push for changes.
6. *Be mindful of the slips:* Do not slip in enforcing what you have decided upon. Pamper your child and provide the best but be sure to not go overboard. Consciously reflect and re-evaluate where you could have done things differently in case there has been a slip. Recognize the reasons for it, to be able to prevent it from happening in the future.

DEMONSTRATE YOUR LOVE BEYOND PAMPERING

You can find other means to show your love and affection, which do not involve pampering your child with things. Over-gratification and constantly meeting your child's demands is not the only way to show that you care and love your child. You can demonstrate the care you have by having good conversations, spending good times together, doing activities together and being available to help your child find her or his way through the varied contingencies of life.

HIGHLIGHTS

- Pampering conveys love and affection, but don't allow it to go overboard as it is detrimental.
- Over-pampering confounds the development of life skills and takes away from the development of personality and character of the child.
- Set firm limits on what is allowed and what is not.
- Help your child understand what is provided by you as a privilege and not a right.
- Encourage your child to be involved with chores and being helpful at an early age.

40

EMBRACE YOUR LIMITATIONS

*Every individual has their own shortcomings and limitations.
This does not make you lesser than another.
Embrace them to bring a change so you can effectively
use your strengths in situations.*

In their day-to-day lives, people attempt to improve and reinvent themselves through changes they incorporate, constantly striving to move in a direction that allows them to err less and achieve more. They wish to be close to perfect, eliminating the errors they make, working with their strengths and transforming their weaknesses. However, the reality is that there is always something that is not okay, can be problematic, be a cause for concern and can act as an impediment in a person's life. Despite all the hard work that may be directed towards bridging the gaps that may exist, there is always something more that can be worked on and modified.

Avoiding the vagaries of the unknown necessitates the building of skills. These form the foundation for all individuals—to be able to take charge and bring situations under their control. People find it difficult to deal with ambiguity and also struggle to comprehend and come face-to-face with their own limitations. However, it has been seen that successful people are those who understand and embrace their limitations. It is then that a person can take effective steps to find creative ways of circumventing these.

This is applicable to parenting as well. Embracing your limitations as a parent is important for you to be able to move past the problems, and also find better ways to resolving them.

DON'T IGNORE YOUR LIMITS—THEY ARE ANSWERS

Your limits as a parent are integral to who you are and your identity. They shape how you think, respond and engage with parenting your child. These limits make you aware of your own boundaries—the rules you need to live by. Emphasis is mostly laid on creating, sustaining and consistently following the rules that you lay down for your child. It is often forgotten that a parent too needs to have some rules put in place. These need to be defined on the basis of the limits, as much as they relate to the strengths you have as a parent.

Being ignorant of your limits exposes your vulnerabilities as a parent. It becomes hard for you to define what may be holding you back or preventing you from parenting your child in the most effective manner. This can be a rather tricky situation, as it does not allow you to know exactly where you need to make a shift to reach the right answers and solutions. This can be particularly frustrating for you as a parent. Being stretched to find time and having to fulfill multiple roles and responsibilities in itself can be challenging and tiresome. If more is added on account of a lack of awareness of your limits, it only increases the stress and pressure you feel. This can lead you to feel angry and disappointed with your own self which can often reflect in your interactions. There is a chance that you snap more at your child or feel helpless, not knowing what to do. Recognize your limits, take active steps to define them, and utilize your knowledge to take the right steps as a parent.

YOU DON'T NEED TO PUSH PAST YOUR LIMITS

Rising to the challenges is a necessity. Various difficult situations get flung at a parent across the domains in which they operate. A parent needs to find ways to stay strong and stable and to find creative solutions. This does not mean that you need to always push your limits. You can let yourself operate within the bounds of the limits that you are aware of. Making this conscious choice makes you cognizant of what you can achieve and what may be lost.

Remember, there is no set or prescribed framework in which you need to fit yourself. It is okay for you to be your own unique self and you do not need to be like any other parent around you. It is more important that you find your comfort zone, stretch yourself a little outside of that zone and keep working towards the goals you have set for yourself, both as an individual as well as a parent.

It is when you pressurize yourself to be a particular type of parent, that you make more mistakes. You may not realize it, but this pressure can inadvertently transfer to your child as well. You may communicate mixed messages to your child that can leave her or him feeling confused and unsure of what is expected.

SHOW SENSITIVITY TO YOUR OWN SELF

You need to start with yourself, before you reflect on your child or your relationship with her or him. It is imperative that you be sensitive to your own self and focus on identifying your needs and desires. Being a parent does not mean letting go of your aspirations. It means finding ways to accommodate more within the framework that you had created for yourself, and expanding the scope of what you had thought of achieving for yourself.

You need to be mindful of your own feelings. Recognize that you too can feel sad, low, anxious, worried, disappointed, angry, happy and tense. You are allowed to go through your own states of mind, and can react to them the way any other person would. Yes, when you have a child there is an additional responsibility, but it also extends to helping your child understand that you can have difficult experiences and finding ways of not letting them affect your relationship with your child.

BE PATIENT AND YOU WILL FIND A SOLUTION

You will make mistakes. There will be times when you will feel unsure of what you are doing, the direction you are headed in, and making the choices you are making as a parent. Give yourself the space to have these experiences. Talk about them and be gentle with yourself. This approach will also allow you to take remedial measures.

> **HIGHLIGHTS**
>
> - Embrace your limits to be able to make them your strengths.
> - Know the boundaries you can operate within to set realistic goals.
> - It is okay to work within your limits.
> - Be sensitive and kind to yourself in deciding how well you are doing as a parent.
> - There will always be things you can change. It is a continuous process. Don't judge yourself harshly for everything that can go wrong.

Section Six

PARENTING WITH A SENSITIVE APPROACH

41

HELP YOUR CHILD FACE FEARS HEAD-ON

Encourage your child to fight fears by conquering feelings of helplessness through acceptance, willingness and building the courage to face them

Like adults, children grow up facing fears and anxieties during the course of their lives. As they move through different phases, they come face-to-face with fears like that of the dark, loud sounds, strangers, exams, stage performances, transitions or relationships. The unknown creates discomfort making them reduce exploration and the joy they derive from it, or impacting their feeling of safety and security. They may resist, cry and avoid facing situations or people as the fear comes to grip them tightly. It is hard to see your child struggle which can push you to either safeguard them, or shove her or him to face the situation head on.

When you look at these fears from your vantage point as an adult, they can be perceived as innocuous or silly. You may find yourself dismissing your child's concerns by saying, 'What is so fearful about this, it's so silly? There is nothing in it,' as you push her or him to face the fear. However, seldom does the child feel motivated to do so. Rather, in most such instances the fear can increase manifold, due to the child's lack of preparedness, and induce anxiety in relation to the feared object or situation. This in turn can make you angry as it is difficult to understand the reason your child is unable to believe your words, making you helpless in trying to resolve it. This may also induce embarrassment, shame and guilt in your child.

Forcing your child to engage with the situation or object may not always diffuse the child's fear as (s)he is not equipped to deal with it. Concurrently, accommodating your child's fears and anxieties is also unhealthy as it does not prepare her or him to face the numerous contingencies of life. Avoidance in turn increases the likelihood of higher levels of anxiety. This predisposes the child to throw tantrums when pushed to face the feared object, especially in a public space. Such a situation can be difficult to manage and more often than not parents rescue the child from the situation.

Ideally you need to strive towards enabling your child to face fears courageously and with confidence. You want your child to be fearless and resilient in the face of difficult challenges and take control of the small and big fears that come along the way. Facing the fear is the only way to deal with it. However, to achieve this goal while keeping your child comfortable, it is important to answer three pertinent questions:

1. Why do children fear certain objects or people?
2. What makes fears worse over time?
3. How can you help your child overcome fears?

UNDERSTANDING FEAR FROM A CHILD'S PERSPECTIVE

Fear is a naturally occurring emotion which plays a protective function, warning against threat or danger. It allows one to gauge potentially harmful consequences and triggers an adaptive response. Such fears are seen to be rational in nature and one understands them as logical. Children find their fears to be real too! Reacting to a fear by wanting to escape or avoid the situation is a means of survival. It protects them from the threat of an unknown external danger.

When the child builds fantasies about fairies and superheroes, fear of the dark and ghosts also finds its place in the child's imaginary world. When the child closes her or his eyes, the imaginary fear-inducing figures disappear. The presence of a parent or switching on the light also tends to provide comfort. As children grow older the fears move into more tangible and real spaces such as of water, loud noises, barking dogs, injuries, accidents or strangers. They are not always able to pinpoint what is causing them to feel fearful or overwhelmed, or what leads to a physiological reaction such as a racing heartbeat or a stomach ache.

While some children jump into a situation and come out victorious taking on the feared entity as a challenge, others see it as a monster that they will not be able to fight. Children do not respond well to being pushed, forced or coerced by others, including parents. This is especially true for those children who are temperamentally more sensitive and tend to think or worry more. They experience behavioural inhibition in unfamiliar situations and find themselves freezing when they need to act. It is crucial for you to not undermine or mock your child's fears. Brainstorming and talking about ways in which to maintain a relaxed stance, in order to encourage your child to not actively avoid fears, can be helpful. The acknowledgment and acceptance provided through such an approach gives your child the scaffolding to try, experiment and push beyond existing comfort zones.

Mild anxiety or hesitation in unknown situations or in circumstances where a child is being evaluated or has to perform, is normal. However, when a child feels upset and withdraws from a situation it is important to observe and talk about what happened and work through the experience. Your intervention would ensure that this does not become an overwhelming experience that prevents the child from engaging with the fearful situation in the future. Mutually developing a stepwise process of exposure to the feared stimuli will help the child overcome them with confidence. It will also help maintain the child's self-esteem and not allow the fear to grow to disproportionate levels.

FEAR, FEAR, GO AWAY!

Courage is not about being fearless. It is about taking control over the fears to face them head on. Parents can help their children get rid of their fears by coaching them and providing guidance to manage their fearful thoughts and emotions. Providing strategies to perceive situations in a realistic manner allow the child to break away from any irrational or illogical fears. Your child needs a gentle push and gradual engagement with the feared situation in a controlled manner. There are simple ways in which you can help your child confront the feared object or situations and gain mastery over them.

1. *I can feel you:* It is important to feel and truly understand your child's fear and worry to be able to help her or him gain control over it. A distant, strong approach does not translate into conquering the fear. For example, if your child is shy and scared of meeting new people and clings onto you or stays in her or his own room, it doesn't help if you respond by saying, 'Why are you so scared of them? They are just Mom and Dad's friends. Make sure you come out to say a hello.' You may even push her or him to greet them by saying, 'Say hello to Uncle and Aunty. I think you can surely say hello to them.' Your child may be tempted to either hide behind you or run away. Later you may find yourself feeling angry at her or him for not complying with such a simple request. In situations like these, the child may feel further ashamed and anxious for not doing something expected from them. What you need to do is acknowledge your child's fear by comforting her or him in such a situation. You can approach the same conversation from a more empathetic standpoint and state, 'Could you wish your Uncle and Aunt today when they come to meet us?' When (s)he responds with 'But I feel scared, because I don't know them very well,' it is more helpful for you to acknowledge it and provide an alternative that (s)he is more comfortable with. You can say, 'Okay. I understand that you need to know them better. How about you just sit with me today and meet them. Today I will not ask you to greet them. You can just observe them and hear what we are discussing and if you feel like it, you could go and play with their child.' This would make your child feel relieved and supported by you to take the first step to

know the unfamiliar people and later engage with them as well.
2. *Provide adequate information about the feared entity:* Orient the child to the feared situation by procuring and providing the right information that also builds mental preparedness. Sometimes children tend to be fearful due to lack of adequate knowledge or information. Having prior information creates a feeling of familiarity. This is particularly helpful during transitions like when going to school. Preparing the child with information about the new place and describing the setting in detail will help her or him feel somewhat more relaxed in the new, unfamiliar surroundings. You should also talk to your child keeping in mind your prior knowledge of what may worry or scare her or him in such a situation, and the skills (s)he can bring into play in a situation like that to feel better.
3. *Let your child observe:* Give your child the opportunity to just sit quietly and observe from a distance the object, situation or activity that (s)he is fearful of. For example, if your child is scared of swimming, just taking her or him to the pool for some days to observe how people swim, and other children play with water, will aid in gathering the courage to experiment. Through observation children are able to address some of the fearful thoughts and gain a better understanding of the situation.
4. *Expose your child systematically to the feared entity:* Systematically desensitizing your child to the feared object is a scientific and effective way of helping her or him overcome fears. It prepares the child and helps them gradually move along the path of complete exposure to the feared stimulus. With each small step that your child takes towards the fear, (s)he develops comfort and familiarity at a slow pace rather than feel pushed to face it all in one go. By gaining control of the fear incrementally at each step the child feels confident and stronger to face the next one. You can also set the pace according to your child as it further enhances the willingness to try.
5. *Use play as a means to distract:* Some children may experience emotional dysregulation while facing fears. For example, the

sound of firecrackers or the fear of injections may cause her or him to get excessively upset, breaking into tears and heavy sobbing. With young children, assuming a playful stance can work wonders as it distracts them from the feeling of being overwhelmed, and makes it funny or silly. A child who is fearful of a fountain, can be distracted by creating a story of a monster changing shapes and colours and how (s)he can grab the monster like a superhero! Make it into a game which you play first and then encourage your child to play with you.

6. *Use deep breathing to tolerate the bodily response upon coming face-to-face with fear:* Help your child explore deep breathing to tolerate the bodily responses that occur when facing a feared situation. This helps your child in better managing the resultant emotions, as slow-paced breathing activates the parasympathetic nervous system which helps in gaining control of the racing heartbeat by pumping more oxygen into the body.

7. *Instil confidence by rewarding each successful step your child takes:* Children often look for a parent's response when approaching a new or feared situation, to gain confidence through the parent's approval. When your child is touching an insect, (s)he turns around to look at the parent's face to gather reassurance to go ahead with the action. This phenomenon is known as 'social referencing.' The reinforcement your child receives through verbal praises and external incentives also encourages the child to feel confident and proud of the self to have dealt with the fear.

BE CAREFUL, DON'T BECOME OVERZEALOUS

A word of caution—in attempting to help your child face fears, it is also pertinent to remember that not every fear needs to be countered. You need to make choices and pick the things that are important and need to be worked, keeping in mind the context of your child's life and what may or may not necessarily impact her or him. Don't become overzealous in your attempts to aid your child in gaining control over her or his fears. It takes time and yet there will be fears that will remain. Perfection is not the goal here and the idea is not to keep working on each and every fear your child may have.

HIGHLIGHTS

- Every child deals with fears and anxieties through the growing years.
- Children can be temperamental to experiencing fear in unfamiliar situations.
- Refrain from undermining the fear and coercing the child harshly to face the fear.
- Do not punish or rebuke the child for not dealing with the fear head on.
- Use a systematic approach to gradually expose the child to the fear by giving adequate prior information, providing opportunities for observation and introducing one step at a time.

42

CONSISTENCY IS THE KEY

For you and the child to hum the same tune,
strive to be consistent.
Create predictability as it ensures security.

A child learns to speak words like mama, dada or papa when you repeat them several times during a day. Everyone in the house uses the same words and the child absorbs them, memorizing them through the process of consistent repetition. This contributes to grasping and learning the language which is being spoken by all. Children are able to process the sounds and words, and to build connections between objects or actions and their corresponding words through rehearsal. Consistency is important. The basic rules of life and family culture are also internalized through their consistency. Consistency defines the functioning of families and society at large.

When it comes to parenting, consistency plays a crucial role. Punishment or negative reinforcement does not teach a child discipline. Consistency of rules and expectations help a child understand and imbibe them to operate within the family constellation and the society. It creates predictability for the child, which is crucial for smooth and stable functioning. Your child feels safe and secure when (s)he can predict how a parent would react to an action, what the father will say or what the mother expects in a situation.

Consistency is not only important in terms of what each parent does or expects but how both parents work together to nurture and raise the child. Parenting needs to be a partnership with both parents operating from the same platform, corroborating their stance with each other. You may have differing personalities but the application of your parenting goals needs to be consistent. Your child will understand limits and boundaries through consistency. This creates a structured and harmonious environment, which promotes healthy self-growth.

KEEP WORKING TOWARDS BEING CONSISTENT

Parents can find it hard to be consistent. When you are in a vulnerable state on account of being stressed, overworked or exhausted, it can be difficult to maintain your balance and be consistent. You lose the importance of your rules in that moment and can give in to your child's demands. As your child keeps jumping and hovering around you, while you have to finish your work or household chores, you can let go of your expected norms to ease the situation. However, the moment you finish your work, you feel angry because your child used your preoccupied state to break the rules. This can make you scream or yell at your child to switch off the TV or stop doing whatever (s)he is occupied with. Your child sees you vacillate in your responses, sometimes being calm and patient while at other times you are at a different goalpost emotionally. The child internalizes that my parent is inconsistent, showing different reactions in a short span of time. This can create unpredictability.

On another occasion you may be repeatedly reminding your child to be responsible and clean the room but (s)he does not adhere to it. You find your patience being tested and after two days of giving reminders you snap. You get angry and yell and also clean up the room. Your need to tidy up and organize overtakes the need for consistency. Your child can learn from this situation that if (s)he causes enough delay, things will be done by the parent. This creates intermittent situations of discord, as sometimes you refrain from doing your child's chore and at other times you do it for her or him. It is not always possible for parents to be consistent. Some situations may warrant that you let go off your expectations.

However, it is important to ensure that the communication made to children regarding the expectation is consistent and as far as possible they are adhered to.

As humans living in a world that is unpredictable, one needs to also learn the art of adapting to unpredictability. However, for a strong foundation, children need to be raised with as much consistency and predictability as possible. This helps them function well by perceiving the world as a place that they can understand and foresee. It is akin to being in a situation where the time for your train keeps changing everyday and you are unable to predict or plan anything. However, if the delay occurs once or twice a week, you adapt to it, as that too becomes predictable, and you are able to do some contingency planning for it.

The harmful effects of unpredictability lie in the anxiety it can cause. Unpredictability in your emotional responses can make a child feel unsure or overwhelmed, not allowing for the development of trust in the parent. This can cause the child to be aggressive, hostile or disconnected with the parent. Predictability in your emotional and behavioural responses and thought process helps the child internalize the same stability as a part of her or his personality. Being able to predict also gives the child the confidence to control situations.

STRIVE TOWARDS CONSISTENCY

To get the desired results, you need to strive for consistency in place of perfection. Consistent efforts driven in the right direction lead to accomplishment of goals. Parenting is a process of consistently striving to teach, nurture, mentor and facilitate the right values and mannerisms to help your child grow into a confident and happy individual. Consistent application of rules and principles will slowly seep into your child to become a part of her or his inner being.

1. *Start with the basics:* Maintain a structured environment at home to bring a sense of predictability in routines. Define timelines for day-to-day activities like sleeping, waking up,

family time, study and play time. Follow them consistently with minimal variation. Don't be rigid. Keep some flexibility in the routine. For instance, during the holidays or on weekends or when some unforeseen events may happen. It is simultaneously important for children to learn how to handle unpredictability as a part of life. Conversations about consistency, while emphasizing the need and ways to adapt in case of unforeseen situations, are helpful in this respect.

2. *Set the rules and regulations together:* Involve your child in the process of rule setting. Participative approaches enhance the will and willingness to follow rules. There will, nevertheless, be times when you may face resistance and tantrums when you draw the boundaries, despite them being understood and accepted. Maintain a calm, rational and consistent approach towards applying them which will give you the desired results.

3. *Discuss consequences when setting rules*: It is important to discuss with your child beforehand, the consequences of not following the rules. It helps her or him to understand and know what to expect in case of deviance from the expected behaviour. Discuss the number of reminders to be provided, before reprimanding her or him straightaway. Decide upon the consequences based on the severity of the problematic behaviour. Also keep in mind that consequences don't have to involve punishments. They include removal of things or activities that a child may enjoy being a part of.

4. *Both parents must be consistent about rules and consequences:* Both parents must be on the same page for rules and expectations to be well understood and followed by the child. Discuss with each other thoughts about regulations, and the consequences for not adhering to them, before talking with your child. If there are any differences, they should be dealt with beforehand. Difference in opinions may sometimes come out in the process of application, which should be handled separately, avoiding any clashes in front of the child. It is also a good idea to talk to other members in the home about the benefits of being consistent.

5. *Apply consistent rules when dealing with challenging behaviour*: To deal with any kind of difficult behaviour, consistent communication of rules and regulations and its application is the key. Your child may test your limits and show worsening of behaviour when you enforce the same rules. Using punishments and time outs may not help, and may instead lead to further feelings of anger and isolation. Parents must maintain consistency in their emotional response and deal with the behaviour with logic and related consequences. It is also important to talk to other members of the family to follow same behaviour guidelines while dealing with the child.

DIMINISH YOUR RESISTANCE

A challenge to being consistent is also posited by the rigidities of your own thinking and behaviour. Every individual is used to behaving in a certain manner, and bringing a change in an existing pattern warrants a need to work on the rigidities within the self. This highlights the need for awareness and understanding of the self, temperament, patterns and beliefs. Equipped with this knowledge you can reduce your resistance to change the approach you currently adopt in parenting your child. This will allow you to help your child modify her or his undesirable behaviour and enhance their ways of thinking.

HIGHLIGHTS

- Consistency creates a sense of safety and security for the child by creating predictability.
- Consistency holds the key to disciplining your child through the application of consistent rules and regulations.
- Having a basic routine brings in harmony and structure to the environment.
- Discuss rules, regulations and related consequences with your child for better adherence.
- Both parents must be consistent in their approach when dealing with problem behaviour.

43

CREATE OPPORTUNITIES TO HONE SKILLS

*Create moments of constructive teaching
and learning for your child.
Your focused attention and time today.
will build a stable tomorrow.*

When you imagine your 6-year old as a 26-year-old adult, what skills do you think (s)he would need to survive in the world? Listening to the success stories of young entrepreneurs and innovators—who design and implement many creative concepts, push for innovation, take on some of society's most challenging issues—you also harbour a desire for your child to take on these roles when (s)he grows up. Though technology has made us more aware of an array of issues from across the world, it has also highlighted the problems posited by the fast-paced nature of the world today. One can often feel ill-equipped to manage the demands that require a particular level of knowledge, expertise and solid skill sets. Through the parenting process, you most certainly aim to equip your child to manage the contingencies of this fast-paced, ever-changing world with utmost confidence.

The challenge of it all lies in finding novel ways of teaching, guiding and mentoring your child through the course of her or his lifespan. It necessitates a marked level of flexibility in you to adapt and accommodate to the changes occurring in your child as well as the world. This also means you need to be constantly vigilant in actively seeking new opportunities for your child to apply and test skills. Your feedback is invaluable as is your presence through the process. Your support constantly encourages your child to not just work on what (s)he has but to build on more.

You play a pertinent role in identifying the requisite mix of essential life skills to inculcate in your child. This you do by understanding your child's existing skill sets, and then working collaboratively, aiding her or him in trying new situations, building on experiences and expanding existing skills. You may falter, as will your child, but remember to keep going on and never give up.

CONFIDENCE BUILDS THROUGH SKILL DEVELOPMENT AND APPLICATION

Skill acquisition is an intensive, long process, which requires varying inputs over time. Communication skills, problem-solving, self-awareness, critical thinking and emotional regulation are key tools for a child to learn how to navigate through life's challenges. Developmentally, these skills start building from the moment the child starts interacting with the world. Your inputs in helping your child build these skills are invaluable, as, it is through direct and indirect experiences with you that the child develops them. Once these skills are in place it is also essential that the child utilizes them to see if and how they work.

Confidence comes through doing things and being a part of the process of getting to do those things. As the child understands and grasps the ways in which tasks can be or need to be completed, confidence grows. Ranging from simple things like learning to tie the laces of shoes to doing chores at home or going to a store to buy something, each act teaches the child some very important skills that contribute to the growing confidence of the child. This happens through recognizing how things are done, the way one needs to think through the doing of things and realization of the fact that they can be done.

The larger the number of experiences in which the child tests herself or himself to see whether (s)he has the ability to do something, the greater the likelihood of it contributing to the child's developing confidence. As the child observes herself or himself doing things, and as (s)he receives your or another adult's appreciation and recognition, the belief in the self grows. It encourages the child to feel assured about how (s)he does things and also builds motivation.

However, you need to balance the ways in which you impart skills to your child and encourage her or him to use them. It is imperative to stay away from being too demanding as well as expecting compliance through preaching, nagging or using forceful means. This makes the child resistant, frustrated and unwilling to engage, as (s)he finds it a burden. Concurrently, it does not help to be too lenient either as it fosters excessive dependency, which is detrimental in the long run. Be balanced, push in some spaces and step back in others.

WAYS TO HONE LIFE SKILLS

How you teach and what you teach your child are important aspects in skills training. You must focus on finding age appropriate, creative ways to impart skills to your child. Innovative ways of modelling skills lead to enhanced learning and motivated absorption. It also stimulates the child's analytical and processing skills, enhancing the possibility for developing the creative process.

1. *There is opportunity everywhere:* Recognize that even small instances and episodes can provide the opportunity to demonstrate or build skills with your child. Be observant and utilize the moments that emerge during your routine interactions, to stimulate skill acquisition. This makes it into a normal part of life instead of having to create a specific time for working on skills.
2. *Use short and specific instructions:* How you deliver what you want your child to learn is important. One must use short, specific and clear instructions when teaching a new skill to your child. Using a visual aid to accompany the verbal instructions enhances the skill acquisition. For example, when you are teaching your child how to set the dinner table, give

one-step instructions, while simultaneously modelling how to do it. Turn it into a routine for the child to learn it well.

3. *Encourage to analyse and solve their own questions:* When your child asks you a question, for example, 'Why does the moon change its shape?', don't jump up to give the answer. Instead change it into a thinking activity of, 'Let's find out why!' Make it into a project for the child to come up with diverse explanations. While with a young child you may have to facilitate exploring, reading and finding answers, with older children you can ask them to search for the different existing theories and come back with explanations. This facilitates the process of self-learning, analysing and finding solutions for themselves.

4. *Make wise use of technology:* Children get exposed to media and technology at a very early age. You can use this technology to help them learn, explore and create. Involve your child in the process of deciding things like which shows or cartoons (s)he should see. There will be times when your child will be on board with your perspective immediately. At other times, (s)he may want to watch a show you think is not suitable. Use this as an opportunity to help your child expand on the ability to think and understand the impact of media and how choices are made. Use rational, logical explanations to help your child think, instead of being prescriptive about what should or should not be done.

5. *Practice, practice, practice:* Give children opportunities to apply the skills they have acquired across various settings. If you are working on your child's organizing skills, turn it into a playful challenge and create various levels to build that skill. Practising any skill leads to greater confidence and automatic processing of the skill in a given setting.

6. *Think out of the box:* Encourage your child to come up with novel ideas to resolve problems. If your child likes puzzles, ask her or him to generate different ways to solve the same puzzle. Don't jump in too quickly to help her or him with probable solutions. Similarly, if your child enjoys art, encourage her or him to come up with their own representations of concepts.

When you ask your child to develop her or his own concepts, it fosters creativity and enhances the skill to think and look at things from multiple perspectives.
7. *Explain the why and how of skills:* Engage in meaningful discussions about why and how a particular skill can be helpful. Ask your child to reflect upon how (s)he thinks it could be beneficial. The more you improve your child's understanding of the need and relevance of the skill, the more enthusiastic and involved (s)he would be to learn and work on it.

YOUR CHILD REFLECTS YOUR CONFIDENCE

Children continuously strive to develop independence. They learn to assimilate and accommodate experiences and world-views, through observation, multiple trials, failing and finding their way again. Parents act as mentors, saviours, observers and facilitators of these processes as they continuously impart life skills. It is an enormous task which requires your patience and persistence. Keep working on your confidence in your skills as a parent, and your child will reflect that confidence too!

HIGHLIGHTS

- Children learn life skills from parents since the time they are born.
- Through the development of skills a child builds increasingly independent interactions with the world.
- Multiple opportunities are available during the course of your day-to-day interactions to impart life skills to your child.
- Consistently work to provide your child with opportunities to apply skills.
- Use creative means to enhance the learning of new skills.

44

TEACH ASSERTIVENESS

*Instil in your children the confidence to talk,
walk and express self.
Help them learn the art of establishing
respectful boundaries for self and others.*

When children step into the real world, start going to school or play in the neighbourhood, they often come back with stories of getting into a fight while playing with friends and peers, or of seeing someone else involved in a nasty encounter. Parents worry about how their child would adjust with peers, whether (s)he will be able to manage if someone gets aggressive, how will (s)he handle an altercation, hope that (s)he will be sensitive to others and not be an instigator of troubles. Peer pressure and bullying is also a reality. As a parent, you would want to intervene and help your child. However, what is really needed is that your child builds the skills to manage such situations and be assertive.

Each child is different temperamentally and has a natural predisposition towards managing situations. Some children are shy, obedient or polite and often you hear praises about their cool, calm and easy behaviour. You feel happy to hear positive things about your child but on occasions you also wonder if your child is being pushed around as (s)he comes across as being submissive. You do not wish your child to be passive when it comes to expressing her or his opinions or needs. Contrarily, some children can be quite bossy or aggressive in their stance towards their peers. You feel frustrated listening to the complaints from other parents, teachers and children about your child's misconduct. You get angry or punish your child or get entangled in arguments with other parents. Both the scenarios create unpleasantness as your child is unable to deal with situations assertively.

Children are not born with an inbuilt ability to deal with the social world. They learn to respond to such scenarios by observing and experiencing methods of resolving emotional conflicts. Their reactions to peer pressure or bullying are a result of the interaction between their temperament and what is modelled in the environment. Both, the child who is passive, and the child who is aggressive struggle with forming or maintaining relationships in the long run, unless they learn to take care of themselves. They either struggle with low self-esteem, or become apathetic towards the experiences of others.

Yes, you would want your child to stand up for herself or himself. Yes, you would like them to deal with conflicts confidently. This can be achieved if you model and teach assertiveness to your child.

THE BENEFITS OF ASSERTIVENESS

Ask yourself these questions: How often do you respond assertively to a challenging situation? How do you respond when a senior colleague requests your help and you already have a lot on your plate? What do you say to your driver when he comes half an hour late every alternate day? These are regular situations which people come across during the course of their daily living. Each of these has the potential to become painfully troublesome if it occurs regularly and unrelentingly. They prompt you to find amicable solutions, and to move forward. Yet there can be times when you feel too pushed and hassled by the occurrence of these episodes.

Now let's take a close look at how you handle the situation when it comes to your child being teased or bullied in the playground. There are two possibilities that commonly occur. In the first scenario, when your child is playing in the park, you see her or him coming towards you crying. The older children in the park teased her or him and called her or him names. Angry and furious, you head towards the children and gave them a piece of your mind. Your child feels relieved, and both of you leave. While on your way back, you either tell your child to give it back to them or to inform you the next time it happens. In the second scenario, you soothe your child and tell her or him to ignore those children as they are bad. Both responses do not teach your child to be assertive.

The core of assertiveness involves understanding boundaries. Your child respects her or his core values and also regards other peoples' rights when (s)he is assertive. An assertive child is aware of strengths and limitations. While we teach our children to be kind and empathetic, it is also important for them to learn the art of saying 'no' assertively. Empathy and assertiveness must go hand in hand. Absence of either can create misperceptions of being weak or rude, which harm the process of building relationships in the long run. Assertiveness helps the child establish safety and trust in relationships.

Assertiveness teaches how to advocate for oneself respectfully. It gives a child the strength to speak up, share and express views confidently. Imparting the skill of being assertive to your child is valuable, as it gives the child self-control and the ability to act assuredly. Through assertiveness, the child learns to disagree without degrading or demeaning the other person's point of view and negotiate respectfully.

TEACH YOUR CHILD TO BE ASSERTIVE

Children express their autonomy early on by saying a loud 'NO' when you push them to do things like going for a bath, tidying up their toys or finishing their meals. Helping your child learn the right way to say 'no' is important. You want your child to make choices that are good and right. The manner in which you react, respond, respect and assert to your child's demands is critical to instilling the same in your child. Let's look at various techniques to nurture assertiveness in your child.

1. *Assertive coaching*: Talk to your child about what is assertive communication and how it differs from being aggressive or passive. Children should understand the concept of assertiveness as it can be quite tricky and difficult to grasp intuitively. Work on your child's ability to stay calm and yet firm while stating what (s)he wants or is not okay with. Encourage her or him through role playing and brainstorming situations from everyday life or observations from cartoons and other media.
2. *Model assertive communication*: Assertiveness should be practised as a mode of communication at home. Parents should give each other, and other family members, the space to express their opinions and share their disagreements respectfully. Children are silent observers and learn their communication style from how you communicate your views and concerns with others. Respect your child's thought process when (s)he says a 'no' and negotiate your demand around it assertively. Regardless of the situation, model calmness and firmness when responding to your child. For example, if your child refuses to finish her or his homework when you are planning to take her or him for an outing, and demands to finish it after you return, you could respond to your child by saying, 'Yes, I know how much you like that place and you want to leave as soon as you can. That is possible if you complete your homework fast because once you come back you would be tired and it would be unreasonable to expect yourself to complete it. Can you please make sure that we all leave quickly for it?' Even if your child persists, continuing to reiterate your point calmly is important. This is an assertive way to communicate with your child, clearly stating your expectations without getting angry. When you consistently use this approach, your child learns to respect your boundaries and understands that tantrums won't work.
3. *Don't just talk but walk the path of assertiveness*: Assertiveness is not just about the words or statements that you use to express yourself. It is also about how you speak. The body posture you adopt plays a big role in asserting yourself. When you are being

assertive with your child, maintain eye contact while bending down to the level of your child and maintaining a calm firm tone. Be careful that your own way of communicating both verbally and physically does not express coercion. This may cause subliminal conditioning and the child learns to comply with coercive demands. Children mirror parents and it is important to demonstrate an appropriate stance.

4. *Practice using role plays relating to real-life situations*: Your child can be a passive or an aggressive person. Giving them the skill of assertiveness, by practising how to communicate assertively, prevents them from being either. For example, in your conversations, enquire from your child about any experiences where (s)he has encountered being pushed, coerced, teased or reacted to angrily. Use the scenarios—which may involve your child, someone else or what (s)he observed—to role play assertiveness with her or him.

5. *Teach the techniques for being assertive*: Some of the most effective techniques of being assertive are using broken record, humour and empathetic statements in a situation. The broken record technique implies saying the same point repetitively till the other person stops putting forth different suggestions to convince you. It helps a child stay on her or his stance, and is particularly effective when dealing with peer pressure. Humour is a mature way of defending oneself without shaking the dynamic between the two parties. Just expressing how you feel about being in a situation, and what you believe about yourself, can be helpful in facing the other person. Empathetic statements help in looping in the other persons' emotions and being respectful, while negotiating between what you want vis-à-vis the other person.

THERE IS A FINE LINE BETWEEN ASSERTIVENESS AND AGGRESSION

You may not realize when being assertive may tip over to the other side and take the form of aggression. It is important to regularly monitor tonality, expressions and body language to ensure that the communication is not perceived as aggressive. Keeping aside personal innuendos and comments is important, and it is imperative that you teach your child to stick with the present situation when being assertive about something. Contextualizing comments to the present helps ensure that the other person does not feel disrespected and targeted which is crucial to the success of being assertive.

HIGHLIGHTS

- Assertiveness is an essential communication skill you need to teach children.
- Assertiveness teaches a child how to say no respectfully and establish boundaries in relationships.
- Model assertive communication at home with family members for your child to internalize it.
- Impart assertive skills to your child by giving them the safe space to share their opinions, respecting them and giving your views as well.
- Give your child the strength and confidence to speak up and stand up for themselves through assertiveness skills.

45

HELP YOUR CHILD BUILD SOCIAL SKILLS TO DEVELOP HEALTHY RELATIONSHIPS

No one can live in social isolation. Children need the right skills to be able to form social relationships which are lasting and contribute positively to their self-concepts.

Adults are social beings who have a strong, basic need for social interactions and forming meaningful relations with friends, family and colleagues. The need to be attached to others begins from the time a child is born and starts looking for a mother's response and reactions. The early parent-child attachment lays the foundation for later social and relational competency in a child's life. As a parent, you play a vital role in helping your child develop trust and security with regard to the outside world. It is an enormous responsibility to help your child develop a balanced view of the world to form healthy relationships. You provide a window by encouraging your child to explore surroundings and engage with people.

As children grow, they mould themselves into different ways of interacting to fit into the social surroundings. Some children can be flexible and more adept at changing in response to the external environment. They are more confident in engaging with social situations. Others can be shy, hesitant and anxious to step into the social world. They may find it more challenging and difficult to open up to unfamiliar and uncertain social situations. They need more prompts from their parents to engage with people. Though children may differ in their levels of sociability, what is crucial is to nurture their ability to connect, invest and maintain meaningful relationships. Social belongingness is a core facet that contributes to happiness.

Social skills are critical not only for developing healthy relationships but also for academic success. Children who are able to understand social cues, adapt well to social structures. They use their skills to form and maintain peer relations. They show greater social competence in both personal and professional life. The ability for social and emotional learning reduces the risk for problem behaviour and marks the possibility of growth for academic learning. The social domain is a key aspect in the development of identity and contributes to self-esteem and confidence.

LAY THE FOUNDATION FOR SOCIAL SKILLS THROUGH PLAY

The key to developing strong healthy relationships is through establishing trust, security and boundaries. Your communication and responsiveness towards your child, as well as mannerisms in the social milieu, affect how your child interacts with the social environment. As children grow, they look for interactions with same aged peers. It is through cooperative play that a pre-schooler attempts to start building peer relations. The desire to explore another child's toys and games or to engage in group activities, acts as a means to initiate interactions. This is further reinforced by parental prompts to share and play together.

It is through play that a child learns to negotiate, share, cooperate, collaborate, resolve conflicts and lay down the rules. These are core elements of social skills that children learn to apply in their interactions with the help of parents at home and teachers at school. These skills are important for children from very early on for initiating, developing and maintaining peer relations.

Let's take the example of a scenario where your 5 year old is playing with another child. They are playing together with Lego blocks. After some time they have an argument about how many blocks should be put together to make a structure, and they start fighting with each other. Your child comes crying to you and you intervene by responding, 'If you cannot share your toys with your friend, I am going to have to ask her or him to leave. You have called her or him to play and now not sharing the toys is not okay.' Your child may feel angry at the friend's need being addressed. (S)He either throws a tantrum or leaves the blocks to play something else. This interaction does not teach your child what to do in order to sustain the play and resolve the conflict. Both of them need to learn a skill that would help them continue playing. If instead, you say, 'Why don't we take turns to build this structure? Let me flip a coin to decide who starts first. Great! It's heads. So, you put your block first and then your friend can do the same.' Here, they both learn to cooperate and collaborate while at play. This helps them stick with the act of building the structure by resolving their conflict. Reinforce their effort by stating, 'Wonderful, you are doing a great job of building this together. You both did your parts really well.'

Another important aspect is the experience of positive emotions through collaboration. Such situations teach children how to move from feeling angry and frustrated because of an unresolved issue, to being happy and joyful by finishing the game through cooperation. Play, as an extensive medium, has great potential to set the right building blocks for social skills in children. Active and mindful use of such moments can play a crucial role in developing effective social skills in your child, which lays the foundation for healthy relationships.

WHAT CAN PARENTS DO TO HONE A CHILD'S SOCIAL SKILLS?

Every child is born with an innate social temperament. Having friends and developing a good bond with them is a natural need. A child may have a large social group or just a few close friends. Without a social circle, a child may experience loneliness and lack of motivation to go to school or to play. Having a peer group at school plays a crucial role in a child's life, both academically and to form the self and social identity. To mould and shape the social temperament, children need to be taught the right social skills. The onus of how to create opportunities to develop social skills rests with the parents.

1. *Assess your child's social needs:* Each child is different and so is the need for social relationships. Seeing a child interact and mingle with people, confidently engaging in conversations with others is a satisfying experience for a parent. However, it is important to understand, recognize and acknowledge your child's comfort and capacity for social interactions. As long as a child is showing developmentally appropriate social and emotional relatedness and understanding of social cues, you need not worry or push your child to respond to social demands.
2. *Move at the child's pace:* Being shy or less sociable is not harmful. It is good to keep pace with your child to develop comfort in diverse social settings. Some children take time before engaging with people in social situations. If you coax them too much, they may withdraw. Provide them the time to develop comfort, and then gently nudge your child. If your child feels anxious in social situations, you can help by first introducing her or him to a very small peer group, and then gradually encouraging her or him to engage with relatively larger groups.
3. *Give your child opportunities for social interactions:* Children should be given exposure to the social world through various means. Whether through art, play, activities, games, sports, social gatherings or even television, children should be provided opportunities to explore and form their schemas of the social world. Using diverse mediums, parents can enhance a child's social abilities by making social interactions a fun process.
4. *Foster interpersonal skills:* Making a conversation does not come naturally to everyone. Be observant to see if your child is able to initiate conversations with her or his peers. If you find your child being predominantly passive in social situations, have an open conversation to understand what holds her or him back. Enquire from your child if (s)he knows how to

commence interactions with friends. Determine if (s)he is able to collaborate in group activities. If you find your child struggling, practise with her or him through role plays and continuously demonstrate the application of communication skills. Work collaboratively with your child to help her or him overcome the challenges (s)he may be experiencing.

5. *Teach your child conflict resolution skills:* Having conflicts within interpersonal relationships is a normal experience. To have successful personal and professional interpersonal relations, children must be taught how to resolve conflicts. Encourage them to begin by calming themselves, and then, listening carefully to each other's point of view. Encourage your child to express how (s)he feels. Help her or him to understand different perspectives and build empathy by pointing out different ways of looking at the same situation. Prod your child to think of alternate solutions to problems, and work together to determine which strategy is most effective.

HEALTHY RELATIONSHIPS WITH PEERS ENHANCE SELF-CONFIDENCE

Sharing stories, expressing emotions and being able to relate to someone, are elements that characterize healthy peer relations or friendships. Healthy relationships add to the feeling of being valued and cared for, and evoke positive emotions to care for those who one feels close to. This mutual sense of belonging enhances self-esteem by making a child feel good about herself or himself. It also contributes to the development of a healthy social identity, which in turn enhances a child's self-confidence. The ability to form good social relationships and networks with people, is critical to personal and professional growth in the long run, making it essential that attention be directed towards this critical skill from an early age.

HIGHLIGHTS

- Forming emotional and social attachments is the core of being human.
- Provide a safe and secure space from which to explore the external world.
- Foster adequate social skills like adapting, collaborating, negotiating, problem-solving and conflict resolution to form healthy relations.
- If your child struggles to make conversations, begin by practising communication skills.
- The ability to develop and sustain long-term, close bonds is critical to self-confidence and success.

46

LET GO OF THE ASSUMPTIONS

Assumptions you hold can alter the realities.
Without knowing, you may harbour misperceptions.

It is natural for humans to make inferences and assumptions about various aspects of their life. These assumptions are a result of the belief systems that are formed through a transactional process between the individual and the family, society and culture. They influence every role that an individual assumes through the lifespan. This holds true for parenting as well. The thinking that guides parents, makes them respond and react towards the child emotionally and behaviourally, is also related to the assumptions they hold. Not all assumptions are bad as they can also be helpful when based on correct facts and figures. It is when one allows incorrect assumptions to rule and influence perceptions, behaviour and decisions that they prove to be a deterrent to the parent-child relationship.

SUBTLE WAYS IN WHICH ASSUMPTIONS OPERATE

Parents find pride and comfort in the belief, 'I know my child well.' Playing a primary role in the child's rearing, you can closely observe her or him grow. You are able to define and characterize your child with certain attributes. For example, you may identify your elder child to be responsible, sociable, expressive, yet rigid in her or his personality. You have always seen her or him being able to take care of her or his problems, evoking less parental involvement. So you believe you can be less worried as you are relatively confident about her or his ability to handle challenges and find a way. With this assumption, you may take a backseat when it comes to checking in with her or him on how (s)he is doing, specifically in times when (s)he may need it the most like transitioning to college, a new place or a new job role. On the other hand, your child may assume that you are unable to understand her or him. (S)He feels compelled to maintain this perfect image of being self-sufficient. These presumptions can build distance between her or him and you.

Assumptions can build a restrictive perception about a person or situation. As the adult who has experience and knowledge, you are likely to hold on to your beliefs and their resultant cause-and-effect relationships. For instance, the common perception regarding a child who is not performing well in exams, is lack of adequate preparation and sincere efforts. You may be predisposed to hold on to the belief that sincere efforts and regularity would have given better results. It can be difficult to look beyond this straightforward correlation. The child's fear or anxiety, which is hampering performance, may go unnoticed. In such situations, the assumptions limit your potential to be attuned to what goes on with your child. It restricts your ability to go beyond the obvious. It is required that you be introspective about your thoughts, assumptions and beliefs, as parenting is a journey of continually evolving with your child.

STRIVE TO LOOK BEYOND WHAT YOU SEE

Children explore. Children experiment. Children get lost in their playful world, often ignoring a parent's request. All children are defined by the nature, temperament and personality they have. Their basic character trait leads to the utilization of specific behaviour patterns causing parents and others to form an image or perception about them. A parent depends upon these perceptual inferences to gauge the child's actions each time. Let's say your 8-year-old child is involved in minor infractions at home. (S)He is naughty—peers and family refer to her or him as mischievous. As parents, you often reprimand her or him for this behaviour.

Recently (s)he informed you about another child troubling her or him at school. In light of your past experiences you ignored the pleas, assuming (s)he must have initiated the situation. This made her or him upset and further contributed to her or his negative behavioural patterns.

Every child makes mistakes, lies, manipulates or cheats through the course of growing up. Each time an incident occurs, it reinforces the existing assumptions. Your response to these behaviours can contribute to the strengthening or weakening of the parent-child bond. You may find it difficult to build trust, and thus, may react on the basis of pre-existing notions about your child. However, as you do continue to respond on the basis of assumptions, your child feels anger, shame and resentment or disconnect from you. It affects the basic trust between you and your child.

Rather than suspicion, interrogation and misinterpretation, a parent must strive towards being mindfully aware and reflective of thoughts and perceptions about the child and her or his behaviour. Asking questions about each situation, developing an understanding and finding the right answers with your child is the path to effective parenting.

LET GO OF THESE PARENTAL ASSUMPTIONS

Parenting beliefs are influenced by how you were raised, your values, culture, family, friends and spouse. In the parenting process, it is important to be in tune with what determines your values and behaviour as a parent. Having an evolving understanding of how you view your child and the perception of her or his intentions, lets you be a sensitive and aware parent. Let's decode some of the assumptions.

1. *I know my child best*: It is true that a parent is more aware of a child's traits and personality. This enables assessment of abilities, coping, ways of responding, problem-solving and negotiating with situations. Yet this overriding assumption can take away from letting you have a continuously evolving

understanding of your child as (s)he goes through experiences and develops cognitively, emotionally and psychologically. Children have the ability to consistently surprise you through their new ways of thinking and behaving.
2. *I need to be strict and stern with my child to ensure obedience*: It is often believed that those children who have strict and stern parents are more successful. Obedience and understanding of what is right or wrong does not develop through pushing a child. Having an approach that is geared towards nurturing and building independence can give the same results. Having a style of communication which is assertive, firm, oriented towards discussions and conversations shall help the child to develop a thought process that reflects the values and beliefs you want to inculcate in her or him.
3. *If I do not constantly remind and push my child, things will not get done*: Overly demanding and involved parenting can be counterproductive and children can become overly dependent or aggressive with parents. Conversely, children do need warmth, love, support and balanced firmness for a strong parent-child bond, that supports the development of a strong self and confidence.
4. *I can always gauge when my child has done something wrong*: When children are young, it is easy for a parent to decipher their playful mischievous acts. As they grow older, children develop well defined mechanisms to show or hide their feelings and thoughts. For any individual to know what goes on in another's mind is not possible. Understanding can be generated through having open conversations, validating the information that is made available and providing multiple avenues to share what is happening.

KNOWLEDGE OF YOUR ASSUMPTIONS IS MOST IMPORTANT

Self-knowledge and awareness underpins your ability to let go of your assumptions. The assumptions an individual holds influences thinking, feelings and responses in an insiduous manner. Letting go of assumptions does not imply not possessing them or not allowing them to emerge. Instead it indicates that you know when they emerge, so you can mindfully modify these in a manner that is effective and contributes positively to your relationship with your child.

HIGHLIGHTS

○ Assumptions naturally emerge in the belief systems without an individual's realization.

○ Assumptions can create mental blocks and perceptual restrictions.

○ Work to build self-awareness to avoid making assumptive beliefs about your child.

○ Let go of the parental assumptions resulting from your upbringing, society, friends or family.

○ Use each instance to know more and understand your child.

47

STIMULATE CREATIVE THINKING

*Creativity is not only about encouraging children
to think out of the box.
It's about letting every step they take be their own.*

'I am going to colour the sky pink and purple because I like these colours. This is my sky.'

'Mummy you go straight, I am going to run up that hill to catch you there.'

'Daddy, I thought you are going to be 36 years old so I drew a tall picture of you. Later you told me you are going to turn 32 years old and I drew another picture with you a bit shorter.'

Children have creative thoughts multiple times in a day. Thinking and acting outside set boundaries, beyond the stated norms, and departing from the given instructions, to explore imaginations comes naturally to a child. Children are not designed to think in a straight line. Expectations and norms for acquiring the right behaviour and learning propel them to think in prescribed ways.

Creative thinking enhances a child's intellectual capacity and enthusiasm to explore. When children engage in creative exploration through art and play, they present an idea or thought which is original. They generate unique cognitive and problem-solving skills to create, design and present novel ideas. Divergent thinking requires clarity of thought process with extensive use of the child's visual-spatial skills to create a unique representation. If you notice a young child walking back from school, often (s)he would prefer not to walk in a straight line. Her or his steps would echo the playfulness of the mind, sometimes walking on the edge of the footpath or running over the ground, pulling down a tree branch or trying to reach out towards the far away leaves. You can enhance your child's creative abilities by being a part of her or his creative world in many such moments.

Helping children delve in creative thinking makes them motivated learners who are invested in understanding what is and what possibilities there can be. It enhances the child's mental growth and also instils confidence in sharing thoughts and ideas with the world.

PRESERVING UNSTRUCTURED PLAY AND ART IS AT THE CORE OF CREATIVE THINKING

The use of art and play facilitates a child's expression of innermost feelings and thoughts that are untainted and pure. This free self-expression can only come through unstructured forms of play. For example, allow your child to use colours in an imaginative way to represent a theme and develop a unique story. Removing limits that are exerted by the presence of rules creates the right environment for unstructured play.

Creativity manifests in many forms like when a child uses a towel to act as a superhero cape, tissues to make snow balls, turns the mattress into a trampoline or pretends the hose pipe is a sword with which (s)he slays a dragon. During young years, children require exposure to as much unstructured play as one can possibly provide. To develop the ability to think laterally, you can remove the drawing book or the art class, the sports or drama coaching and instead let the child make her or his own rules and play. Shape these over a period of time to help your child gradually learn to reign in the creativity and apply it in specific contexts, while adhering to the rules in others.

Communicate and tutor your child about values and life skills by encouraging her or him to think creatively. For example, when you want to teach your child about the environment, pose a question when (s)he is at play acting like a superhero in the park deriving superpowers from the plants. Ask her or him to imagine the park with only one tree and discuss how it would look or feel like, how it would affect the game or impact the people. As you wait for your child to share her or his answers, don't be in a rush by providing directions or nudges to respond. Instead, become a part of the child's creative process, engage with the statements (s)he makes and help develop the thought process by asking the right leading questions.

WAYS TO HONE CREATIVE ACUITY IN YOUR CHILD

Children have an innate ability to imagine, create and play, and there is always room for more. Building on creative thinking capabilities enhances the mental agility of the child to act in a given situation. Parents can further harness a child's creative thinking capabilities by encouraging them to widen their imaginary world through thoughtful strategies that focus on sharpening the creative skills.

1. *Be cognizant of your child's creative fantasy flights*: Children embark on their fantasy journey multiple times in a day. While sitting on the table drinking their milk, your child may pretend that an alligator comes out of the paper and is going to eat her or him. Given the tight schedule in the morning you may be tempted to respond by saying, 'Stop playing now, finish your milk and get going.' When (s)he is back from school and pretends to be a rabbit hopping around the house, you nudge her or him and say, 'Change your clothes quickly. I have to feed you and then you have to finish your homework.' When (s)he sits down to do the homework, you sit with her or him to ensure it finishes on time and keep prompting to focus. When (s)he gets ready for the activity class, (s)he hums a tune and dances to it, which is followed by a quick comment from you, 'Seriously! Every time you get lost in your world and start doing whatever comes to your mind. Please get ready fast, we have to go.' A child can go on and on in the fantasy world. Of course, it may be difficult to keep pace with it or let her or him be there every time. However, to enhance your child's

creativity, indulge a bit, and become a part of the fantasy that (s)he creates.

2. *Make some time for unstructured play and use your creativity to engage*: Keep play unstructured and think of new ways to engage your child. For example, give her or him a few colourful sheets, glue and some sparkles. Ask her or him to make five different things that (s)he can think of using these materials. Sometimes a child may be hesitant to start on their own and you can aid in initiating the play. Get involved in your child's play. Ask your child to choose a favourite animal and let her or him act like that animal for the day. You can choose to respond to the child by being the animal mom or dad.

3. *Think of unconventional, diverse teaching methods*: Creativity and teaching don't need to be two separate entities. You can always use unique and creative ways of teaching children. For example, you can use forks and plates to teach addition, while laying the table for dinner. Integrate your surroundings when teaching concepts to the child. This makes them understandable, relatable, applicable and brings a sense of undiluted learning, that can happen anywhere and anytime in a fun way.

4. *Pose open-ended questions without prompting for answers*: Ask open-ended questions that take your child on a creative journey without providing answers yourself. You can ask questions like, 'If the colour of the leaves was something else, what could it be' or, 'If cars could be of different shapes, what would they look like?' Make sure to pose age-appropriate questions to your child. Pretend you are thinking with them but don't feed into their imagination. Wait to see them release their creativity in their responses.

5. *Provide exposure to creative excursions*: Based on your child's interest, provide opportunities to explore creative skills by going for field trips to museums, art galleries, drama, or theatre. Art and entertainment provide a larger window to nurture creative minds. This expands the understanding of diverse aspects of situations and helps children see various forms of creative knowledge present in the world.

MAKE CREATING, DESIGNING AND INVENTING YOUR CHILD'S MANTRA

Creative thinking enables a child to accommodate and integrate complex thinking. Higher levels of comfort with ambiguities reduces judgements and creates openness to diversity and subjectivity that the world can present. Creativity should be fostered in a child as an approach to thinking, perceiving and heuristic problem-solving. It cannot exist in an either/or way and is contextually driven. Creativity allows the child to synthesize a dialectical understanding of situations. Make creative exploration a part of your child's daily life by providing an unstructured environment.

HIGHLIGHTS

- Every child has innate latent creative abilities.
- Build your child's imagination by asking open-ended questions that propel her or him to think differently.
- Provide space for unstructured play to harness your child's creative imaginations.
- Consciously make time to engage in your child's imaginative world, and integrate teaching with creativity.
- Encourage divergent thinking as part of your child's daily routine and interactions.

48

DEVELOP CRITICAL THINKING IN YOUR CHILD

Give children the skills to see the world through their eyes, form connections through their thoughts and create their own belief system through their inquisitiveness, questioning and finding solutions.

A child is curious to see, play, observe and try new things, which sets the tone for the development of critical thinking from the beginning. It takes effort and mental processing for a child to analyse and assimilate new information that (s)he comes across on a daily basis. Whether it involves learning language, imbibing skills to eat or wear clothes, or making simple choices about what to play—enormous information processing happens in young minds to understand, acquire and implement these skills and actions. As they grow, the complexity of information increases and children require complex skills to analyse, assess, assimilate, realign or accommodate the new knowledge on a daily basis, with already existing reserves.

It takes hard work, effort and trust in your own self to make choices for your child. For example, when choosing a school for your child you gather information about schools from various sources. You invest time to understand the curriculum, evaluate their philosophy and systems to see if it matches your beliefs and ensure it is a good fit for your child. Critical analyses help you make decisions independently, think them through properly, and have the satisfaction and confidence in implementing them. Rather than being complacent with your reasons, or absorbing hearsay information, you are likely to apply a comprehensive methodology to think through and do a critical analysis to reach a rational, logical conclusion.

You would want your child to be able to adopt such a methodology that allows her or him to critically think through the situations (s)he faces. This can be harnessed from an early age to help your child have good problem-solving, decision-making and interpersonal relationship skills. It augments academic learning and sharpens the analytical thinking of a child for its easy application in day-to-day life. Keeping pace with today's times, children need to think independently about issues and challenges and find novel ways to navigate towards their life goals.

UNDERSTANDING CRITICAL THINKING

Critical thinking is a complex intellectual process that entails conceptualizing, analysing, applying reasoning, synthesizing and evaluating skilfully, the problem or information at hand. To be able to analyse critically, one must acquire information from various sources to understand the question or the problem well. Information gathering could be through observation, reading, experiencing and listening to various sources. Having gathered the requisite information, the individual reaches the next process of analysing the information to derive the meaning and break it down into chunks for processing.

These processes do not always work sequentially. Even while the information is being gathered, the mind attempts to analyse and reach answers to the questions of why, what, how and from where, simultaneously. This helps in creating an extensive understanding and comprehension of the core problem, along with its relations with various sources, through the emergence of more aspects during the simultaneous gathering of information and its processing. This finally leads to the next step of synthesizing all the information, to be able to move in the direction of finding possible solutions or alternatives to the problem.

This process of information gathering, reasoning and

synthesizing, stimulates the individual to think. It reduces the impulsiveness of actions and allows for thinking through problems, instead of being reactive towards them. Critical thinking instills good decision-making over time, which in turn boosts a child's self-confidence.

CRITICAL THINKING—A VALUABLE TOOL IN LIFE

Critical thinking skills are essential. They should be fostered in children to help them make informed choices. In today's technologically driven world, much information that is being circulated—both through reliable sources and other channels not backed by research—reinforces the need for, and importance of, giving children the right tools to analyse, evaluate and make decisions/judgements.

As the parent, you can encourage your child to question, think and rethink several messages as a part of the filtering process, by changing the style of communication. Rather than simply imposing your beliefs or judgements about certain information, it is helpful to engage children in the exercise of thinking it through critically for themselves. This allows children to generate and develop their own belief systems through a process of critical analysis.

Critical thinking is also crucial to developing an independent thought process in your child. Furthermore, it reduces the probability of a child taking adverse risks and engaging in undesired or disruptive behaviour, as the child is able to question the need or utility of the behaviour, recognize the limits it places, the impact it has on perceptions and the negative influence it has on relationships. Concurrently, it makes thinking flexible, ensures open-mindedness and the willingness to consider alternate possibilities.

FOSTERING CRITICAL THINKING SKILLS

You can enhance your child's power to think and act by fostering critical thinking skills. By employing some simple strategies, you can make your child learn and practise these skills. Let's take a look at some of these.

1. *Pose thought-provoking questions:* You can start building critical thinking in your child by posing some high-quality questions that provoke her or him to think. Stimulating the higher-level thinking process in the child provides the scaffolding for better critical thinking. For example, posing a question about why leaves fall during autumn to a 5-year-old, or what (s)he likes about a character in the story you are reading together, doesn't just let your child absorb experiences as facts; it stimulates your child to look and think beyond the obvious. It is important to plant the seed of critical analysis and reflection as a way of thinking and processing information.

2. *Encourage decision-making by providing information and reasoning:* It is natural for parents to make daily choices and decisions for a child as you may consider many of them to be trivial. It also saves time and allows you to apply knowledge gathered through previous experiences. But you can change the way you approach many of the decision-making processes with your child by providing information and encouraging your child to reason. It is also important to understand that critical thinking is a process. The earlier your start, the more you prevent a child from engaging in risk taking behaviour, and ensure well-informed decisions.

3. *Make connections with real life experiences:* When you interact with your child and explain a concept, it is helpful for the child if you make connections with pre-existing knowledge. For example, it is helpful if you can link the explanation of a traffic rule to a question your child asked or a game you played. This contextualizes the information and allows for developing a more comprehensive understanding. Create more opportunities for experiential learning at an early age for children to make more meaningful connections with the world.

4. *Support the child's curiosity:* Children enjoy asking many questions. Whether they seem purposeful or meaningless, it

is important to promote and support their 'why's.' Encouraging their questions today will make them lifelong learners. Also, seek answers to their questions with them, rather than immediately providing them with the answers. Ask more questions that relate to the why of a problem or situation to keep them engaged and motivated to look at multiple perspectives.

5. *Use tools like reading and writing for developing critical thinking:* Reading is a great tool for harnessing critical thinking. It provides knowledge and material for analysis and synthesis of various types of information and paves the path for rich critical analysis. With young children, picture books and storytelling can be used to develop critical thinking, by asking questions from the story about the characters or the scenes. Similarly, writing is also a great means to enhance critical thinking.

6. *Think out loud with your child:* A parent can model thinking aloud to the child by using phrases like, 'I was wondering', 'I think it could be', or 'That makes me think about.' These provide the child a language to use in order to support their critical thinking process.

CRITICAL THINKING—A LIFELONG PROCESS

Building skills like critical thinking is not a one time learning experience. It is a lifelong process which teaches children to work in more meaningful ways through situations and with people. The development and enhancement of critical thinking is dependent upon the continued provision of opportunities and means for applying and testing the skills. Providing corrective experiences that simultaneously highlight areas of modification or improvement to these skills are equally important in their continued acquisition.

HIGHLIGHTS

○ Critical thinking is an essential tool for children to navigate towards their life goals.
○ Critical thinking augments understanding and filtering of valid and real information.
○ The process enhances good decision-making and reduces the risk of impulsive actions.
○ You can encourage critical thinking by asking thought-provoking questions, using stories and reading as tools and making learning experiential.
○ Critical thinking results in the creation of an informed, independent thinking process which promotes self-confidence.

49

EVALUATE PERFORMANCE, NOT YOUR CHILD

*A child doesn't need your constant evaluation of who (s)he is.
Your support, encouragement and constructive mirroring
is good enough to shape what (s)he can be.*

Life examines us all at various junctures. Evaluations are inescapable—whether big or small. Any role that one plays entails an evaluative component. We reach an understanding of our growth and success by engaging in realistic evidence-based assessments to measure performance in the context of our professional, personal and social spheres. Despite being a core component of life, evaluations induce feelings of anxiety and restlessness in most people. Take a moment to reflect on the day of your appraisal at the office or when you organized an event at home. You can possibly recall the jitters and apprehension that flooded you at the time. When you take a deeper look, you would recognize these to be evaluations of the self.

EVALUATIONS AFFECT US

Across generations, examinations and evaluations have been perceived as fear and anxiety-inducing elements. The most direct form of assessment—that an individual has early exposure to—is through the medium of academic evaluations. In that case, the emphasis on scores and their meaning represent who a person is and what (s)he is capable of in the future. Harsh remarks often follow a poor performance, while good performance is reinforced with an equally abysmal, 'Could have been better.' This practice unintentionally creates a cascading effect of self-doubts and poor self-concepts.

The beginnings of the evaluation process can occur much earlier than we may realize. From the early developmental years, a parent begins to instil healthy virtues in the child by helping her or him understand a clear demarcation between 'good' and 'bad' behaviour. Despite the best of intentions, this often gets miscommunicated or misinterpreted—taking the form of 'good child' and 'bad child'. This develops associations with the constellation of the child's self. As children grow, academic evaluations become an inherent part of the self-evaluation process. Children tend to link their level of self-esteem with their academic scores. Linkages are also formed with the number of friends a child has or the perceived popularity within school—all of it acting as markers for assessing the self. This is why there is a need to focus on changing how parents approach the evaluation of behavioural and academic performance, as well as the attributes and traits a child displays.

Be mindful and take a constructive approach to appraise the child's performance. In discussions with your child about her or his performance, communicate the distinction between the self, behaviour, academics and social characteristics clearly. Help your child understand that outcomes are the result of the actions and not due to who (s)he is.

BUILDING A COGNITIVE APPROACH TO EVALUATIONS

Evaluations are important. A goal set by an individual needs strategizing, planning, organizing and implementation. A big chunk of this process also includes evaluating the progress after implementation. This helps in assessing the strengths, flaws, hindering factors, and how to reach the goal in a cost and time effective way. Measuring one's progress helps in finding meaningful ways on how to improve performance.

Parents can work towards building a more self-aware and cognitively based route to evaluating the child's performance. The way you shape the perceptions and communicate to the children about their performance helps them develop a practical approach to understanding failures and success. Children become aware of various connotations relating to results and are likely to form maladaptive belief systems, unless otherwise guided. For example, children commonly feel that they are not intelligent if they are unable to score a certain level of marks. Here, intelligence is equated to obtaining high scores. With the academic domain determining a major chunk of their self-concepts, this correlation between scores and their selves leads to vacillating self-esteem and a fragile or fragmented self. This often leads to a spill-over effect in other domains.

A conscious effort from the parent to keep the child's sense of self separate from scores or behaviour—focusing on the why, how and what of subpar results—can lead to a healthy performance evaluation process. Brainstorming about the outcomes helps a child approach flaws and barriers from a problem-solving viewpoint. Continuous self-evaluation can cause cognitive clogging, as it triggers emotions such as guilt, shame or anger. This compromises the ability to think through a situation. It is equally important for you to set aside your emotions while evaluating outcomes with your child.

WAYS FOR KEEPING EMOTIONS ASIDE WHILE EVALUATING PERFORMANCE

Measurement of performance is a continuous process, and it is natural for children to experience highs and lows during their assessment of performance. Supporting your children during these moments is important as is the need to adopt a non-judgemental approach to help them review their performance.

1. *Refrain from using emotional or demeaning words when evaluating performance:* On hearing about a bad performance, parents may often remark impulsively, 'What! But how come? I told you to focus more. Now, see what happened!' Children can sense a parent's disappointment and interpret it to be anger and

unhappiness—this makes them feel emotionally overwhelmed, resulting in withdrawing from the discussion. They internalize negative thoughts and emotions, and associate these with who they are. It is important to be patient and open to hearing what your child has to share. Focus on just evaluating the how and why of the performance while ensuring that global assumptions about the self are not being made. At the same time, reinforce the good parts of the performance to maintain a balance.

2. *Maintain a calm demeanour when talking to children:* Parents must ensure they are in a state of emotional calmness when talking to children about their performance. A parent may feel let down, disappointed with the self or be confused about how the child was unable to perform—thereby being unsure about the approach to be taken to ensure a better performance the next time. It is important that parents deal with their own negative emotions related to the performance before helping the child analyse why they struggled to achieve the desired results. A rational state of mind creates the space for a meaningful and goal-directed discussion.

3. *Conveying disappointment is okay, but only as a factual piece of information:* Parents must communicate and share their disappointment with children in ways that resonate with them. You can always begin by asking, 'How do you feel about your performance in this?' When the child says, 'Not good or disappointed,' you can also share your opinion about the performance... 'Well I feel the same too. Could we discuss what led to this and how we can improve further?' While at it, reinforce the need to not be stuck with the performance, encouraging the child to focus on upcoming challenges and ways of finding success.

4. *Use the evaluation process as a problem-solving approach:* Explain to your child why evaluation is necessary and how it helps in restructuring the goals or the approach if they were not effective. This will help the child assume a constructive approach to the evaluation process and not feel apprehensive or overwhelmed by it.

PRAGMATISM IN THE FACE OF FAILURES

Emotions that emerge from experiencing failure, if not curbed after a point in time, can lead to complete derailment from the goal. It is important to assume a more pragmatic stance after working through the initial emotions that can disturb you. Analyse the various components of a problem to see it for what it is, and then reach a conclusion on what needs to be done further—this can be facilitated through a pragmatic approach. It is a skill that needs to be transferred to your child so (s)he avoids succumbing to negative self-evaluations on account of the problems faced in reaching goals.

HIGHLIGHTS

- Evaluation is a natural process of life.
- Assessing performance is necessary to measure growth towards achieving goals.
- Parents must consciously take the cognitive route to evaluate the child's performance.
- Work towards building a cognitive understanding of the connection between self-concepts and evaluation, and their mutual exclusiveness as entities.
- A child's ability to adopt a constructive approach towards evaluation keeps their self-esteem intact and enhances self-confidence.

50

SHARE YOUR STORIES

We can live through stories
Of ours and others.
Give your child an alternate space
To know more about the world.

A child's best friend is a book full of stories. But what's even more exciting and thrilling for them is to hear your life story. We all love to hear about our parents' or grandparents' funny tales, mishaps, mischievous school days, their troublesome habits, again and again. 'Dadi, could you tell me that story again when dad slipped and fell in the cow shed?' Hearing real life stories of your own family gives children a sense of belonging and joy, by getting to know their parents and grandparents more closely. It builds connections with the past and to the times before they were born. 'Mom, what did I do when I was in your tummy?' For children, stories are always fun and can be a great source of learning.

Parents understand the benefits of reading to the child. They place a lot of emphasis on reading to them everyday, particularly at night before sleeping. This expands the child's vocabulary, enhances language skills, listening skills and provides information and knowledge about the world. Stories trigger imagination and creativity and provide a window to understand the mechanisms of the outside world. By hearing stories from your past, children characterize, identify and associate their selves with that of your younger self. They look for similarities and share excitely, 'I also do the same na, Mama!' or feel validated for their own life experiences —'I also had a similar experience with my friend, Daddy, I will tell you all about it!' Through your stories, connections are built with the previous generations, which contribute to the shape and structure of the child's developing identity.

Family stories provide cultural rootedness to the child's identity, as the historical narrative of the family plays a strong role in defining who they are. Through each story, the child tries to link personal characteristics or traits, like adventure, creativity, professional achievements, failures or resilience, to the family. The parent-child relationship can be significantly strengthened through sharing of life stories.

BENEFITS OF SHARING YOUR LIFE STORIES

During the course of daily work, conversations with children can become prescriptive or overwhelming for a child, which impacts the level of connection and motivation to bring change. Telling stories itself is a creative process, and the tone and approach of everyday conversations can involve too many rules or be loaded with expectations. Despite the reservations you may have about sharing family stories, worrying about the impact they could have on a child, they serve many important functions.

Sharing stories helps create a record of events and keep memories alive through generations. It allows family members to convey values and share their learning across experiences. It helps create connect between you and your child, aids in imparting life lessons and instilling virtues. They provide the child the knowledge about family customs and traditions which becomes embedded in the child's personality. It gives them a sense of clarity about who they are, where they have come from, where they belong and where they would like to go from here. These are critical to a child's self-concepts, thereby building strong esteem and confidence.

Life stories can act as a problem-solving tool. The child is able to observe the story being narrated as an outsider, which helps in building a third-person perspective of the situation being presented. This helps them identify the problem and find a solution to it. Being surrounded by a problem can make cognitive processing of it difficult, in contrast to when you see it as an outsider. Stories provide the child a director's perspective, that allows her or him to understand the critical points and choose what to take away from it.

In the early years, life stories are particularly important for emotional and cognitive development. Given the interest, attention and willingness with which a child listens to an adult's reminiscence, evokes a deep emotional response and develops a strong attachment, utilizing such narratives is important. Sharing the memories of the past evokes images, and the child immerses herself or himself in your life experiences, feeling a sense of joy, comfort and safety. At the same time, life stories inspire a child to achieve goals and develop a sense of control by transformational learning that occurs through such moments.

KNOW HOW TO BOND OVER STORIES

Life stories are powerful tools to create strong connections between family members. A good laugh over old stories, during family time, creates good memories for a lifetime. Learning happens by looking at past mistakes, and the path can be laid to move ahead in life. Let's look at ways in which you can share and bond over stories.

1. *Choose your life experiences age-appropriately:* Young children like to hear dramatic and action-packed stories. Sharing short, funny, explicit memories with a lot of detail and description would make your child want to hear more and laugh with you. It enhances the emotional bond you share with each other. When children grow, the nature of stories needs to be more purposeful, conveying a certain meaning through the course of its narration.
2. *Share stories of failures and success in a non-preachy way:* It is important to gauge the right context and approach in which you share your story with your child. Especially during the teen years children may not be very open to listening to others' stories of success, as they are moving through their own phase

of identity formation. Avoid using a tone that may undermine their problem or struggle. While sharing your story, focus on your emotions, hardships and failures, for them to take comfort from your experiences. It makes them realize that they are not alone in negotiating through hardships and challenges.
3. *Encourage talking about family stories:* During family time over the dinner table, share more stories that are fun and positive. Reminisce about good memories from the past to create an atmosphere of love and warmth. Children should be encouraged to talk and ask more about their family history. It enhances their confidence and builds self-esteem.
4. *Create a family story box:* Create a box with pictures and various articles that are of great value in terms of the associated memories or events. This can qualitatively enhance your conversations when you retell family stories, your history or any memorable moments.

BE GENEROUS WITH YOUR STORIES

More is less when it comes to the stories you share with your child. Don't be shy and don't hesitate to share your experiences and those of others. Help your child learn more about you and the family. Answer the questions that arise and take the extra step to satisfy your child's curiosity. Be generous with your stories and also in your stories. Pass down the values you want your child to imbibe through the stories you share.

HIGHLIGHTS

- Children feel joy and excitement to hear family stories from parents and grandparents.
- Family stories give children a sense of belonging and rootedness, and shape their identity.
- Life stories create relatedness and enhance the parent-child relationship.
- Children feel comforted and safe in knowing they are not alone in their experiences of hardships and challenges.
- Children should be encouraged to talk about family history and ask more questions to different members, as it builds positive self-esteem and confidence.

51

BE A GENDER-SENSITIVE PARENT

*Eliminate the gender from defining who a child is.
Focus instead on qualities and traits
to create the right environment
for a happy and confident child.*

The first thing that a parent hears when the child is born is the gender of the child. People around rejoice in sharing, 'It's a boy!' or, 'It's a girl!' At birth itself many associations occur with the gender of the child. Parents are flooded with colour-coded gifts and clothes which are pink or purple for girls and blue or grey for boys. Gender stereotypes and gender associations are deeply embedded in our belief systems, culture, society and community. These make it almost impossible for people to be objective about gender in their attitudes, perceptions and belief systems, specifically when it comes to raising children.

SOCIALIZATION EXPERIENCES OF CHILDREN

A child's gender-related expressions are largely shaped and influenced during the early developmental years. Children come to understand physical differences between the genders from the age of one and one-and-a-half. Further to this, they are able to express their preference for toys and activities in accordance with their gender by the age of three. They absorb gender differences based on their observations, the interactions that occur around them and the media they are exposed to.

Children learn gender stereotypes from multiple sources. Yet, the immediate and most impactful gender related experiences occur at home. These begin with how one perceives the presence and acceptance of gender-biased notions within the home. For instance, if a parent displays the idea of a girl controlling her anger and being polite, while a boy is allowed to express his anger, the acceptability of gender-related stereotypes is passed forward. Such seemingly simplistic situations have a huge potential to influence and structure a child's gender identity and its expression. It also creates a favourable or unfavourable gender image that evokes a child's conformity to what is acceptable.

It is a known fact that rigidly held stereotypes and prejudices create restraints, reduce openness and have a negative impact on the individual. This same holds true for children who may develop low self-esteem if raised within the restriction of gender stereotypes and gender-based roles. Recent times have seen greater levels of awareness and conscious attempts by parents and society to shift towards being more gender sensitive.

To build a gender-sensitive approach, parents need to give children a safe and free environment that provides the opportunity for free exploration of play, clothing, expressions and roles, regardless of the gender of the child. This helps build an atmosphere that is not rigid in gender expression but encourages a child to be inclusive and respectful of diversity.

TALK ABOUT THE EQUALITY OF GENDERS WITH YOUR CHILD

Children observe and begin to understand gender specific roles at home. For instance, when they see a mother investing more time in household chores as opposed to the father, whose primary role is seen to be to focus on work, a child unconsciously imbibes this and internalizes it. Consistent messages and responses that attribute direct or indirect qualities to men or women—men being more direct, harsh and aggressive in their reactions, while women being soft, warm and emotional—contribute to the gender-based stereotypes and role assignments. These gender-based norms are further reinforced by constant media messages, which leads to subliminal conditioning predisposing individuals to naturally conform to these norms and qualities.

Gender-based norms, roles and stereotypes make experiences with people prescriptive, predictable and constricted, going against the very idea of providing an explorative and creative environment. It affects a child's ability to fully explore her or his potential. Concurrently, gender roles can affect a child's mindset negatively.

For instance, encouraging girls to be tolerant of negative emotions or experiences can make them less assertive in situations, and reduce communication about their feelings and thoughts. In contrast, remarks and reinforcing messages to boys about being tough and strong, highlights the underlying rejection for the qualities of being gentle or emotionally expressive. It impacts a boy's ability to express feelings through words and puts a maladaptive coping mechanism in place, like abusing substances or showing physical aggression.

Gender norms create the pressure to fit in which can force boys and girls to act a certain way even when they want to experience things differently. It is not uncommon to hear experiences of how a young boy became a laughing stock amongst his peers for putting on nail colour, or a girl being labelled a tomboy for wearing boyish clothes and having a boy-like haircut. Experiences like these emotionally scar the child, making her or him conscious and sensitive about her or his own expressions of gender.

Strong gender stereotyping teaches girls and boys about cultural expectations that are placed on their belonging to a certain gender. To build a society which is diverse and inclusive, it is important that adults question and dismiss such notions and ideas in children's thinking. Each step taken towards demolishing stereotypes and negative associations with gender lets children experience their true capacities and be confident individuals to tackle the challenges posited by the world.

CREATE A GENDER-SENSITIVE ENVIRONMENT AT HOME

A change in society can result by empowering the young, and this needs to begin at home. Children are not born with gender-based notions firmly wedged in their patterns of thinking. Instead, they are shaped to believe and identify with these thoughts. Parents can play a crucial role in dislodging such belief systems by initiating gender-sensitive conversations at home. Being more self-aware in your attitudes, beliefs and perceptions about gender roles and expectations at home, will sow the seeds for raising children who are gender sensitive.

1. *Create a basic gender-sensitive structure at home:* Begin in a simple manner by creating basic gender-neutral structures at home like colours of the rooms and clothes, keeping mixed bunch of toys for a child to explore, reading books to your child that do not rigidly define gender qualities or stereotypes, or, introducing them to shows on television that present boys and girls in varied roles. Encourage playdates by pairing them with children of opposite gender as much as you do with same gendered peers. Get out of your existing comfort zones that relate to gender-based norms and create structures at home that view gender in a neutral manner.
2. *Consciously avoid making gender-biased remarks*: The language you use reflects your thoughts and beliefs. Parents must use gender-sensitive language at home. Gender-based remarks like, 'Naina, please sit like a lady' or, 'Rahul, be a man!' can really pierce and get lodged in the subconscious mind of a child, becoming an inherent part of their thinking and identity. This makes the child more conscious of who (s)he is in terms of gender identity. Parents need to work towards using less gender-defined comments.
3. *Critically evaluate gender biases that may reflect in various media:* While watching television, listening to songs or even reading a book that showcases gender stereotypes, parents must encourage children to identify them and help them understand

how these emerge. Encourage children to think critically about how gender stereotypes impact their perception of how boys and girls should be, and the pressure they feel to fit with certain existing norms.
4. *Introduce children to role models that represent unconventional gender roles:* Children must be exposed to men and women who challenge gender stereotypes, like a male dancer, female cricketer, a male chef or a female rider. Engage in discussions and conversations about assuming healthy gender roles and focusing on who a person is and the qualities (s)he possesses. Reinforce the acceptability of assuming roles that may be atypical to the gender your child possesses.

WALK TOWARDS CULTIVATING A LESS GENDERED SOCIETY

For generations, gender stereotypes have ruled society, which has had a substantial impact on the lives of both men and women across generations. The current debates and restlessness which is prompting individuals to question age-old gender norms and encouraging whole societies to think critically about the existing stereotypes, is an important step forward. The idea is not to erase gender but make it less relevant.

As a parent you can contribute to this change by raising children in a gender-sensitive manner. An important facet of raising a confident child is to first raise your child as an individual of the society!

HIGHLIGHTS

- Gender stereotypes are pervasive within homes and society.
- The way gender-related concepts are taught to children reflects how culture expects them to be.
- Gender stereotypes and gender-based roles pressurize and restrict children, negatively affecting their self-esteem.
- Create a gender-sensitive environment at home by giving your child the opportunity to explore interests, roles and activities in a non-gender specific way.
- Encourage critical thinking around gender stereotypes by engaging in healthy discussions.

52

BE ACCEPTING OF WHAT COMES YOUR WAY

Parenting is a lifelong journey.
Its success is not merely measured by the control you gain.
Be accepting and mindful of what comes your way.

A friend: 'So, how is parenting coming along? You seem to be such a good parent!'
You: 'Ah, I wish! I don't know, actually. You know what I mean. It seemed easier with the older one but it's a lot tougher with my younger one. They are so different that I often feel lost. I wish parenting was easy!'

Parenting is not about raising a child in a controlled environment where everything is predictable. It involves a complex interplay of what the child and the external environment bring into the context of parenting. Despite trying your best to prevent troubles or negative consequences such as your baby's colic, a child's playful injury or sickness or a teenager's experience of failure, you will face challenges that are not in your control. It can seem like a long journey in which you feel love and joy along with exhausting questions that raise doubts about what you did and how you did it. Managing the uncertainties you face is also integral to the confidence your child builds within the self.

THERE WILL BE WORRIES

Every parenting journey will make you experience a new set of anxiety, worry or fear. Though the journey may be seemingly smooth, there will be times when you face rocky turns and slippery roads. What comes your child's way is what you must accept and deal with. As a parent, you want to ensure comfort and a pain-free journey for your child. Yet, part of parenting is accepting what comes in the way. Life is a continuous process of experiencing success and working through challenges that impact your child and yourself. New things will come up that will test your patience—be it moving to a new place, going through a financial crisis, or dealing with a traumatic experience or a major illness.

Therefore, this enormous process called parenting necessitates that you are aware of your needs that arise due to the problems you face with your child or by yourself. It is important to develop resilience and indulge in your own emotional care as well. Parental responsibilities and stress can impact your mental well-being, affecting your parenting as well. Imagine a day you woke up to after a good night's sleep, when you ate well, attended fewer phone calls and your work was smooth—how would you feel? While you cannot escape the negative situations that come your way, you need to invest in self-care and develop the resilience to keep fighting the upcoming battles.

VIEW YOURSELF FROM AN OBJECTIVE STANDPOINT

Who you are and how you parent a child is influenced by your belief system and, in some ways, by how you were reared as a child. You may or may not imbibe the parenting strategies that were adopted by your parents. Some people can follow patterns of parenting similar to their own experiences while others may apply strategies in accordance with the perceptions and understandings garnered through personal experiences and other interactions with the world and environment.

Adults carry a significant proportion of their past into their present and future approaches. While constantly appraising the environment around, it is natural to project one's own subjective ways of thinking and feeling in situations, people, decisions and activities. This subjective perception is the result of the internal cognitive schemas you possess. Your beliefs and ideas make you truly believe the same about the world and it defines your reality. However, you must strive to build an objectivity that enables you to look at yourself first as an individual, then as a parent and then within the context of the world in a less judgemental manner.

THE MANY BENEFITS OF BUILDING OBJECTIVITY

Your perceptions about yourself and the world have a direct impact on your parenting. It is pertinent for parents to understand themselves and the parenting process more objectively. Objectivity is the ability to recognize and accept things 'as is' and respond to the situation, person or context thoughtfully and deliberately. It helps you question your beliefs and the underlying assumptions in relation to the context of parenting while making decisions. To be able to objectively perceive the context, it is important for you to first accept what is in front of you.

Acceptance means to know and understand who you are without constantly rejecting or dissociating from parts of yourself. For example, a parent who has an internal belief of not being good enough tends to experience moments of dissatisfaction with efforts—this reflects on the child as well. The need to keep pushing and proving oneself in this context greatly influences the parenting goals. Similarly, a parent with an ingrained self-doubt would have difficulty in taking parenting decisions or may vacillate in trying to reach a conclusion. This can create an atmosphere of uncertainty and instability for the child.

Being able to perceive the context objectively would help you detach your self-beliefs from the context of parenting. It would also result in greater awareness about the self to be able to take the next step of developing a fresh perspective towards the child and parenting. Objectivity gives you clarity and helps you see the interconnectedness of things around you. How stress at work affects your mood and makes you react at home differently is a knowledge that you can gain by being more objective in how you perceive situations. When you distance yourself from the situation to see it more clearly, you can develop a deeper understanding, enhanced self-control and healthier mechanisms to adapt to the same situation.

To know yourself as a parent and gain an objective understanding, you can ask yourself the following questions:

1. What are my belief systems about myself?
2. Have my belief systems influenced my parenting approach? Can I recall any incidents where I can see their influence?
3. What are the five core beliefs, assumptions or ideas that have created a strain in my relationship with my child?
4. What approach, response or behaviour have helped me and my child feel more closely connected?
5. If I must change something about myself as a parent, what aspects would those be?

OBJECTIVE UNDERSTANDING BUILDS RESILIENCE

Building objectivity and acceptance develops the power of positivity in you. It gives you the strength to acknowledge and accept the situation as is. By acceptance, you are not giving in to situations or giving up. Instead, it allows you to reassess and look for alternate approaches allowing you to operate from a position of strength. Through this process, you have a context with a sense of detachment and rationality, being fully aware of what can be controlled and what you need to let go. You are able to take on the challenges that come your way during the course of parenting head-on with confidence—this is eventually reflected in your child. Even in times of distress, this sense of objectivity would give you the strength, resilience and coping skills to deal with situations in the best possible way. To be able to raise confident children, parents must perceive themselves with confidence. Your children will mirror the qualities you demonstrate!

HIGHLIGHTS

- Parenting entails many uncertain turns and challenges.
- Parents must work towards building an objective approach towards the self and the environment.
- An objective perspective enhances the ability to accept who you are and the situation at hand.
- Objectivity helps in perceiving situations in a less judgemental way and in building a fresh, positive perspective.
- Objectivity allows you to develop resilience to take on challenges that come in the way of parenting your child.